I Choose You

For Amanda

Also, special thanks to my dearest friends Laura Partsch and Doug Froggatt, and my mother and father for raising me to love.

I Choose You

Charles A. Bush

ISBN 13: 9781500107130
ISBN: 1500107131

I

Emily

The coruscating lamp, hovering above the operating table like a guardian angel, stung Emily's pupils, quickly reminding her of rule number twenty-six from her Procedures and Forms course: 'Never look into the light. Your focus at all times should be on the patient.' She knew the rule as well as she knew her name, along with the 12,754 other procedural aphorisms. But still she looked, wasting precious time in the midst of havoc.

"Her vitals are plummeting," shouted doctor three. "Doctor Robertson, we are going to lose her if we don't act fast."

Emily looked back down at the patient. Her hands were, protected in latex and coated with blood, and equipped with only a chest tube passer and a pair of cardio scissors to cut the built up tissue. The woman's chest was split open like a hot dog bun, exposing her sternum. It was because of moments such as this that Emily told inquiring people, 'being a doctor isn't glamorous.'

"Give her the iloprost now…double dose! We need to stabilize the pulmonary arterial hypertension. If the blood pressure rises any more in her vessels she'll be out of our reach."

Emily's voice was austere and confident. This is what she was trained to do; it was what she lived for.

"Applying iloprost," shouted the adhering doctor to Emily.

As the patient's vitals plummeted further, Emily's heart began to race, her nerves beseeching her hands to remain steady. She would get only one shot at saving this woman, and she knew it. Her jittery hands guided the sharp head of the scissors down through the patient's exposed caverns, stopping next to the inferior vena cava. She had to remove the excess tissue from the cava to reestablish proper flow of the de-oxygenated blood cells to the right atrium, a procedure she had studied countless times in medical school. But the rush of adrenaline assured her that this was no longer spoken words in a classroom, but the exigent reality of life and death. She took a deep breath, releasing it as she cut. And *snip*, the sound of the flatline filled the room with melancholy song.

"I cut too deep," she whispered to herself out loud, her hands now appallingly still and frozen in aghast shock.

The three other doctors stood in a state of panic, awaiting Emily's next command. All she could see was the patient's unresponsive heart, lying there as if it were a trophy for her failure.

"Doctor Robertson!"

Emily didn't answer, glued to the mess she had made and the life she had just ended.

"Doctor Robertson!" inquired doctor two in post haste.

And as Emily stood there frozen in fear, only three words left her mouth in obsequious reply, "I'm sorry, mom."

Sweat. The sweat keeps pounding through her pores like tiny vents into her soul, consuming her body every night like a disease. Emily Robertson had inherited many traits from her mother, such as a keen intellect and poor eyesight; however, Stephanie Robertson's, ability to receive a full night's rest was not one of them. The night terrors were becoming too much for Emily to bear, despite having to have coped with them for the past sixteen years. They have always been a nuisance, inexplicably the one where she maligns the most important surgery of her life to fatal proportions. Her ex-boyfriend, Kevin, used to get frustrated with her when she awoke in the middle of the night, petrified from fear. Truthfully, she wasn't entirely certain that was the reason for his frustration, as he seemed to always be cross with her for one reason or another. He constantly harped: "You're so dull, Emily— we have to do something."

The burning red lights from her alarm clock beside her bed read 2:45 a.m., so she figured she might as well sit up and study some more for her final exam tomorrow. Last night, like the majority of her nights, was spent at the Yale library. On the rare occasions when she wasn't at her field study, she would be tucked away in a vacant desk in the corner of the library, studying for hours on end until her roommate would beg her to return home for some well deserved sleep or the librarian would kick her out. Her mother had always preached to her the importance of books, telling Emily in her elegant voice, which made her sound like a benevolent schoolteacher,

"Books can take you anywhere you want to go, Emily."

But even her mother could not have predicted the myriad of hours Emily would choose to spend between the pages of a book.

Emily tucked her legs cozily beneath the comforter before putting on her thin-rimmed spectacles and turning on the lamp beside her bed. The front door creaked open and then closed, signifying the return of her roommate, Melissa Hall, from her ritual pre-exam party. Emily directed her attention back to the pages, which gave off a strong sense of déjà vu, unsurprisingly because she had read them two days prior, when Melissa had talked her in to taking a few hours off from studying to attend the premier of the new Ben Affleck movie. A film which Emily didn't even see because they arrived so late and were forced to sit in the front row. Emily used their tardiness to her advantage by pulling out her textbook from her handbag and using the magnified light from the movie screen to read for the length of the film.

"Are you seriously reading in a movie theater?" whispered Melissa irritably. "You could at least be reading a novel and not one of our textbooks. Or, I don't know, be watching the film like a normal person."

And as usual, Emily didn't speak, but accepted the criticism and plunged back into the pages as if they were pulling her by the neck.

She wasn't naive to the fact that her aberrant behavior left her socially inept, for it had been doing so since she had first picked up a Nancy Drew book in third grade. Her youth was far less littered with sleepovers and play dates, than most girls at such a curious age. In a way, she pondered if her mother found her lack of social skills to be at all a hindrance to her ambitions. Perhaps they would be if she inspired to be a talk show host or D.J., but becoming a doctor didn't really require one to be well transverse in the art of 'being the life of a party.' Not to mention Emily had grown quite fond of the person she had become over the years. For as far as she was concerned, in no way was her unquenchable thirst for knowledge a bad thing.

'*Haemophilus influenza genome*' as she came across the phrase again in her bed she couldn't help but smile at how funny she thought it sounded. She had said it once outside of class to Melissa when they were waiting for coffee and she swore the gentleman behind them thought she was having a stroke. But it was surely going to be on the exam, so she burned it into her memory banks for tomorrow. A thunderclap interrupted her studying and she gazed out into the dreary night's sky at the lightning that followed. Like the two nights prior, it was raining—most peculiar for Connecticut this time of year—and she pondered whether she would again know the luxury of a good night's sleep. Her head dropped down to the textbook with the faintest hint of dolefulness, as she wouldn't object to having someone to talk to about her lack of sleep. Melissa was completely out of the question, because there was a hundred percent chance that if Emily walked down the hall to her room, she would be passed out in a despondent state of alcoholic fulfillment.

The thought of spending another sleepless night studying was beginning to annoy her in more ways than one, so she closed the book and attempted to will her way into a slumber that wouldn't spark another abhorrent night terror.

The alarm clock's cry blending with the smell of pancakes lured Emily from her bed. Her room was fairly empty, consisting only of a generic calendar from Staples, a wardrobe, her nightstand, a petite desk with an assortment of medical books piled on top, and a Yale pennant hanging alongside the calendar. Her desk was always coated in books, mainly educational textbooks, with the occasional literary fiction, such as Jane Austen and Charles Dickens, which she read for pleasure during the minuscule free time that she did have. She grabbed her spectacles from next to the alarm clock and slipped into her slippers, while she nonchalantly tied up her hair and made her way into the kitchen.

Melissa was flipping pancakes in a rusty iron skillet while her iPod played Taylor Swift low in the background on the *Bose* sound dock by the toaster. They had managed to squeeze in a breakfast bar despite their petite kitchen being just beyond the size of a large bathtub.

Emily drug out her words while yawning and stretching in harmony: "smells good."

Melissa turned towards Emily, while shaking her hips to the rhythm.

"Well, you know what they say? Breakfast is the most important meal of the day. We have to have a full tank if we're going to pass Dr. Emerich's final." Melissa placed two pancakes on the plate, coated them in butter and syrup, and slid them down the counter to Emily. She received it, spilling a driblet of syrup that dangled off the side of the plate like a teardrop, on the tip of her index finger.

"Thanks," replied Emily, sucking the syrup from her finger. "But I'm not sure pancakes will help me differentiate between a clogged artery and a heart murmur. Especially the way Emerich writes case studies."

Melissa stationed her plate across the counter from Emily and proceeded to drown her pancakes in syrup, squeezing the bottle until it puckered with emptiness.

"Trust me, when your stomach is not growling in oh, let's say… the middle of a huge final today, you'll be thanking me."

Emily laughed and began cutting into her pancakes, thinking there may be some truth to Melissa's words.

"Well thanks again, they look delicious. Well, at least mine do. You sure you don't want any pancakes to go along with your syrup?" mocked Emily.

"Hey, I happen to like maple syrup. Is that such a crime?"

"I guess not," she smiled. "Honestly though, Melissa, thank you, this is great. You're such a good friend. I'm almost embarrassed to say it, but I'm going to miss you when you head back to New York."

Melissa replied with an encouraging look on her face, as if preparing to talk Emily into something:

"Yeah, I am pretty rad aren't I?" she said cockily shaking her head in agreement. "That's why we're all meeting at Riley's after exams to see everyone off before summer. You are coming right?... NO! Let me rephrase that, YOU ARE COMING!"

Emily smiled tauntingly before taking another bite of her pancakes, pretending she was about to say no, which was her usual response to such a question. Although Melissa had succeeded in talking Emily into going to the movies last week, it was beyond a rare sight to see her partaking in social activities. In fact, besides Kevin, she had never had a boyfriend. Even in high school she had been obsessively focused on her studies and becoming class valedictorian, all so she could attend an Ivy League school like her mother and have a better chance at becoming a doctor. Her lack of a relationship was not from the lack of interest from boys however; quite the contrary. Boys would ask her out all the time, but she always had an excuse—debate team practice, too much homework, Class council meetings, in the middle of a good book—the list was endless.

"I guess I'll go. Besides, who else is going to carry you home after you're five martinis in and singing *You Belong to Me.*"

"Very true, but don't act like you don't love my singing voice." Emily looked up from her plate immediately, catching Melissa's eye to make the point that she was absurdly crazy for thinking anyone liked her singing voice.

"I don't."

"See, you say you don't, but I happen to know for a fact that you do." Emily shook her head in laughter and continued to finish her pancakes.

Melissa and Emily hadn't always been the closest of friends. They had been assigned to room together freshman year at Yale, and on nights when Melisa was well past intoxication, she found it easy to inform Emily how annoying her obsessive studying was. Emily would just sit there on her bed engrossed in whatever textbook they were analyzing for class, and no matter how much Melissa exhorted her to attend a Harvard frat party or a freshman mixer, Emily graciously declined. But Melissa's feelings quickly faded when she put two and two together: an always sober roommate equals a free designated driver. Not to mention, some of Emily's academic habits did rub off on Melissa—well, maybe they didn't completely rub off on her, but she was able to graduate with a rather decent GPA.

After breakfast, Emily washed the dishes and took a quick shower before squeezing in some last minute studying. She didn't usually use flash cards to study, but knowing the final would be definition heavy, she added them to her usual routine of reading the textbook multiple times. Her first flash card was ironically, '*Haemophilus influenza genome*' and again she got a kick out of seeing the phrase. As they walked over to the medical building, Melissa tried to fill Emily in on the hectic night she had experienced. But obstinate to the task at hand, Emily kept her head planted firmly between her textbook's pages. Melissa, used to it, rambled on and didn't even become upset at Emily's inattention, but instead found Emily's skill of walking and reading to be rather impressive.

Once in the classroom, Emily breezed through two chapters in seven minutes before the class commenced at one and Dr. Emerich began walking down the rows of students passing out exams as if they were raffle tickets. She placed her textbook in her bag and kicked it under the desk out of sight. She knew the material inside out, but she still became a bit flustered before any big exam. She turned her head briefly, making eye contact with Melissa, who sat in the back of the room attempting to hide from the class all together. Melissa made a hanging gesture with her tongue dangling from her mouth, as if she'd rather be dead than take the exam. Emily smiled and mouthed the words, 'You'll be fine' to her. Melissa replied, mouthing 'I hope so.'

The exam lasted five hours with a fifteen-minute break at the top of each, leaving Emily appreciative of her pancake breakfast, though she would never admit that to Melissa. After the exam, Emily and Melissa walked back to the apartment together, both mentally drained and physically enervated.

"So what did you think of that second case study?" asked Melissa, examining her phone for any missed text messages or calls.

"I don't know; I thought it was pretty straight forward."

Melissa's eyes shot up from her phone's screen in amazement. "Are you kidding me? I almost put down 'see Doctor House' it was so insane. How on God's earth were we suppose to decipher that shit he called a case study?"

Emily laughed lightly; always amused at the way Melissa could over-dramatize any situation.

"You're exaggerating. It was practically identical to the Bradley vs. Milton case in chapter sixteen of the textbook. I'm sure you did great." Emily's smile had a way of making anyone who saw it feel better, no matter what it was they were going through.

"Yeah, you're probably right. Well let's pick up the pace; I cannot wait to dive into those martinis. I am going to be so wasted!"

Emily rolled her eyes in beguilement.

"I was half joking when I said that earlier. Must you get drunk? All you're going to do is end up making out with some random guy at the bar again." If there was one thing she had learned from their six years of friendship, it was that Melissa acted as if she couldn't survive without some drunk guy's tongue exploring every crevice of her mouth.

"Hell yeah I am! It's called living for a reason, Em. You should try it sometime."

Emily gave in, knowing she was fighting an uphill battle. "Suit yourself. I guess I better bring my carrying shoes."

"You better bring two pairs, because since the semester's over things may get a little weird…just saying."

"Well, they can't get any weirder than that time I picked you up from Robert Zeke's party."

Emily was right. No matter how much Melissa drank tonight, things couldn't get that weird. Robert Zeke had been the head of the Sigma Phi Epsilon fraternity at Yale their senior year. When Emily received the call from their mutual friend, Rachel, to come and get Melissa, she was surprised to find Melissa passed out in a baby pool of chocolate syrup drenched with, what she could only make out at the time as pillow feathers, and sporting a homemade dunce cap.

Melissa laughed at her past misfortune humbled enough to know it were not one of her finer moments.

"God, isn't that the truth. I can't believe you still remember that night."

"I was sober."

"Oh yeah," she said laughing. "Thankfully you'll be there to monitor me from the start tonight."

"Well, lucky me," replied Emily sardonically.

As usual, it took about two hours for Melissa to get ready; as she always indulged in extra preparation time whenever she left the apartment. Any time they even contemplated going out in public, Melissa felt it necessary to put on a fashion show for Emily. She would mix and match an assortment of shoes with shirts and twist and turn in the mirror trying to see which outfit better showed off her figure, inquiring every several minutes, "How does this look, Em?" Emily often asked Melissa why she put so much effort into going out, and Melissa usually answered,

"You never know who you are going to meet. How am I supposed to impress Mister Right while wearing sweatpants and no makeup?

No offense, Em." Naturally when people say, 'no offense' they, in fact mean, offense, but in Melissa's case she did not. Not to mention it was true, Emily did wear sweats more often than not and had worn makeup only six times in her life, four of which came when she was seven and she got into her mother's makeup drawer.

"Right, because heaven forbid he would actually like you for your intellect," replied Emily. Both girls shared a laugh at Melissa's expense.

"Have you met me? And come on, Em, we are talking about guys here. You know as well as I do they wouldn't know intelligence if it hit them in the face. Unless of course that intelligence was wearing a mini skirt and had D cups."

Melissa finally settled on an outfit, a dark jean skirt that rode up a few inches past her knees, along with a black halter-top that matched her long black hair and black and gold open-toed Steve Madden sandals. Melissa had mischievous green eyes that seemed to attract every drunken guy's attention and glazed tanned skin from the several hours a week she spent at the cheap tanning salon in Chinatown. Although she was a few inches taller than Emily, they both had slim figures, so Melissa often tried to convince Emily to wear some of her clothes; her convincing success stood at a resounding 0 for 245.

Within ten minutes, Emily was promptly dressed and prepared to go. She cared little what people thought of her appearance. She was always herself and would rather be comfortable than feel as if she was going to sprain an ankle wearing high heels or have a breast pop out while wearing some provocative dress. She artlessly threw on a pair of light denim jeans that she bought last year from the GAP, a Yale medical t-shirt, and her spectacles. She brushed her hair several times to straighten it before effortlessly tying it up. In spite of how hard Emily tried to disguise it, she was beyond a doubt her mother's daughter and exceptionally beautiful. She had inherited her mother's long free-flowing brown hair and engaging hazel eyes, both complementing her slender frame, which she worked out vigorously every morning on the Yale track. She had a tiny assortment of freckles, including a peculiar one on her left nostril that in the proper light made it look like she had a nose piercing. And although she hated wearing them, her spectacles gave her an exceedingly kind and elegant look, as if she were a conservative model posing as a librarian. Many of her friends would joke and tell her that in a few years she will easily be able to pass as Tina Fey, even though she disagreed with them immensely.

They arrived at Riley's Pub at half past nine. Riley's was not your typical hole in the wall. The bar wrapped around the dining room, which sat slightly above the floor plan holding over eighty people. Flat screen televisions oversaw each section of the bar like spotlights and a vibrant orange, white, and green Irish flag hung in the center of the room with an abundance of pride. The walls were decorated in a collage of photos of celebrities that had previously visited, many of them Red Sox players with the occasional movie star like Matt Damon. There was even a photo of Senator John Kerry wearing a Tom Brady jersey and posing with the owner. The several large windows looked out into the main street and provided a view to the small outdoor lounge area that is utilized in warm weather. Most people came for the incredible dollar drafts on game nights, while others came for the large dance hall upstairs. There were many nights where Melissa had made a fool of herself when drunk by abusing that very dance floor. Emily had even been forced to call the paramedics once, when Melissa accidentally tore her ACL while doing the Thriller dance on Halloween Junior year.

As Emily and Melissa entered, they saw Lilly's arm shoot up from a long table near the middle section of the bar. Lilly and Melissa were the co-masterminds behind the get-together.

"Hey *girlfriends!*" shouted Lilly. Lilly seemed to have this idea in her head that they somehow resembled the girls from Sex in the City, little to her knowledge, they didn't. But that didn't deter her from talking like it.

"Hey everyone," Emily and Melissa replied while waving to the table. The entire Yale med school gang was present, Emily, Melissa,

Lilly Thompson, newly engaged Rachel Lowe and Scott Brooks, Sharon Gallagher, and Denise Reynolds.

Emily managed to enjoy herself, despite the fact that she didn't care much for pubs or even going out. Everyone shared stories of exams and reminisced about funny tales of medical school. Scott even joked that if Emily kept up her obsessive studying regimen, she would be valedictorian again, just as she had been for their Yale undergrad class two years ago. And although her reserved demeanor would never show it that was precisely her plan—to become the best doctor she could be.

When the waitress stopped over to check on them, Melissa commanded everyone to order another drink so she could propose a toast. The girls ordered another round of Apple Martinis, Emily kept an eye on how many Melissa consumed; she was at three about two away from her tolerance, and Scott ordered another Sam Adams Summer Ale. "I'll have another ginger ale please," said Emily softly, like a shy schoolgirl. Everyone at the table moaned,

"Come on, Emily," scolded Scott. "We all know you don't drink, but at least have one. We're celebrating! No more Emerich!"

Emily gracefully smiled and placed a loose strand of hair behind her ear.

"No thanks, guys. You all drink enough for me."

They all started to boo as if she played for the opposing team, and Melissa jumped in,

"Hey, leave Em alone! There's a reason she is head of the class and will probably be making more money than any of us someday." The mob adhered to Melisa's demands and backed off. When the drinks arrived they all raised their glasses in unison and Melissa gave her long awaited toast.

"To finishing year two, may we never have to take an exam as hard as that one again!"

They all replied, "To year two!"

"Now, to the real reason we are all here." Melissa raised her glass and turned towards Emily.

"Em, you are such a great roommate and friend to us all. You're there when I pass out in the middle of dance floors, and when Denise needs help on a case study. You even managed the miracle of hooking the two most unfit people up." She motioned her glass towards Scott and Rachel. "With that being said you are also, and don't take this the wrong way, Em, you know I love you, the most boring person I know. But all that changes tonight. You are finally going to relax, enjoy life, and not think about school for more than five minutes for once in your life." She noticed the complex look that inhabited Emily's face, "I see you look a bit confused, and I'm glad you asked. All of us here have pitched in and got you a little gift. Instead of you just going back to your grandmother's for the summer, you will be going to stay at my Aunt's inn in England. And we are not taking no for an answer missy!"

Scott again interjected, "and before you answer, know we've already paid for the ticket. So if you don't go I sure as hell will."

Emily was bowled over beyond comprehension. Her complexion morphed into a ghostly white umbrage at the thought of her spending a summer in Europe. In her mind, Europe was a place reserved for girls with 90210 addresses on weekend vacations and actresses looking to purchase the newest fashions. Not a twenty-five-year-old medical student that couldn't tell *Prada* from *JCPenney*.

"Thank you. I…I, don't know what to say."

Lilly yelled from the opposite end of the table, smiling in amusement at Emily's reaction. "Say you'll go!"

Emily sighed, trying to hold back her loathing initial reaction. Any other time, on any other day, in any other place, she would have said no because she needed to continue studying to be prepared for next year. Vacations, no studying, this was not part of her well scripted plan, a plan that was sixteen years in the making, one that was being executed without any hiccups or afflictions. But for some reason, she could never afterwards explain, she decided for once in her life to take a chance.

"Okay, I'll go."

II

Jude

Jude Macavoy awoke to kisses on his cheeks, which slowly moved to his neck, and then lusciously down to his firm stomach. He didn't stop the girl, but instead laid still with an beatitude grin on his face. The room smelled of week old latex, booze, and expensive cologne. His shelves were littered with football trophies and medals, most of which he had won with the youth team at Blackpool Football Club when he was seventeen. Although his room wasn't the biggest for a professional footballer, he still managed to fit a poster of David Beckham and Eric Cantona on his wall, hanging alongside his two Blackpool FC jerseys that he had framed after his hat tricks against Derby County and Cardiff FC in the league last season. He also had a huge Manchester United crest plastered on the back of his door, constantly reminding him of his dream club. Next to the bed rested two empty bottles of vodka, an empty case of Newcastle Ale, a condom wrapper, and a small plastic bag containing a powdery white substance adjacent to a scratched up *Star Wars* DVD with the powder aligning its rim.

The girl's head was now fully submerged under the covers as she lay on top of him gyrating back and forth below his pelvis. The grin on his face expanded in unison with each of her movements. Just as he was about to fully give into her carnal seduction, his bedroom door flew open. The girl's head quickly emerged from beneath the covers and she embarrassingly wrapped herself in the white satin sheets in an effort to keep her naked body from being exposed to Jude's teammate, Michael Vaughn, who was now standing in the doorway with a judging leer plastered across his face.

"Piss off, mate! Can't you see we're busy here? And you scared the piss out of? Um...Um...What's your name again, love?" asked Jude in his thick scouse accent, that he inherited from his Liverpudlian parents. She returned his question with a glare that would frighten a grizzly bear.

"I reckon you may want to get up. We have to be at the pitch for pregame in under an hour," barked Michael, his London accent thick, like he hadn't spent the last eleven years in Blackpool. The girl retreated from the bed enraged, putting back on her clothes with authority, no longer caring if Michael saw her naked.

"Don't worry, Michael, I'm leaving anyways!" She grabbed her pink high heels from under the bed, briefly losing her balance upon stepping on the used condom from the previous night—this made Jude laugh wholeheartedly. "You're a pig! And my name is Susanna, you dick!" she yelled, storming out.

Jude called to her from the bed as she exited.

"Ah come on, love, don't be like that! I can get you tickets to today's match… Oh well, I didn't truly fancy her anyway. She had this whole Emily Blunt double chin thing going on that didn't quite do it for me."

Michael's disparaging look morphed into dismay as he picked up the plastic bag from the floor.

"Are you serious, Jude? What is this?"

"Ah, there it is. I've been looking for that bag of flour everywhere. I was planning on making a pie later. Would you suggest rhubarb or a custard?"

"You and I both know that's rubbish! Honestly, Jude, the pints, the birds, you're twenty-five-years-old so I cannot stop you, but drugs? Who are you Tony Montana now?"

Jude, still half covered in his bed, felt a pain shoot through his head, partly caused by Michael's scolding and part by his hangover.

"Who's Tony Montana?"

"Bloody'ell, I don't know if I'm madder that you have resorted to taking drugs or that you are a grown man that hasn't seen *Scarface?* Wake up and get your shit together. You have five minutes; I'll be in the motor."

Jude stumbled to his closet and grabbed his Blackpool FC football bag. His ocean blue eyes were still bloodshot from the pharmacy's worth of illegal substances in his body and if asked, he wouldn't be able to recall what happened last night. He sluggishly tossed in his new Nike Mercury boots that had his initials engraved in the soles, a pair of shin guards, socks, his trusty hair gel and comb, and a pair of spandex shorts. He put on his tracksuit and brushed his teeth quickly before grabbing a banana and energy bar from the counter on his way out. To Michael's frustration, Jude then returned five minutes later to grab his forgotten keys and to safely lock the door, which he rarely did, since more often than not there was a party being held.

Michael lived in the same upper high rise in Blackpool as Jude, granting him the pleasure of being able to wake Jude up for practices and matches on a daily basis. They lived only fifteen minutes away from the stadium, but often found themselves rushing due to situations just like this. Michael would never question Jude's ability on the pitch. Both he and the rest of England knew Jude was one of the brightest young footballers in the country. However, it was Jude's off the field antics that catechized Michael daily. He had a bit of sympathy knowing Jude had never been the same after his parents had died when he was sixteen, two days after he had signed his contract with Blackpool. They never even had the opportunity to see him play a game as a professional. So Michael made it a point to look after him.

They listened to *Sports Talk Live* on the BBC's 606 on the way to the match. Alan Green and Robbie Savage were previewing the match, predicting a Blackpool win with Jude scoring both goals. Every time

Jude was mentioned in high regard on the program, Michael could see Jude's head expanding and beginning to spill over into his lap.

"Have I mentioned how much I admire 606's take on football? These blokes are spot on."

Michael abruptly switched off the radio.

"Jesus, Jude, can you be serious for one moment?" Jude sucked his teeth like an ill-tempered teen, turning towards the passenger side window as if no longer listening. "How are you to manage a good impression with Manchester United next season if you are out partying every night, shagging anything that moves, and now doing drugs? Seriously, Jude, you need to give that rubbish up. You are a professional athlete, and soon to be an overpaid one at that. They will do nothing but hurt your body. " Jude didn't answer and continued to sulk out the window.

Michael has been looking after Jude ever since he had signed with Blackpool nine years ago. He had noticed him on the first day of training, a small scrawny teen with a baggy kit, a rebellious innocence, and a true passion for football. Being ten years older than Jude, Michael naturally became an older brother figure to him once his parents had passed, attempting to teach him the ins and outs of both football and life. It was plain to see that Jude had a good heart; always the first one to volunteer to attend PR functions at local children's hospitals and made it a point to sign every autograph, no matter how in a hurry he was. He was just a young misguided soul that had turned to the wrong outlets to vent. And his temptation would be even greater next year on the heels of having been offered a 30-million pound contract from Manchester United for the next three seasons.

"You mustn't squander this opportunity. With a massive club comes massive responsibility. You cannot act like a child anymore. At this rate the fame, the media, the supporters, and the boardroom will eat you alive."

Jude gave an effortless rebuttal, seasoned in the art of making excuses.

"First, the blow wasn't mine. It was that bird's...What's her name?"

"Susanna—"

"Right, Sarah. And second, as long as I score goals they won't care. You watch, I will score two goals today and everyone will forget that little skirmish in the *Daily Telegraph* last week. Seriously, mate, come on, we're playing bloody Portsmouth today. I can score two goals without even playing."

"That's not the point! When you join Manchester, you will be held to a much higher standard, it's time to grow up. I can assure you that if you don't focus on and off the pitch, you won't last more than a year."

They pulled up to a red light a block away from the stadium. Jude frowned sulking with his arms crossed, shaking his head in disagreement. Michael aimed to break the tension.

"Come on, mate, I'm just trying to help." Jude remained stubbornly silent. "I know what will cheer you up."

"You'd better not, mate!" demanded Jude. Michael started to sing a key out of tune.

"*Hey Jude, don't let me down…*"

Jude cut him off abruptly, "Bloody'ell, I swear to God!"

"*Take a sad song and make it better.*" He stared at Michael tickled, reluctantly breaking into laughter at his foolishness.

"You are such a twat you know that? You know I hate that bloody song. And don't quit your day job either, because you sing like a mauled animal."

"Shows how much you know, animals can't sing."

"Me point exactly."

"Well you better laugh it up now. Because next week when you join the Reds the real work will begin, and trust me, mate, it isn't going to be easy."

"Will you stop worrying so much; you're like a daft mum. There's a reason I was nominated as the young player of the year. I'm going to run circles around those blokes."

Michael gave him an off base smirk.

"If you say so, but don't' say I didn't warn you."

Jude turned his attention again out the window and imagined how he would out play the Manchester players next week.

"Don't worry, I won't. But I will say I told you so. Because I'm going to dominate, you watch…you just watch."

Blackpool went on to win one nil with Jude scoring the game's only goal from a free kick seventeen meters out in the eighty-seventh minute. When he scored, the cameras flashed, illuminating his ocean blue eyes sparkling in the afternoon's glow. He tore his shirt off over his head, ruffling his precisely gelled and groomed dirty blond hair that always took him at least forty-five minutes to perfectly mold into place. He received a yellow card, but any excuse he had to show off his tightly developed six-pack abs, or the plethora of tattoos that covered the majority of both arms and his back, much like is hero David Beckham, he took willingly. He just got the sleeve done on his right arm two months ago; it was a picture of several angels floating towards the sky, meeting at the top of his shoulder, the Virgin Mary on a cloud. Above Mary's head was a banner with his parents' names *Benjamin* and *Margaret*. The other tattoos were pictures that he had seen hanging from the walls of the parlor or a popular saying like Carpe Diem, that was on the inside of his left arm. Though he had quite a number of tattoos, besides his right arm the remainder of his body was visible and chiseled. Making many female supporters unhealthily obsessed with his cut vanilla skin and statuesque features. He also secured further female admiration, by donning the rule of never wearing a shirt during his famous parties.

Once the match ended, the fans gave Jude a standing ovation, fully aware it would be the last he would play with the club. Jude trotted around the pitch applauding the supporters in appreciation and becoming slightly choked up in the process. As much as he hid, he had grown quite fond of Blackpool over the nine years he had played there, and not just because he threw some of the most legendary parties the town has ever seen. The club, along with Michael, had taken a chance welcoming an emaciated kid from Blackpool and without them taking that chance he would have never had the opportunity to sign with Manchester United. At the press conference following the match, Jude thanked all the supporters, teammates, and management for allowing him the opportunity to play for the club. He held nothing back, naming everyone all the way down to the custodians and lads that fetched the balls on the touchlines. Jude had the unique trait of making everyone feel important, no matter their status. During the rare moments of the day when he wasn't drunk, he welcomed everyone and often made whomever he was speaking with feel as if they were the celebrity and not him. He had become a fan favorite after giving away his 2011 Mercedes Benz last year to some random guy that attended one of his parties. When the gentleman inquired what he did to deserve such a gift, all Jude said was, "Nothing, mate. You're just guest two-hundred tonight," and then he guzzled the Dom Perignon in his hand and two hours later gave away his flat screen television to the three-hundredth guest.

The string of celebratory questions came to a halt when a reporter from *The Guardian* felt his journalistic duty take over.

"Jude, how do you plan on justifying the photos of you and those rather ambitious women from the *Telegraph* last week to your new employer?"

Jude dallied in a response, he was honestly too drunk to remember that night let alone articulate a befitting response to the ardent journalist.

"I don't know, Jerry. I reckon United and I will cross that bridge when I show up for training next week. But I can tell you this; they probably won't take it nearly as bad as your misses. I told her those girls meant nothing to me. Tell her I'll be home tonight to make it up to her."

Pseudo laughter filled the room and the journalist sat back down in shame, like a kid being embarrassed on the playground. Notwithstanding the question's intent, it was nevertheless a good question, and got Jude thinking. He had not even considered what his new boss, Sir Alex Ferguson, would say, but he suspected it wasn't going to be, '*Well done handling four prostitutes at once.*'

III

Emily & Jude: The Arrival

Emily arrived at the airport filled with nerves and a youthful exuberance. She could hardly believe she was moments away from being off to England. It was only five days ago when her friends had surprised her with the tickets that left her shell-shocked. She had written them all robust thank you cards before they left to their prospective places for the summer, and was elated at the thought of having an adventure and taking some time for herself. But as elated as she was, the thought of leaving the country still concerned her. She had been to only three states in her life, Connecticut to visit her grandmother, Massachusetts where she went to school, and, once when she was eleven, her grandmother took her to New York to see the *Nutcracker* at the Radio City Music Hall. Much like any inspired young person she had always wanted to travel, but between her four years at Yale, medical school, and when she would complete her residency, she would have little opportunity to do so.

An attendant at the gate came over the speakers, "At this time we will now begin boarding all first class and club member passengers for flight 729 to Manchester, England." When the attendant finally called for coach passengers, she grabbed her knapsack stuffed with two medical books *The Advanced Cardiovascular Life* and *Discussions of the Human Anatomy*, a medical textbook for her advanced surgery class, her laptop computer, and a DVD of season three of her favorite television show *House*, and boarded the plane. She claustrophobically walked down the crowded aisle, seeking the seat number on her ticket, *34F*, apologizing as her bag brushed up against passengers' foreheads and knees, and made her way to her window seat at the back of the plane.

She spent the first three hours of the flight rereading her textbook. It was the tenth time she had read it in its entirety; at this point having a better grasp on the material than her professor. She finished just in time for the in-flight meal. The perky flight attendant smiled after every word and gave Emily the choice of chicken parmesan or salmon with vegetables. She kindly chose the salmon but refused the in-flight movie, which was some new horribly generic Katherine Heigl romantic comedy. Instead she popped on her iPod headphones and listened to some seminar lectures on blood cell counts. After her meal, she managed to get about an hour of sleep off and on due to the midflight turbulence. Once she realized that the plane was not going to let her sleep, she took out one of her medical books, *Discussions of the Human Anatomy,* and proceeded to read it for the remainder of the flight.

When the plane's wheels skidded across the Manchester pavement the reality of actually being in England struck her with forthwith consternation. Just hours ago, she had never been on an airplane, had never taken a vacation, and now all of the sudden she was in a foreign country. She would have pinched herself to make sure she wasn't dreaming, but was afraid it would leave a mark, on account that she bruised so easily. She made her way to the baggage claim, waiting several minutes before the flamboyant pink Juicy Couture luggage bag that Melissa had lent her came tumbling down. She thought, '*If I didn't stick out like a tourist before, I certainly do now.*' She waited outside the terminal for Melissa's aunt, taking in the little scenery she could see. It was a sunny summer day, the temperature settled at a warm eighty-two degrees and the sky clear and blue as far as the eye could see. She noticed the peculiar way the cars were driving on the opposite side of the road and the police walking by in tiny helmets complete with chin straps just like at the Royal Wedding. After waiting nearly half an hour, her legs were becoming increasingly tired, when a 2004 green Mercedes Benz station wagon pulled up in front of her. The young woman in the driver's seat rolled down her window,

"Are you Emily?" the woman's British accent was thick, reminding Emily that people here had one.

"Yes." She remained still, looking into the car confused as if not certain what the woman meant by her question.

"Well, come on then, get in. We don't want you catching a tan on your first day in the English sun. You're as pale as a ghost." Emily's second grade teacher would be so disappointed, because losing all control over her body she placed her bags in the back seat and sat up front with the stranger, completely disregarding her teacher's infamous words, 'stranger danger.'

They got on the M56 heading towards the inn.

"Pardon my manners; I'm Veronica Mae, Melissa's cousin. My mum wanted to pick you up herself, but the inn became rather busy this morning." Veronica resembled one of the girls from Melissa's celebrity gossip magazines. She had long blonde hair and enchanting green eyes. She was dressed in a lovely pink and white sundress with matching sandals.

"That's okay; I figured you weren't a serial killer. I'm Emily Robertson."

Veronica took one hand off the steering wheel and shook Emily's.

"A pleasure. And again you must forgive my tardiness, United won the treble last week and the parade was today. I simply couldn't have missed that."

Emily responded with a perplexed look on her face.

"Treble? I did some research on Google before I left, United is the soccer team right? But I didn't read anything about a *treble*." Veronica laughed hysterically almost swerving the car into the opposing lane.

"Yes, United is our 'FOOTBALL' team. What is it with you yanks and the word soccer? You do realize that you play 'FOOTBALL' with your feet? But the treble is when you win all three major trophies, the Champions League, the domestic league, and the F.A. Cup."

Emily shyly replied, "Sorry, I'll make a mental note 'Football' not 'soccer.'"

Veronica smiled at Emily's shame.

"It's quite all right. Just don't let the lads at the inn hear you call it that, they will be taking the piss for a fortnight."

"Taking the piss?"

"It means they will be making fun of you more or less. I know, it does sound rather raunchy, but its harmless trust me. Don't worry I will be sure to schedule you and I private translation studies every night. You will be a proper Brit in no time at-tall."

"So do you and your mom live at the inn?"

"We do, but it's more of a bed and breakfast than a Radisson if that's what you're thinking. It's a fairly well off living situation. Everyone has their own room, I've had mine since I was a little girl; I still have the pink wallpaper to prove it."

"Well, that's great. You and your mom must really be close, because none of my friends would be caught dead still living at home."

"Yeah my mum is alright, she's a mum you know. Truth is I rather enjoy staying there. My babe from university wanted me to get a flat with her in London last year, but I turned her down. I get three free meals a day, no rent, and no bills, as far as I'm concerned I will be living here until I land a footballer to buy me a house as big as the inn."

"So what do you do for work? You must be saving a bundle not having any expenses."

Veronica laughed sarcastically.

"Me? Saving a bundle? Ha, don't let my mum hear you say that. I just work around the inn currently, so between the nights out in Manchester and my taste for high fashion I have little to nothing saved up. I studied marketing at university, but then I realized I'm pretty, so I thought why work when I could just marry a rich bloke?" Emily couldn't fathom the thought of planning her life around some boy coming to rescue her with money. The idea alone made her squirm.

"What about you? Are you a doctor like Melissa?"

"Well, we're not doctors yet, but we are studying to become one."

"Brilliant, you're like proper smart then! I used to study hard as well, but then I noticed blokes don't want birds with brains. They fancy the type like Kim Kardashian or Keira Knightley." Emily had no problem seeing the family resemblance; Melissa and Veronica were clearly cut from the same cloth and, knowing them, that cloth was probably *Dolce and Gabbana.*

Twenty minutes later Emily and Veronica arrived at the inn. During the remainder of the ride they discussed the flight and Veronica enthusiastically described the Manchester nightlife. The inn was located a few miles outside of Manchester in a quiet country town in North West England. Veronica turned off the main road onto a narrow gravel strip that was half a mile long. Emily stared out the window astounded at what lied in front of her. The large oak trees shaded the car from the sun, slowly passing them off to one another as they guided them down the gravel drive. The grass was exceptionally green as if painted with watercolors, each blade leaping from the ground in resplendent mystique. The long gravel path led to a circular cobblestone driveway in front of a large white Victorian home. The banks of the circle were lined with vibrant daffodils and vivacious long stem red roses. Off to the side of the property, a petite parking lot held space for about twenty-five cars. A faded vintage sign with antique lettering hung below the front door reading, 'The Queen's Inn at Manchester'.

Emily, accompanied by Veronica, who carried her bags, entered the house. To Emily, the inside was superior even to the outside. A huge center hall provided a dramatic entrance, with two exquisite flowing staircases that wrapped around the room like golden snakes, leading to the second floor balcony. As Emily followed her deeper into the main hall, they passed a black grand piano that blended in perfectly with the glossy white and black marble floors. They continued on pass the dining room that was inhabited by a long luxurious walnut table, to the Lilliputian concierge desk, where a charming blonde hair woman in her late fifties, dressed in a blue dress shirt and matching blazer, stood smiling, prepared to make their acquaintance.

"Well, have a look at you! She is lovely isn't she, Veronica? Just like the photos Melissa showed us. I'm Linda Mae, Melissa's aunt and this crazy girl's mother. We are so glad you are here." Linda, much like her daughter, had a heavy London accent. She leaned in giving Emily a hug.

"Emily Robertson. It's a pleasure to meet you, Mrs. Mae. This house is beautiful; it's like something out of a fairytale."

"Thank you! It actually served as one of Queen Victoria's summer homes, or at least that's what we tell our guests. It's been in our family for generations. My mum ran it before me. And please, call me Linda. That *Mrs.* stuff is for old people and I am what you would call experienced." Emily could already tell that she was going to get along fine with Linda. She reminded her very much of her grandmother, sweet and elegant.

"You must be exhausted from your journey; Veronica shall show you to your room. Dinner is in an hour and will be located in the dining room, which is right down there off to your left. And please do not hesitate to phone the front desk if you should need anything at-tall."

"I will certainly do that. And thank you again for having me. All of this is truly amazing."

Linda gave her another hug this time holding on tighter.

"It is our pleasure, deary."

Emily's room, much like everything else to do with the house, was vintage, quiet, and quaint. She immediately noticed the brown mahogany antique desk in the corner, and imagined Jane Austen sitting there writing *Pride and Prejudice*. The room had no television and overlooked the luscious backyard garden. There was a couple sitting hand in hand on one of the white stone benches overlooking the rose bushes, while the groundskeeper pruned some azaleas behind them next to the walking path. The majority of the room was taken up by the king-sized, regal bed and the overly sufficient rustic wardrobe by the bedroom mirror. She unpacked her clothes and books before heading down the hall to the bathroom to freshen up before dinner.

At supper, Linda introduced Emily to the other guests before joining her husband, Ron, and Veronica at the table. The couple that was sat in the garden an hour prior was a young French couple on their honeymoon. They didn't speak English well, but nonetheless were endlessly equipped with matching smiles for the length of their stay, as young romance seemed to warrant. The other guests were made up of an old skinny Irishman and his grey dog who were relieving themselves from their homeland after the recent loss of his wife, an American family from Chicago who had a bizarre fixation on visiting the platform in King's Cross from the *Harry Potter* movies, and several other American families that were on summer vacation. On top of Emily constantly firing compliments at Linda in regards to the house and the landscaping, they discussed the royal family, medical school, and Ron's job as an insurance broker for a small firm in Blackburn. Ron Mae was a proud man with enough self-assurance for both his charming wife and tenacious daughter. Between Linda discussing the inn's books with him over the freshly served tilapia, and Veronica expressing her need to borrow his credit card for a new dress, his spirits remained playful and he would just smile in-between bites of tilapia and say,

"You women are going to be the death of me. But I love you both."

A charming family, anyone could see, and they were the most hospitable of host to make Emily feel as much at home as one could feel in a foreign country.

Emily was exhausted from her travels, so she returned to her room and went to bed. She was so relieved when her head finally hit the pillow. It took everything she had to stay awake during Veronica's speech at dinner, about why Cristiano Ronaldo is the hottest guy in the world; unsurprisingly it came down to him being worth over 90 million pounds. The moon's smile crept in through the window eclipsing her body. Normally she would have drawn the drapes, but the view overlooking the moonlit garden was so peaceful and comforting that she decided to bask in it. Everything about the day gave her hope that this was going to be a great summer.

The refreshing night's breeze beat up against Jude's body as he jogged through empty downtown Manchester. With his headphones blaring rock tunes, he took the time to notice the street sign and realized that he had been running for over seven miles. He couldn't quite put a finger on why he was running. Was it because he was nervous to join a new team tomorrow? Or the opposite, he was excited? His pride had him believe the excited option, but his head was fully aware of his heart's betrayal. As he jogged back to his new apartment in Moss side, thoughts of his childhood ran through his head. Reminiscing on the times his father would push him during training, encouraging him to do one more lap and repeat, 'United wants players that are fit.' He recalled all the hard work that had gotten him to this point in his career, the late hours on the training ground with Michael, where they worked on free kicks until he couldn't stand, the mornings spent running five miles before training sessions when he was with the Blackpool under 21s, and the first time he scored a hat trick against the Tottenham reserves. But most of all he thought of failure, what if he didn't live up to everyone's expectations? In theory everything seemed perfect; he finally reached his dream club and was getting paid millions of pounds to do what he loved, but that's what scared him the most.

He reached his apartment at 2:15 a.m., jumping into the shower for one last effort to clear his head. The place was bare with boxes scattered everywhere, still waiting to be unpacked. He slurped down a noodle of low mien out of the half eaten Chinese container on the kitchen counter, following it up with a swig from the open beer bottle. A proper midnight snack for any athlete, he was sure. By 3 a.m. he could no longer stay awake. He set the alarm clock on both his mobile and digital ticker, being exceptionally cautious, knowing Michael wouldn't be there to wake him up. Before falling asleep, he looked up to his mother and father asking them to watch over him on the pitch tomorrow.

IV

Emily & Jude: Second Impressions

E mily felt she put more effort than usual into getting dressed, coming downstairs to the dining room in a pair of worn down grey sweatpants and a yellow Yale t-shirt. So it surprised her immensely when Veronica joined them at the breakfast table looking as if she were attending the Academy Awards. She was wearing a creamy white dress with her hair curled to perfection, topped off with a tinny yellow daisy accenting her vibrant golden hair.

"Good morning, Darling," said Linda.

Veronica replied with an affectionate wave, "Good morning everyone."

The other guests at the table caught themselves admiring Veronica in-between their biscuits and eggs. Emily let her curiosity spill out.

"Wow, you look nice. Do you have a date this morning?"

"Something like that. I'm going into town to watch United's first training session."

"Veronica has this impractical fantasy that if she clicks her red pumps three times then a player from the pitch will magically appear in her arms. It's all rather daft if you ask me."

"*Ha-ha...*" replied Veronica in fake laughter, "very funny, mum. But Maureen Francis landed a player from Tottenham's training session last week, so if it can happen to her then it can very well happen to me."

"Darling you are really not doing yourself any favours. Audrey Francis, much in resemblance to her mother Annemarie Francis, is what you would call, a whore."

"Mum!" Veronica joined in-laughter with the rest of the table.

"What? Is it not true? She's been through more husbands than we have guests."

"Mum, I can't even talk to you right now, you're ridiculous. Emily, do you fancy going—if for no other reason than to get away from this crazy lot? I could take you down to the shops and we could do a little sightseeing as well."

"Well I'm not really into socce…I mean football, but when in Rome, right?"

Veronica replied joyfully, clapping her hands as if discovering a new idea:

"Brilliant! We are going to have so much fun."

"Veronica, try not to corrupt this lovely girl's mind with your never-ending search for a shallow man."

"I'm still not listening to you, mum, so I haven't heard a word you've said. But if I had, I would say I don't look for shallow men at-tall, but rather mature gorgeous ones."

Emily interrupted the family feud, "What time are we leaving?"

"In about an hour, so you still have time to change." Emily looked down analyzing her attire, thinking there was nothing wrong with it.

"You surely weren't planning on wearing that today were you?"

Emily thought 'Yes, what's wrong with this?' but replied: "Of course not, this is just some old stuff that I slept in last night. I was planning on changing after breakfast anyway."

Emily was not entirely sure what to expect. Part of her wondered if it would be like the movies with a bunch of drunken guys chanting and beating the snot out of one another, or just an assortment of kids cheering on their favorite heroes. It took only seconds upon arrival for her to notice it was the latter. There were several drunk guys shout-ing at the players for mistakes they had made last season, fathers with their kids scattered through the crowd wearing little kits with the name Rooney or Macavoy on the back, but all of them were few in comparison to the barrage of screaming women like Veronica, all dressed to impress, and screaming at the top of their lungs as the players warmed up. Emily thought, '*this is madness.*'

Jude has never witnessed a crowd this big for training. He surveyed the crowd while running his warm-up laps, spotting a few of his number nine kits, arrogantly admitting to himself that his name never looked better on a shirt. But in addition to the wow factor of seeing his name on a Manchester United kit, he was in paradise among all the women. There were short ones, skinny ones, fat ones, tall ones, blonde ones, red haired ones, emo green haired ones, and even one wearing a Liverpool shirt. Jude tugged at his teammate and new hallmate, Steven Frye's, shirt, who was also a new signing from the youth academy at Everton.

"Oi, look at that bird in the Liverpool kit. I reckon she won't last long when people realise she's wearing the wrong red."

Steven trotted beside him looking up at the woman.

"She must be mental. However, I will say I would still shag her."

Jude smirked in agreement.

"Yeah, she is quite fit. I wouldn't mind having a go meself. This is bloody mad! All these birds, it feels like a buffet."

Jude continued jogging, finding himself a tad winded, '*maybe I had one too many fags last night, I need me second wind,*' he thought.

"You alright, mate? It's only warm ups, you can't be tired yet."

Jude tried to play off Steven's inquiry as if it were all part of his plan.

"I'm alright, just had a long night is all. A few fit birds kept me up if you know what I mean?" They jogged a few more feet, "and since when does a football warm-up require running a bloody marathon?"

"Since today—you're in the big leagues now, mate. Welcome to United..." yelled Steven as he sprinted off ahead of Jude.

Emily turned to Veronica, who was practically hanging over the rail shouting down at the players on the pitch, pleading for someone to look her way.

"How can you hear yourself think with all these girls shouting?"

"*What?*" Veronica shouted. Emily leaned in closer, yelling with all her might.

"I SAID, HOW CAN YOU STAND ALL THESE GIRLS SHOUTING? I FEEL LIKE WE'RE AT A JUSTIN BEIBER CONCERT!"

Veronica's eyes were still transfixed on the pitch and all the eye candy.

"I know! All the players are so gorgeous. Look," she shouted, not hearing a word Emily just said, "Especially that new one over there, Macavoy, his body is delicious." Veronica howled as Jude placed a perfect volley past the keeper in one of their shooting drills. Emily thought to herself, '*why do I even bother?*'

Midway through the training session, the coaches split the players into two nine apiece sides for a training match. Jude was placed on the side heavy with new signings and second team players. About ten minutes into the match Emily rose from her seat.

"Hey, Veronica, as much as I enjoy listening to girls scream for hours on end, I think I need a little break."

Veronica laughed.

"I understand. I forgot you yanks are used to boring sports like baseball or whatever. There's a café down the road if you want to walk there? They should only be about thirty minutes longer."

"That sounds fine. I will meet you back here in a half hour."

"Alright, cheers!"

Just as Emily began walking away from the pitch, the entire crowd stood in awe as Jude went on a long run. He stripped the ball from the left-winger Nani and began storming down the left flank, whizzing past one, two, and then three defenders. Cutting inside onto his right foot and tapping the ball around the right back in stylish fashion, focused on nothing but scoring. He made his way to the final defender performing a series of stepovers, then placing his body weight on his left ankle before exploding past the centre back on his right, deceiving the defender and cracking a shot with his right foot into the upper ninety. As the ball flew past the keeper and into the back of the net the crowd cheered and the manager blew his whistle profusely. Sir Alex was standing in the middle of the pitch with his blood pressure rising and the whiteness of his eyes morphing over to enraged.

"Come here, son." Jude a bit confused began walking over.

"NOW!" He turned his walk into a sprint.

"Yeah boss?" he said mildly winded attempting to quickly catch his breath.

"How many players are on your team, son?"

"Uhm...nine?"

"Precisely, so when there are two of them open ahead of you pass the bloody ball, yeah!"

"But sir, I score..."

Sir Alex didn't let him finish: "You scored? Perhaps you haven't noticed, but we have been scoring goals, the correct way, long before you arrived. The name on the front of the shirt is more important than the name on the back. So pass the bloody ball to your teammates when they're open!"

Jude turned his head in discuss.

"Aye, sir," he said in a maddened tone.

"Son, come back here."

"I said *aye*, sir."

"I heard what you said, go get yourself a shower."

"What?" Jude's bewilderment at the situation dissolved into unmitigated anger.

"You will learn quickly how we do things around here. Not only do we pass to our teammates, we also show respect."

Jude trampled into the locker room, kicking a chair in the corner, screaming curse words, and slamming his kit in his locker in tantrum.

He didn't even bother taking a shower; at this point all he wanted to do was return to his flat and finish the case of beer in his refrigerator. He put on his tracksuit and placed the hood over his head so no one could recognize him. He was in no mood to sign autographs or speak to the press.

Emily was enjoying her afternoon stroll to the café. People were outside jogging with their dogs and sitting under large dining umbrellas having early lunches. Upon reaching the doors of the café she realized that she had left her pocketbook back in Veronica's car. She had been so anxious to get out of there that she completely forgot to grab it. Not minding, because anything to kill time was welcomed, she headed back towards the training ground. She took out her mobile thinking it would be a good time to update Melissa on her first football experience. Her head was firmly planted in her mobile's screen when a sharp pain rushed from her hand to her chest, sending her mobile flying through the air, and placing her on the edge of misplacing her wind.

"Bloody'ell, watch where you're going!"

Emily lay on the ground squinting up at the hooded figure, patting the concrete blindly in search of her spectacles.

"I am so sorry! I was just looking down at my phone for a second and…I'm just so clumsy."

Emily continued rambling apologetically, but Jude didn't hear a word she said. He stood overlooking the most blind and beautiful girl that he'd ever seen. Her smile reminded him of all that was beautiful in the world, and as he gazed upon the corky expression on her face as she frantically searched for her spectacles, he couldn't help but feel a connection, as if he had loved her in lifetimes before. He handed her the spectacles before offering his hand to help her up.

"No… me apologies, I should have been more conscious of where I was walking. It's sort of been one of those days you know, when you're mind is elsewhere. Are you alright?"

Emily brushed off her jeans and shirt, placing on her spectacles and bringing the hooded figure into full focus.

"I'm fine thank you. You wouldn't have happened to have found my cell phone too would you?"

"Ah, yes. Here it is. It's a brilliant cell phone as well might I add. I too fancy Verizon…really brilliant coverage…really brilliant." He had no idea what he was going on about, 'really brilliant coverage,' was that seriously the best he could come up with? I mean you would think he had never spoken to a girl before. She awkwardly shook her head in agreement, eagerly awaiting the end of this encounter.

"That's nice. Well, again I'm sorry for bumping into you."

"Don't be, it's not every day a bloke bumps into such a lovely woman." She turned to walk away, but Jude pursued her persisting nervously.

"I'm not saying I bump into people every day, I'm actually quite a competent walker, I mean competent enough to chew gum at the same time. I'm just saying if I did have to bump into someone I would prefer it be someone like you as opposed to some fat bloke with a hair piece…" Jude laughed, 'Christ,' he thought, he had become one of those people who laugh at their own horrible jokes, everything that was coming from his mouth seemed to have the word pathetic written all over it.

"…I'm sorry, I'm not usually like this, usually I'm rather good at this bit, but that's beyond the point. How, uh…Do you, um…Look, what I'm trying to say is, can I have your name and number?"

She found his mumbling nerves a bit charming and was intrigued to the point to stop walking.

"I don't think so, I don't even know you."

"Oh how silly of me, I forgot I even had this bloody thing on." He removed his hood in dramatic fashion, flipping his hair flamboyantly, "Well?"

She went from collected to flustered all within a glimpse of him. His dirty blonde hair was just long enough to run fingers through, and teamed with his faultless cheekbones and blue eyes, she almost collapsed from the butterflies. As if his handsomeness weren't enough, she could see his toned chest muscles through his jacket, wanting nothing more than to reach a finger over and touch one.

"Well, what?"

"You mean you honestly don't know who I am?"

"No, I can't say that I do. Sorry."

"Oh the accent, right. You're a yank."

"I beg your pardon!"

He put up both hands in defense.

"I'm sorry, you are *American*. Well, how can I put this? I'm kind of a big deal. I play for a little club you may have heard of, Manchester United, I'm practically the star of the team."

They stood face to face in an eerie silence, Jude waiting for her to fall to her knees and praise his social status.

"That's nice. Well if you'd excuse me..." She began walking away again; he scurried to catch up to her, softly touching her arm to slow her down.

"Alright, alright...hold on a second, let's start over yeah? My name is Jude Macavoy, sorry for almost killing you earlier." He smiled and she couldn't help but blush.

"It's okay, I'm fine. And I'm Emily Robertson." He shook her hand while softly licking his lips and the butterflies began rushing back to her stomach.

"Well it's a pleasure to make your acquaintance, Emily. Listen, me flat's not too far from here, do you fancy accompanying me? I have a massive bed and any drink you could imagine."

She frowned and let out a huge sigh of frustration as her tone took form of someone irritated and unimpressed.

"Jesus! No, I would not. Now excuse me I have to get back to my friend." She rushed off at an angry brisk pace, never looking back.

"Was it something I said?" She had put distance between them now. "...Well, good talk, I'll see you around then, yeah!"

Emily rolled her eyes.

"I hope not," she called back to him.

As Emily flipped through the pages of her *Discussions of the Human Anatomy* book on her desk, she found her mind wondering off to her earlier encounter with Jude. She overlooked the same page ten times lost in thought, *'The nerve of that guy, thinking I would fall all over him because he's some big shot athlete. Who does he think he is?'* However, despite her appetent protest she could not deny how handsome he was. The way his soft blue eyes captivated hers and how he majestically licked his soft lips had the hairs on her neck rising in bliss. Only if she could put the brain of a competent human being in his head, then she may have reconsidered giving him her number. But it didn't take her graduating medical school to know this idea was implausible. Her thoughts were broken when Linda walked into the room taking a seat on the edge of the bed diagonally across from the desk.

"So? How was your first day in Manchester? Did you enjoy the shops and the football?"

"It was interesting. I liked the soccer, but I think I will stick to the Red Sox; I wasn't too sure what was going on. But the shops were great! A little too pricey for me, but it made for some fantastic window shopping."

Linda laughed, "That is Veronica—she enjoys the finer things in life to say the least. I keep telling that girl, 'you are not a film star, so stop trying to spend as such.' But does she listen? *No.*"

"She did insist I let her buy me a dress."

"You don't say. Under what stipulation provoked such a kind gesture?"

"I had to agree to go out with her tonight to some nightclub, and I also have to let her wear it out first. I believe she used the words *test drive.*"

Linda's disappointing headshake and half smile read of one of amazement and calamity.

"I swear, that girl. If it makes you feel any better all she will do is sit at the bar and let lads buy her drinks all evening. She would not be caught dead on the dance floor. So it shouldn't be sweaty when she finally does give it to you."

Emily shared a smile with Linda.

"Well that's good to know."

Jude was hunched back on his long Italian leather sofa playing a video game of *FIFA Soccer* on his seventy-inch flat screen television. He was getting annihilated five nil and contemplated tossing his game controller across the room in frustration after the fifth goal went in. This was the precise reason he steered clear of playing video games when he had other pressing matters on his mind. It was all he could do to not think about Emily. There was just something different about her that piqued his interest to the max. *'What a girl. What a beautiful sweet girl,'* he thought to himself. She didn't care about what club he played for or how much money he seemed to have, she didn't even fall for the, 'me flat's down the street' line, which worked every time. For heaven's sakes, he shagged a nun from the 37th convent in Bristol using that line. And the spectacles, in a weird sexy teacher way they made her more attractive. As the sixth goal went in he lost all encumbrance for the video game, instead focusing his efforts into dreaming up another meeting with Emily, where this time he would tell her how beautiful she was and ask her out properly instead of horribly trying to impress her with things she didn't care about.

His thoughts were broken up by a soft knock at his front door.

"Come in!" Jude announced from the sofa, too drunk and apathetic to attend to the door. Steven walked in casually, shutting the door behind him.

"You little wanker! Have you been here all day sulking since the gaffer kicked you out?"

"No, I took a thirty minute break to eat. Wait...and another five minutes to have a piss."

"Cheer up, mate, you'll do better tomorrow. It was a brilliant run after all; you just have to remember to pass next time."

Jude stayed firmly locked on the video game, not breaking his attention for any of Steven's words. He took a final sip from the current beer he was drinking and placed it beside the six other empty bottles on the dining room table.

"Oi, I know what will cheer you up so you're not sitting here looking like some emo bloke ready to cut himself. Two words, 'Top Ten!' Come on, mate; let's go get some pints and some birds. You know you want to."

He thought about Steven's proposition for only a second, *'yeah, I should go out. There's no use in crying over spoiled milk. And I'll find a well fit bird to take me mind off Emily.'*

"Alright mate, just give me a tick to get ready."

Steven pumped his fist in celebration.

"Yes! And Christ, man, six nil? Who taught you how to play *FIFA*, you're bloody rubbish," said Steven, who was now fiddling with Jude's paused game.

"I'm Chelsea, I'm *winning* six nil. And stop touching shit."

"Really? That's why it says player one is controlling Liverpool. You're rubbish, just admit it."

Jude yelled from his bedroom while changing clothes: "You're lucky we have to leave; otherwise I would beat you six nil."

"In your dreams, mate. Just hurry up and get dressed I'm ready to start drinking."

Emily and Veronica were latched to one another in the middle of the *Top Ten* dance floor. She kept repeating Melissa's words in her head hoping they would give her strength, 'Have fun, take some time to yourself, try not to think about school.' She was making a valiant effort to enjoy the night, but she just did not care for nightclubs. In her mind they were just far too crowded and left her surrounded by obnoxious drunk people. On the other hand, watching Veronica in the club was like watching a fierce lion preparing to tackle a gazelle. The only thing missing was an intense narration from Morgan Freeman or Steve Irwin. The way Veronica scoured the premises for single, rich men, was nothing less than comical.

"I love this song!...*And the bass keeps runnin, runnin, and runnin, runnin,* WOHA, THE BLACK EYED PEAS!"

Emily could see the look in Veronica's eyes; it was the same look Melissa got right before she would make a fool of herself on the dance floor. So much for not sweating up her dress, she thought.

"Hey, I think I'm going to get a drink," she said. "Do you want anything?"

Veronica was still lost in the song and her off beat drunken dance moves.

"No, thanks—I'm still working on this one! *WOHA! LET'S GET IT STARTED IN HERE!*"

Emily slipped off to the bar and spent the next fifteen minutes attempting to get the bartender's attention. A small town, shy, and quiet girl didn't mix with an overpopulated, dark, and musty club, she noted.

"Excuse me? Hey...Excuse me?" Her pleas were to no success as the bartender constantly walked passed her accepting money and shouting out drink orders like some punk rock auctioneer. She felt an affable tap on her shoulder, getting her attention.

"Perhaps I can be of some assistance." She looked up at Jude's six-foot frame, distraught and surprisingly excited.

"Oi, mate! Couple of drinks here! What would you like?" he asked, turning from the bartender back to Emily.

"Oh you really don't have to..." He gave her a look as if she didn't have a say in the matter.

"A ginger ale is fine," she said timidly.

"Are you serious?" She shot him an honest but intense look and he could hear her intentions over the blaring music. "Bloody'ell, you're not joking are you? Alright then, one ginger ale coming up. Oi, a pint and a ginger, mate!"

He handed her the glass of ginger ale and tenderly gazed into her soft eyes. His face oozed confidence with an abstruse faculty of handsomeness. And even though it was too dark to see, he could tell she was blushing.

"Thank you, how much do I owe you?" she asked, digging through her wallet. She pulled out a crinkled five-dollar bill. "I'm afraid I only have American money though..."

"Don't worry about it, love. Consider it an apology for how I acted earlier to-day."

"Yeah, you were kind of a dick." She laughed and then quickly caught herself, "Oops, I'm so sorry I can't believe I just said that. That was so mean."

"Don't be, I very much deserved it. Would you mind if we start over again, one more time?"

Ignoring her head's better judgment, she decided to side with her heart.

"Okay, but this is the last time. After three strikes you're out." Jude placed his pint on the bar and stood up straight, brushing off his shirt and straightening his collar.

"I'm not entirely sure I get your reference, but either way I will be sure to do it right this time. Well, as we already established, me name is, Jude Macavoy and I have to say, I think you are the most beautiful woman that I have ever seen and I would love the opportunity to get to know you better." If Emily's face was any redder she would be able to stop ongoing traffic.

"Thank you and that was much better than your previous attempt. As you already know I'm Emily and I do not go home with strange men—even rich ones."

"Well, how about a walk with a strange, rich man? I promise my intentions are pure, I just want a chance to talk without having to shout."

She smiled before taking his hand, "I'd like that."

They made a detour to the dance floor to inform Veronica that she was leaving. When she saw who Emily was leaving with her jaw plunged to the floor bewildered beyond comprehension. Unable to move or form coherent words, Veronica stood in the middle of the dance floor speechless. Emily nonchalantly played off her date and acted as if Veronica was not in the middle of some sort of mental break down.

"Okay, well don't wait up. I'll find a way back to the inn." They walked pass Veronica on their way to the main entrance and she still hadn't moved, her jaw now permanently planted on the floor like an anchor. Jude placed his hand on Veronica's face placing her jaw back in place.

"Cheers, love. You wouldn't want anyone to come by and slip something into it."

Outside, the hot summer day had transformed into a cool summer night. They walked several blocks into the downtown Manchester streets, neither talking, and both filled with nerves and questions. The summer wind made for great walking ambiance, surrounding them with a sense of charm and wonder. Jude took off his Polo blazer and placed it around Emily's shoulders as the wind began to whisper.

"So not that I'm not a fan of awkward silence, but someone needs to break the ice."

"Agreed, but I must forewarn you that I'm not very good at these things," replied Emily softly.

"No worries, I'll start. So what brings you to England?"

"I'm on vacation. My friends concocted a plot to get me away for the summer. They think I need to relax and have more fun."

"Well, do you?"

"I guess so, but after factoring in school there's not much time for fun."

"Then you've chosen the right bloke because fun is me middle name. Well, not really, it's actually Joseph, but trust me I'm proper fun."

"We'll see," she replied playfully, giving him a pleasant smile.

"So you go to university, where about?"

"Yale medical, I just finished my second year."

"Bloody'ell, you're a doctor? That's quite impressive."

"I'm not one yet, but it has been a dream of mine since I was a little girl."

Jude looked upon her as if witnessing the next big thing. Her eyes occasionally found themselves staring at her feet as they walked; embarrassed from his attention. She had never experienced a guy that kept his eyes on her as much as he did, every time she spoke his eyes found a way to wander into hers.

"I reckon you are going to be a brilliant doctor."

"Oh—and how do you know that?"

"You see, I had a broken heart before I met you and now I'm magically cured." They both began abundantly laughing.

"I do apologize. That was a bloody dreadful line. I don't know what it is but I seem to only possess the words that make me sound like a complete idiot whenever you are around."

She looked down at her shoes again, attempting to hide her blush. As the street light reflected off her spectacles and onto her soft heavenly smile, his thoughts were consumed with how beautiful she was. He studied her warm hazel eyes and sweet pink lips as she spoke, wanting so badly to kiss them. Her voice was soft and alluring, making him wish he had never heard another.

"Well I think it's cute, so don't beat yourself up too much."

"You do? I never thought I would say this, but hopefully I can continue to make a fool out of meself."

As they continued walking Emily realized that she had not once thought about schoolwork. She couldn't even recall the last time she had gone this long without stressing over an exam or homework, nor could she remember the last time she had spoken to a boy for this long, other than Scott of course, but that was always about Rachel. The more she and Jude spoke, the more she found herself blushing. He was deceivingly charming, and with each strategically selected word out of his mouth she became more captivated by his agreeableness.

They sat down at a bus stop bench a mile from the *Top Ten Club*.

"So what's your story? Do you always go around trying to use your stardom to pick up helpless American girls?"

"Ouch," he said, clutching his chest, like she had just broken his heart. "Don't be cheeky. I really don't even try; the accent does all the work for me. It's not even fair. It's like fishing with dynamite."

She nudged him playfully, trying to hide the fact that he was at least partly right; his accent did indeed make him somewhat irresistible.

"Is that so?"

"But seriously, I suppose when you are in me line of work women just tend to come along with such propositions. If I am to be completely honest, I don't particularly prefer it. I am just a footballer. I've been kicking it about since I could walk; it is the only thing I could ever do well. If I could just play football every second for the rest of me life, I would. It's the time in-between playing that I haven't quite figured out yet."

"I see," she replied softly smiling at him.

"How do you do that?"

"Do what?"

"Whenever you smile it makes me mind go numb, and all I can do is think about how lovely you are." Emily looked towards the ground embarrassed, her face now bright as a cherry. He stared directly through her spectacles into her eyes, "I mean it. You have no idea how beautiful you truly are." She began leaning in craving with her entire body for a kiss. Just as she got close he rose up from the bench pulling her along. "Come on I want to show you something." Not waiting for her response they began running down the street.

"But it's getting late and don't you have practice in the morning?" She attempted to collect her breath in-between strides.

"Oh don't be posh. That's your problem, you have to learn to live a little, you know enjoy the moment and all of that. Besides, me manager already hates me."

A few blocks later they arrived outside a small local football ground. Jude looked over his shoulder suspiciously; making sure no one was watching and proceeded to squeeze through the cold iron chains wrapped around the main gate.

"What are you doing?" she whispered, scared someone nearby would see them.

"Well, come on then. Do you want a bloody invitation?"

She instinctively shook her head in disagreement and he quickly rebutted with a headshake of his own. She shook her head once more, suppressing her instincts like a child preparing to steal bubble gum from a candy store, and slipped through the gate after him.

The stadium was pitch black, so Jude used the light from his mobile phone to guide them to the centre of the pitch. Jude lay in the middle of the centre circle with his hands behind his head, staring up at the night's sky as if it was a painting.

"Are you going to join me?"

"This is crazy. You can't just break into a soccer stadium and have a nap in the middle of the field."

"Will you just trust me? You must stop over-thinking everything or it will eventually drive you mad."

She sighed adversely and joined him on the ground.

"I don't overthink everything," she argued.

"Will you just be quiet and look up."

She looked up into the midnight sky, to the miles of stars that somehow appeared to be multiplying right in front of her. The crystal sparkles, shining endlessly in the black forever of space like infinite promises.

"They're beautiful." Her voice now enchanted and dazzled.

"This is the best spot to see the stars in all of England. Me dad used to bring me here when I was just a young lad. He'd make me train all day until the sun went down. Then when they were about to shut down for the night we would hide in the loo until everyone had gone. Eventually we'd kicked it about so much we could no longer stand, that's when we would just lie here and look up at the stars trying to see what shapes they made."

"Does he still bring you here?"

"No, me mum and dad died in a motor crash when I was sixteen."

"I'm so sorry."

"It's alright. Somehow I know they're with me whenever I step on the pitch. I can't really explain it, it's like I can feel them or something, like they are cheering me on. That sounds weird doesn't it? Sorry, I know you probably think I'm like that bloke from the *Six Sense* now."

Emily was silent. Her look compunctious and her voice dejected.

"No, I understand where you're coming from. My mom passed when I was nine from leukemia, I never really got a chance to know her. I remember how beautiful she was, my dad used to tell me that she was the talk of the boys' bathroom and all the boys in school dreamed of dating her. She graduated from Yale with a journalism degree but had me shortly after so she put her career on hold, and she was a great person. My grandmother told me there wasn't a person in the world who didn't like her."

Jude smiled at her, the crickets singing in the background as if trying to set the proper mood.

"It sounds like you're a spitting image of her."

She returned his smile.

"Thanks."

They lay next to one another for the next hour gazing up at the stars and talking about their childhoods, ambitions, and the ridiculous look on Veronica's face when she saw Jude. He wasn't exactly sure what it was, but he first noticed it when she mentioned her mother. There was a hint of melancholy in her voice, as if she were masking her tone from some irrefutable pain. He only knew this because he too would get the tone, it was uniformly present when he'd become blackout drunk when reminiscing over his parents.

Jude offered her a ride home but Emily kindly declined. Instead she hailed a taxi, which Jude paid for. Before ducking her head into the backseat Jude planted a kiss on her cheek.

"Have a good night, Emily Robertson. Forgive me if I'm being forward, but could I see you tomorrow evening as well?"

She leaned forward mimicking his kiss on the cheek, "I would love that."

As he closed the door the taxi slowly began to roll off, she yelled from inside, "Oh, your jacket!"

He winked, "You keep it."

V

Emily & Jude: A Beginning

When Emily returned to her room she was met by a bubbling Linda and Veronica who were in the middle of nursing a bottle of pinot grigio.

"What are you doing coming in at three in the morning, looking like you just had tea with the queen?" said Linda with a sly grin on her face, already knowing the answer from a babbling Veronica. Emily replied cautiously, crinkling her nose as if unsure whether her words were good or bad.

"I met a boy?"

She took a hint from Linda and Veronica's jubilant screams that it was a good thing. But she'd seen enough movies to know that after joyous screams always comes gossip, and if there is one thing she hated more than nightclubs, it was gossip. She always made it a point to keep her feelings to herself. She had dated Kevin for four weeks before anyone found out and had been broken up with him for six before Melissa caught Kevin making out with Theresa James at the *Roxy Club*, frantically putting two and two together. But with Linda and Veronica already settled in her room partly buzzed off wine, she feared there was no way to avoid this pow-wow.

Emily walked them through the entire night, only leaving out details of her and Jude's personal conversation. Linda spat out a mouth full of wine in laughter when Emily impersonated the look on Veronica's face when she saw Emily leaving the club with Jude. For the length of their sleepover gossip session, Veronica had appeared envious and resentful towards Emily, but by the time they were saying good night, she had come to terms, assuming that the only reason Jude had chosen Emily was because he hadn't seen her first.

Linda stopped in the doorway facing Emily, her motherly instincts kicking in like aftertaste.

"Just be careful, deary. Young love, albeit magical and new, can also be heartbreaking and tragic. We mustn't take it lightly."

Linda's last words weighed heavily on Emily's mind. She didn't know what she was feeling; all she knew was she had never felt this way before.

Jude, a new man, welcomed the morning sober and alive, inspired by the unfamiliar feeling he now possessed. He was sure to arrive at the training pitch several minutes before his manager's usual 6:15 a.m. arrival time. He sat at the foot of Sir Alex's office door, dressed in full training gear, with a determined and inspired look on his face. He stood as Sir Alex came down the hall carrying his leather brief case, a copy of the morning's *Daily Mirror*, and his stainless silver travel mug.

"Boss, I wanted to send me sincerest apologies for me behaviour yesterday. It was unprofessional and childish. You have me word it won't happen again."

"Very well, son, it's behind us now. Do your talking on the pitch. Now if you would excuse me I haven't had my morning cup of tea yet."

Jude stepped aside, letting his manger enter his office.

"Of course, boss, I'll see you out there."

Training that day began well physically, but mentally, it was another story. Running sprints, he thought of her; passing the ball, he thought of her; scoring a goal, he thought of her; and even taking a water break, he thought of her. If he thought yesterday was bad because his thoughts were consumed by Emily, today was much worse now that he had actually spent time with her. He managed to get through the morning weight session with a sparkling performance, and by the time the afternoon session came around, he discovered his thoughts of Emily were a breath of fresh air, placing an extra pep in his step and an enduring smile on his face. In the single evening they spent together she had managed to engulf him in ways he never knew possible. As soon as training finished for the day, he casually sprinted back to the locker room. He grabbed his mobile and checked the time before calling Emily.

Emily was in the middle of a heated chess match with one of the elderly inn guests in the foyer when her mobile rang. The instant she saw Jude's name flash across the tiny mobile screen she broke into an apprehensive smile.

"It's a boy isn't it?" the older woman said in her Tennessee drawl. Emily smiled in reply before walking to the corner window for a little privacy.

"I was young once too!" the woman announced still trying to force her way into Emily and Jude's conversation.

Emily answered the phone, trying her hardest not to let her nerves translate through the receiver.

"Hello."

"EMILY! You alright?" He instantly thought he was much too extravagant with his *Emily*, cursing his nerves for getting the better of him.

"I'm fine, how are you?"

"Bloody tired. We just finished training and I am quite certain me legs are going to fall off." They both shared an icebreaking laugh, suppressing their nerves. As Jude opened his mouth to speak again, the rest of the team walked in. Steven and a few of the others began teasing him from the background. "Ooh, Jude's in love…muah, muah, muah." The locker room erupted with laughter and several other players joined in with kissing sounds of their own.

"Piss off, mate!" said Jude while attempting to fight off Steven who was trying to give Jude a taunting kiss on the cheek.

Emily couldn't help but overhear the ruckus, "Where are you? A fifth grade classroom?" she laughed.

"I might as well be, these twats act like they're six. *Seriously*, I swear I'll batter the lot of ya!" They all began laughing again at his unconvincing threat. "Well, as you can tell this isn't exactly an ideal place for us to talk, so I'll get straight to the matter. I would love to see you again tonight if you're up for it? Can I pick you up at, say seven tonight?"

Emily was beaming ear to ear and turned giving the thumbs up to her chess partner across the room. "Sure, that's sounds fine," she replied attempting to hide her excitement.

"Alright, I'll see you soon. And sorry about these blokes."

"That's okay, boys will be boys. I'll see you soon." As she ended the call she caught the tail end of his background conversation, "Oi you wankers, I'm gonna...." She found his embarrassment cute. It reminded her of elementary school when kids would teasingly sing *Emily and Austin sitting in a tree, k..i..s..s..i..n..g*. She looked at her phone and noticed it was already 5:00 p.m. so she darted upstairs to get ready.

Upstairs on video chat, Melissa was pleased to see that within a few days Emily had already begun relaxing and had even spoken to a member of the opposite sex. She was doing her best to help pick out something for Emily to wear, but the tiny laptop screen was making it hard for her to facilitate. Under normal circumstances she would just walk into Emily's room and hand her a dress from her own closet and demand she wear it.

"I think the blue dress looks nice; trust me you don't want to come off too easy. The trick is the perfect balance, not too much prude and not too much sexy."

"So you like the blue one?"

"Yep, I think you'll knock his socks off."

"Well that settles it; I'm going with the white."

Melissa laughed, "Okay, suit yourself. But you look like a soccer mom who hasn't been on a date since her last Bon Jovi concert in 1984. I'm trying to get you away from the whole Joan Cusack look, remember?"

"Whatever, I don't dress like Joan Cusack. I like to think of my style as more of a Julia Roberts kind of look."

"Just the fact that it's 2013 and you're proud to dress like Julia Roberts proves my point. You're a sexy young piece of tail, Em. You should be aiming to dress more like Emma Stone or Olivia Wilde."

"Thanks for that in-depth analysis of both me and my tail, but I 'm still going with the white one." Emily continued getting ready as Melissa rambled on about her first few summer days in New York. Emily was partly tuning her out with her attention transfixed on Jude and what they would do tonight. The only bit she remotely comprehended from Melissa's New York shenanigans had something to do with a handsome stock exchange broker, a Lionel Richie album, and a turkey baster.

"Em, are you even listening to me?"

Emily turned away from the wardrobe mirror to face the computer on her bed.

"I'm sorry, what were you saying?"

"I was saying I can't believe this is your first date since Kevin. How long has it been, like three years?"

"Gee, thanks for the reminder! You certainly know how to give a pep talk, in no way am I nervous now." Her sarcasm thick, feeling more pressure from Melissa's added words.

"Oops, sorry. Just don't do anything I would do and you won't scare him off. Oh, and mention parliament and tea, English people go nuts for that stuff, it's like their cat nip." Emily laughed, hoping no one was walking by her room to hear Melissa's stereotypical comment.

"I will be sure to keep that in mind."

At 6:55 p.m. a car pulled up outside the inn. Both Linda and Veronica rushed towards the windows to see who it was. Jude was walking towards the door styling a pair of dark denim jeans and a tight black v neck t-shirt that highlighted not only his arms, but his rock abs as well. Behind him in the circular gravel driveway sat his new silver Audi A8. Veronica pouted to her mother, "It's not fair."

"Oh hush up, Veronica. You should be happy for Emily. I believe she's falling in love."

As Jude reached the door, Emily opened it, stopping him dead in his tracks. "Wow! You look lovely, Emily," he said in awe.

She was wearing a slim white sundress, fitting her curves like an old country road, with matching flats and a light yellow shawl.

"Thank you," replied a blushing Emily.

Jude remained as still as a deer caught in headlights, Emily following suit stood awkwardly in the doorway.

"I'm sorry…It's just, I can honestly say that you are the most beautiful thing that I have ever seen." Her cheeks grew even rosier. "But pardon me manners I could be here all night telling you that. Shall we get going?"

She followed him to the car where he opened the door before letting her in. She felt she would never get used to the passenger side being on the left; it was as if everything had been turned upside down.

They drove for twenty minutes. He told her about training and again apologized for his teammate's immaturity on the phone earlier, while she went over her day and how she had been bested in chess by a seventy-year-old countrywoman. They arrived at a local forest with not a building or car in sight. The sounds of crickets singing and frogs wailing dominated the night's voice.

"Are we going hiking?" she said with a baffled look on her face.

"Not exactly. Follow me, it's not too much further." She took his hand and they walked for several minutes. Emily was not a nature girl, but she could at least appreciate how nice the night was. The gentle breeze brushed across her peachy skin and the moon's smile illuminated their path as it swept through the valley.

"Alright, now close your eyes."

"Why?"

"Just close them please, trust me. I had this all worked out in me head." She closed them cautiously as he led her slowly a few more feet.

"Alright, open them."

Her face rested for a moment in a state of shock, searching for the appurtenant words to say.

"Jude, this is amazing! But how could…"

He interrupted, "I know a guy."

In front of them lay a tall, long, cream tent, the kind that would be used for an outdoor wedding reception or party. The ceiling was made of clear plastic so you could look up into the stars, and dim lanterns lit up each corner, giving the room a romantic glow. Inside a table was set for two, fully equipped with plates, utensils, wine glasses, a lit candle, and a petite vase containing a long stem rose. A gentleman greeted them at the entrance, dressed in a black and white tuxedo with a clean white towel draped over his forearm like a butler.

"Dame et le monsieur, your dinner awaits," said the gentleman while motioning his hand towards the table elegantly. Jude pulled out her chair and then rushed over to his, anxious to start the date.

"You hired a French waiter too?"

Jude laughed, "Heavens no, that's Patrice. He plays left back for us. He's the only French person I know, and come to find out the French are suckers for romance, so he offered to help."

Emily's head continued to swerve back and forth surveying the room, still attempting to take in her extravagant surroundings.

"This really is amazing, Jude, you didn't have to do all this."

"The pleasure is all mine. I figured I may only have one shot at taking you out, so I might as well make it special."

"Well, you did. Everything is beautiful!"

"From the looks of you, that seems to be tonight's theme." She thought if he makes her blush one more time her face would turn into a cherry permanently.

"A bottle of your finest wine please," said Jude to a hovering Patrice.

"Why, Jude Macavoy, are you trying to seduce me?" she said playfully.

"Why, are you seducible?"

She shook her head no slowly, giving off an impish grin.

"Ah, I thought so, that is why I made sure they stocked the finest ginger ale as well."

Jude raised his glass of seventy-six crisp pinot grigio toasting Emily, "To us. May you have a wonderful stint in England, and may I not get kicked out of training again."

For dinner they enjoyed a delicious serving of Cordon bleu that Patrice had prepared earlier that evening. Being French fine dining seemed to be in his blood, as he also prepared a nearly perfect strawberry soufflé for dessert.

"So what made you want to become a doctor?" asked Jude, taking a bite from his soufflé. "God, this is brilliant. Well done, Patrice." Patrice gave him a thankful bow from across the tent.

Emily couldn't make eye contact with him, and instead stared at her dessert with a lugubrious glaze.

"I try not to think about it," she said softly.

He could hear the tribulation in her voice and didn't want to pry.

"No worries, you don't have to talk about anything you don't want to. How about this? How do you like medical school?"

"I love of it, the knowledge, the people, and the exams. Don't get me wrong, it's extremely stressful at times and I practically have no free time whatsoever, but I couldn't imagine spending my time any other way."

"Yeah, I've been meaning to ask you about that. I never met someone who revises as much as you. You're like, proper nerdy."

"Hey, I'm not nerdy," she defended in laughter, pushing up the bridge of her spectacles while doing so.

"No, I suppose you're not. But you are quite lovely, Emily." She smiled, flattered by his rapturous observation. "And, you are a little nerdy…you must admit." They both laughed again, this time becoming lost in each other's smile.

"Well, what do you mean by revising?"

"Revising, it's like…like, to study. I guess that's what Americans call it."

"Oh, well then if that's your definition of nerdy then, yes, I am one…because I love to study."

"Why is that? That's a rather peculiar attribute to have."

"I think it began when I was eleven. I started idolizing Gandhi and Florence Nightingale."

"Wait, me apologies, but you idolized Gandhi and Florence Nightingale? You certainly are the most unique girl I've ever known. But then again, perhaps if I idolized them instead of David Beckham, then maybe I would be as smart as you. Okay, please continue."

"Yes, Gandhi and Florence Nightingale, I had this idea that if I could change the world through medicine and live to write about it, then maybe I could leave my stamp on this earth and make my mother proud."

"I don't even know how to take the piss out of you for that. That's a bloody good answer."

"What about you? Do you love being a pro-soccer player?"

"I love being a 'pro-footballer,' if that's what you mean. As God is me witness, I will get you to call it football."

"…Sorry, 'Football.'"

"Well, what's not to love? I get paid millions of pounds to do what I love, free fish 'n chips from *Harvey's* in Blackpool, and it gives me the means to throw some wicked parties. You must come to one, Emily. It's a bloody good time. I would even be so chivalrous to keep you away from the alcohol and narcotics. "

"I'm not much of a party girl."

"Bollocks, we met at the *Top Ten.*"

"I wasn't there by will," she assured him.

"Well, that's alright, no parties then. Besides, I'm fully content just spending time with you alone."

Their dessert finished with further conversation of school and football, the stress of balancing medical school and the constant pressure from supporters and media to perform. They continued talking and becoming better acquainted for over an hour when Jude noticed Emily gazing up through the tent at the stars, slowly becoming lost in their beauty.

"Would you fancy a dance?"

"But there's no music."

"Hm, that is rather odd." He winked at Patrice who took the cue, pulling out a small stereo from under the food cart. The composed voice of Frank Sinatra's *Moonlight in Vermont* furnished the air as Jude stood from his chair offering his hand. She graciously accepted as he pulled her close, swaying left to right to the subdued melody. She willingly gave in, falling coolly into his soft embrace. She could feel his muscles tighten with each step and the sensational feeling that rushed through her spine as he placed his hand on her lower back, feeling as if they somehow wandered onto a cloud drifting towards heaven. She safely rested her head on his strong chest, closing her eyes and hearing nothing but the music and his steady heartbeat.

They danced silently for the next two songs, both becoming trapped in the moment and whishing it could last forever.

"Emily?"

"Hm," she said still lost in his arms not bothering to look up. He removed his hand from her back and used it to bring her face to his.

"I know we've only just met, but I feel it necessary to tell you that I really fancy you."

She returned his comment with a concerned glare,

"I like you too, Jude, but you just signed a new contract and I have to go back to school…It just wouldn't…"

He cut her off, "None of that matters, all that matters is you feel the same, the rest will take care of itself in due time." She gave him a bereaved look wanting so desperately to believe him, but she had read enough books to know how summer romances end; with forgotten promises and tears. "But Jude..." He again cut her off, this time leaning in to kiss her, and she could resist no longer. Her lips felt at home pressed up against his, moist and enduring. He felt their passion spread through his veins like wildfire leading him to the only logical explanation; simply, his lips were meant to kiss only hers. Emily pulled away slowly, smiling in a state of euphoria.

"Sorry, I haven't kissed someone in a long time," she admitted bashfully.

"It's quite alright, it was perfect," he assured her, sealing his words with a kiss on her forehead.

Around 10:30 p.m., long after Patrice had gone, Emily lay in Jude's arms under the tall peaceful oak tree by the riverbank, watching the fireflies as they kindled the night's sky. He kissed her once on her forehead then on the cheek, "Can I ask you a question? You don't have to answer it if you don't want."

"Of course you can. Shoot—"

"Why don't you drink? Not that it really matters, I'm just curious is all. Is it because you don't like the taste? If so, I have a mate that bartends at *Gilligan's Pub* in Chester and he could whip up a drink that taste just like taffy, you wouldn't even know your were drinking alcohol."

"No it's not that, I've never even tasted alcohol."

He motioned for a high five as if proud of her statement.

"Well done! I don't know anyone that can say that, well, no one over the age of ten anyway."

She half-heartedly smiled, giving Jude the notion that she was being serious.

"You remember when I told you that I was raised by my grandmother?"

"Yeah—"

"Well, before my mom died, my mom, dad and I were, as they say, one big happy family. I remember my parents would always read me a Dr. Seuss or Berenstain Bears book before bed. My dad would do the different voices for the characters and act out whatever they were doing on the page, my mom and I would laugh at him. Whenever he finished he would always tuck me in, kiss me on the cheek, and say 'goodnight princess.' He once took us to Disney on Ice and arranged for my mom and me to skate with Belle and Ariel. He would have done anything to make us happy, especially my mom. But when my mom died, he slowly stopped reading to me. I noticed he would hire a babysitter and come home in the middle of the night drunk and after the sitter would leave he would sit on the couch and drink some more." He could see her eyes beginning to water; he kissed her forehead and held her closer while letting her continue.

"As soon as I was old enough, he stopped hiring babysitters. After school I would be home alone until he'd eventually stumble in around midnight drunk and half aware of where he was. He would pull me out of bed yelling and scolding me for not having cleaned the dishes right or for not folding his clothes properly…I remember one day he called me into the kitchen at three in the morning to heat up his TV dinner, I misjudged the time and burnt it pretty bad. He said, 'You know I love you, so why do you do things that piss me off? Sometimes I think you do them because you want to see me upset.' I'll never forget how hard he struck me. I had to have been blacked out for at least several minutes because by the time I came to he had already fixed himself a hot pocket. He always made it a point to apologize after he'd hit me, I knew he was a good man who was just going through a lot."

Jude's fists began to clench in rage. He wanted to fly to America and give this guy a piece of his mind and fists. Any man who would lay their hands on a woman disgusted him. They were the ultimate scumbags in his book. Emily continued, her tone becoming more and more melancholy.

"He would keep me home from school for a few days after he'd hit me, worried that someone might question me about the bruises. Keeping me away from school hurt more that his fists, even though I was only in junior high I still loved school more than anything. After this kept going on for a few more years into my freshman year of high school, I realized it wasn't just a phase and this was the man my father had now become. So one night when I knew he was at the bar I gathered my things and took the train to my grandmother's house where I told her everything. And I've been living with her ever since. That was the last time I saw my father. He was sentenced to fifteen to thirty years in prison for killing two college kids when he was drinking and driving. " As she finished her last words she noticed she was crying, not sure for how long, she became embarrassed and tucked her head into her hands in shame.

"I can't believe I just told you all of that. The only person I've ever told those stories to was my grandmother." He wanted so badly to say something comforting, but knew from his own experience when he lost his parents that there was nothing anyone could ever say or do that would make him feel better.

"Jude could you please…" He interjected, unclenching his fists and wiping the tears from her eyes.

"Your secret is safe with me, love."

The night finally drew to a close and Jude dropped her back off at the inn. He walked her to the front door under the well-lit lamp that was being attacked by the nighttime moths. They stared into each other's eyes for what seemed like an eternity, before Jude bid her goodnight, taking her lips and kissing them slowly and passionately. As the front door shut behind her Emily collapsed into it, melting with affection, feeling every part of her fall into absolute bliss. Two things were certain, she was falling in love and this was not part of her plan.

VI

Emily & Jude: To Leap is to Fall

For the next several weeks Jude and Emily were inseparable. She introduced him to the whole gang, Linda, Veronica, Ron, and, Charlotte Wagner, her new found southern chess partner. She did her best to keep Jude and Veronica separate, as Emily noticed every time she brought him around Veronica became more and more jealous, like one of the evil stepsisters from *Cinderella*. It never got to the point where she would try and sabotage Emily and Jude's newly discovered relationship, but she still possessed the bitter taste of resentment because she wasn't being escorted to the finest restaurants in London and paparazzi weren't dying to get a picture of her for their new cover story. And despite her humble nature, Emily couldn't help but enjoy the attention, for she had never had someone envy her life before.

They often took walks through the gardens, which led to evenings of peace while entangled in each other's arms under one of the oak trees. Their more challenging evenings were spent teaming up to try and take down Charlotte in a game of chess. They came to realize their two twenty-five-year-old brains were no match for her seventy-year-old wisdom. Emily even spent time at Jude's flat, meeting several of his teammates, and was occasionally, when she played her cards right, treated to a showcase of cooking skills, or lack thereof, when Jude would make one of the only two dishes he knew how, grilled cheese or jam and toast.

Jude knew he had fully succumbed to his feelings for her when he found himself getting talked into watching a romantic comedy marathon at his flat. Although he found the movies to be positively horrible, each film seemed to have the same plot and starred either Sandra Bullock or Rachel McAdams, he didn't mind because it gave him an excuse to lie next to her all day. They would make a giant bowl of movie popcorn, sprinkle some salt, butter, and mozzarella cheese over it and curl up on the sofa. On the occasions they did go out, they found themselves creeping through back doors of restaurants and movie theaters to avoid the paparazzi. One persistent photographer managed to snap a photo of them walking out of *Harwood Arms Restaurant* in London. The photo made a small headline on the cover of a British tabloid magazine that read, *Macavoy Spends New Contract on New Girl.*

After roughly their thirtieth date, Jude called Emily with a question.

"I can't believe you're going away tomorrow," said Emily, saddened by Jude's future departure.

"I know, but it's going to be proper fun. I always wanted to go to Italy and play in the San Siro. You know, I've been thinking—"

Emily laughed, "Oh no, I know how you hate doing that."

"True, but hear me out. We have a few days off before the friendly on Tuesday night, so I was wondering if you fancy a trip to Italy?"

Emily was flattered at the offer. "I couldn't. I wouldn't want to impose and I'm sure they don't let just anyone travel with the team."

"Awe, come on… it will be so much fun. And if you don't come I won't be able to enjoy meself because I will be thinking of you the entire time. Besides, players bring their wives and girlfriends to matches all the time, this is no different."

Emily had a shot of glee run across her face, but then quickly remembered her policy of no boyfriends.

"Oh, so I'm your girlfriend now? Don't I have a say in any of this?"

"Of course—"

Emily was so confused, her mind locked in an intense debate with her heart. On one side she had a man with whom she was falling in love while on the other she had the kryptonite to her one rule, the very rule that had the potential of interfering with her dreams; no boyfriend. She didn't know if it was the foreign country, a brief state of vulnerability, or perhaps true love, but again she gave into this new sensation.

"Well if I'm going to be your girlfriend, you do know this means no more groupies, picking up girls whenever little Jude feels like it, and no more partying to the break of dawn with super models and God knows what else?" She was surprised, and truthfully so was he, at how fast he replied, not hesitating for a second.

"Emily...that part of me died the very moment I laid eyes on you."

She hesitated briefly, reconfirming her next words were actually what she wanted to say.

"Well, since you put it that way, I guess you can be my boyfriend."

Jude's words were true. He hadn't thrown a party or thought of another woman since they started dating. On several occasions he had to turn people away who showed up at his flat unannounced, fully equipped with booze and sandwich bags full of narcotics, expecting to attend one of his infamous gatherings. However, Jude was always sure to confiscate the cartons of booze. He thought, just because there would be no party, didn't mean he couldn't put the beverages to a quenching personal use.

"Brilliant, nothing would make me happier. Now stop mucking about, pack your things and tell Linda, because your ass better be on that plane with me tomorrow morning."

The flight the next morning had Emily feeling a little out of place. She sat next to Jude glancing down the aisle, seeing some players with their headphones on nodding their heads to a tune, some next to their wives engaged in conversation, and some playing cards. She couldn't believe she was among them; it was all happening so fast. Just a month ago she was arriving in England, now she hadn't picked up a medical book in over two weeks, and was dating a millionaire athlete who took her on trips to foreign countries on a whim. Her mind could barely keep up. It wasn't that all of this wasn't wonderful, she enjoyed every minute she spent with Jude, it was the frightening fact that she was falling hard for him and there was not a single thing she could do about it. His charm, those hypnotizing blue eyes, the way he could get her to try new things, and most importantly the way he made her feel as if she was the most important thing on earth, all left her defenseless. He lived his life free and adventurous, with a sense of not knowing what crazy thing he would do tomorrow, and the funny thing was all that did was make him more attractive in her eyes. She viewed him as this handsome, daring, and kind-hearted athlete who held an air of confidence, and some would argue arrogance, matched only by the likes of Muhammad Ali. She knew the deeper she got involved the harder it would be to say goodbye at the end of the summer.

"Are you alright?" asked Jude, interrupting her thoughts.

"I'm okay, just tired is all."

"Don't worry; you're going to love Italy. From what I hear it's lovely this time of year. I Googled a bit before I went to bed last night and I think I found some places we can visit that you will surely enjoy."

"It's not that, it's the summer. All of this is so amazing, but what's going to happen when the summer's over? ...I'm sorry, I just wasn't expecting all of this; maybe I'm just overthinking things?"

He saw how perturbed she was at their situation, but he felt now was neither the time nor the place to have the discussion, nor did he really what to have it in the first place.

"I told you, love, don't worry about the future. Just enjoy yourself and everything will fall into place. Trust me; I'm good at these types of things."

"Oh really? When was the last time you were plopped in a foreign country not knowing anybody, broke your biggest rule, were whisked away by a millionaire, and had to come to grips that in a month you may not see that person again? All while experiencing ninety-nine percent of the things you did together for the first time."

"I see your point." He studied her emotions briefly before speaking again. "I can't predict the future, but I can tell you that I'm crazy about you and that I love calling you me girlfriend. So let's not deal with that right now, let's just enjoy the moment for however long it may last."

Emily took a breath, regaining her composure and newly discovered adventurous attitude.

"You're right, like I said I was probably just overthinking things. Let's just have fun."

As soon as they landed, Emily phoned Melissa. And for the first time in their friendship, Melissa could barely get a word in. Emily raved on for over an hour about how magnificent the city was. She described in extraneous detail the European charm of the architecture, the stone roads, the petite cafés, and the surprisingly hospitable people. One of the first things that came out her mouth was, "It's even better than they show in the movies." Emily's joy was met by Melissa's mild disappointment in her own city. "Consider yourself lucky. I just finished wiping down that cute top that I got at *H&M* because a rude New York Pigeon decided it looked like an ideal place for a shit." However, in spite of Melissa's fashion emergency, she found herself thrilled with Emily. All the new things she was trying and places she was seeing— if it weren't for their occasional video chats she wouldn't have believed it was really Emily doing all these things. She ended their conversation asking only one thing from Emily, to bring her back a handsome Italian man. She went on to say, "But I'll settle for an ugly one if that's all you can manage."

Emily and Jude checked into a penthouse suite in downtown Milan. There was a narrow hallway that filtered into the main room, the floor coated in caramel colored marble and the walls aligned with several seashell shaped lighting fixtures. A balcony with a lucid view of downtown Milan overlooked the living room, consisting of a pool table, a large sofa, a gaudy television, and a robust minibar, which was filled with overpriced bottles of Perrier mineral water and one of Jude's favorites, Jack Daniel's whiskey. The bathroom was the size of Emily's apartment, fully equipped with twin sinks, a large vista steam shower, and a bathtub-jucuzzi. The only downside, to Emily, was that there was only one bed. Sleeping arrangements had completely slipped her mind. For the past month she had spent a lot of time at Jude's place and he at hers, but they never spent the night together or made love. They spoke about it only once when Emily told him she was a virgin. Jude completely respected her choice and, having already suspected such, he wasn't surprised by her confession.

Jude didn't even notice the bed situation, already scrambling to regroup with his team in the lobby.

"Alright, love, I'm off to training. I should be back in two hours, so be ready because I have a big surprise for you." He gave her a kiss on the cheek and was out the door, and then was back in the door, "Oops, I forgot me bag. Cheers!" And then was gone again, only to return seconds later, "Bloody'ell, I forgot me key. Alright, this time I'm gone for good, cheers love." He returned thirty seconds later. This time, Emily was standing at the door holding his wallet. "I forgot me wall... ah brilliant, thanks love." She swapped him the wallet for a kiss and he finally left the room for good.

Not sure what to do in a foreign hotel, Emily did what any tourist would do, go out and explore. She put her room key in her purse and headed out to the busy Milan streets. People roamed the streets in a dreamlike state as if everyone had been told good news; money constantly changing hands, and the smell of fresh pasta floated through the air, reminding her stomach how hungry it was. The city had a unique charm, one she couldn't quite put her finger on. It reminded her of Boston, but at the same time held the mannerisms of a small rural town like New Haven. She walked a few more blocks, taking in the sites, stopping briefly to examine the flowing canals and placing her fingers on random buildings touching the ancient architecture. A couple of men walking by shouted at her from across the street.

"Sei, bella! Essere fidanzata mio favore. Io ti amero per tutta la notte."

She smiled attempting to ignore them, skeptical of what they were saying. A young Italian man in his late twenties, wearing dark denim jeans, a collar shirt that exposed his chest hairs, and loafers that matched his curly black hair, walked up beside her.

"They say you are very beautiful."

Emily turned looking at the gentleman, initially taken back by his handsomeness.

"I have a feeling they said more than that."

The gentleman laughed at her observation.

"They do say more than that, but that was, how you say?...The main part. You are very beautiful, you are American, no?"

"Thank you, and yes I'm just visiting for a few days."

"I see—benvenuto! My name is Francisco. I am from Napoli. Come si dice? Um… how long are you here in Italy?" His accent was thick, making some of his words hard to follow.

"Only a few days and, Francisco…is it?"

"Si," he said, nodding his head in humble fashion.

"Nice to meet you, I'm Emily," she replied, shaking his hand.

"Piacere, Emily. If you like I am not busy; I can show you Italy and all of its beautiful places."

"Thanks but I really should be getting back. My boyfriend is probably waiting for me."

"Oh, accidenti, he is a very lucky man." He took her hand and planted a kiss on her knuckles, "Ciao mia bella. I hope he tells you, you are beautiful every moment of every hour."

His parting words made her giggle, as she recalled Melissa forewarning her about such poetic advances from Italian guys. Melissa watched *Under the Tuscan Sun* one time, and now she acted as if she was an expert on Italian men. She giggled some more, amused that, for once, Melissa was actually right about something she had learned from a movie.

She made her way back to the hotel with enough time to get a cup of coffee and for the first time in over three weeks look over one of her medical books. By the time Jude arrived she was dressed and ready for her surprise. Having used up all her "nice" dresses, as Melissa put it, she resorted to her more comfortable attire of jeans and a Yale t-shirt.

During the taxi ride to Jude's surprise, she tried every trick in the book to get him to reveal their destination. She flirted with him profusely; mocking the way women threw themselves at him, and played Twenty-one Questions, but still couldn't unmask his secret. They pulled up in front of a large Victorian building in the centre of Milan. The massive collection of steps led up to six large chalk stone columns that provided a foundation for the entryway. The title of the building was in Italian, *La Biblioteca di Milano Per la Ricerca e L'apprendimento*, keeping her further in the dark until they made their way inside. Upon entering, Jude once again asked her to close her eyes in anticipation.

"You know, we really have to stop beginning all of our dates like this. There are only so many surprises a girl can take."

The room was deathly silent and for a brief moment before opening her eyes she thought it to be a funeral home. Her eyes opened skeptically to a world of wonder, hesitating for only a brief moment to soak in her surroundings before she turned to him leaping into his arms with fulfillment.

"I reckon you enjoy it then? They told me it's one of largest libraries in the world. "

"It's unbelievable, Jude. Look at all the *books*!" The librarian at the front desk shushed her obediently.

"Sorry," she whispered to the librarian.

Jude followed her as she made her way through the barrage of books. It was an open floor plan with over seventy long rose hardwood library tables in sequential order filling the main floor's reading area, with three more floors of bookshelves overlooking that. The library consisted of 15 million books spread across approximately 410 miles of bookshelves. In the middle of this massive structure dangled a 780 lamp Bohemian crystal chandelier that burnished the room in an omnipresent glow. It resembled a castle cathedral more than a library.

She was convinced the library had every book ever made. Not wasting a second, pointing out each one like some sort of well-informed tour guide, she went on enthusiastically, sparked by each word on the bindings. "I can't believe they have this one, my professors can't even get a hold of this." And, "You see that one, Jude? That's a first edition. Those sell for around twenty-two thousand dollars on the Internet." He coasted behind her analyzing the way she rummaged through the mountain of books like a kid in a candy store. Each book was like an epiphany, lighting up her face with magic. He found himself overjoyed at her happiness and losing his breath in her smiles. As she picked up a first edition of Jane Austen's *Pride and Prejudice* examining each page as if it were some sacred artifact, Jude snuck up behind her, placing his arms seductively around her waist.

"Do you like it? I know the library isn't the most romantic place to bring a woman. But then again you're no ordinary woman." She blissfully smiled before placing the book back in its place, hugging his arms and welcoming the warmth of his touch and his breath on her neck.

"Is that so? Well, if I'm not ordinary then what do you see me as?"

"The fittest bird I've ever pulled." She playfully jabbed him with her elbow, catching a good chunk of his right ribcage. "Oi! That actually hurt a bit."

"Serves you right. I may not understand all of your British terms, but I know that wasn't remotely romantic." He turned her in his arms as if they were doing a dance, looking her in the eyes so she could see and feel his sincerity.

"I'm sorry, love, in all seriousness you are the most special girl that I have ever met. I struggle to remember me life before you were in it and can't imagine a life without you."

"That's more like it, good save." She kissed him slowly.

"Thank you so much for bringing me here. I love it. I feel like this is all a dream and I'll wake up tomorrow back in Connecticut." He pulled her close continuing their kiss.

"As far as I'm concerned you should be kissed everyday and reminded how special you truly are. So if bringing you here makes you feel special then me work is done, because there is nothing I wouldn't do to make you happy."

"Okay Romeo, you don't have to suck up anymore. You already managed to save yourself from another rib shot."

"I'm serious, Emily, there's nothing I wouldn't do to make you happy."

"Well, you know what would make me really happy?"

"No, but I hope it involves you and me topless." She jabbed him in the ribs again, this time ferociously.

"OUCH! I thought you said I was safe."

"That was before you made another grotesque comment."

"I was only taking the piss. Honestly love, what would make you happy? And please don't hit me." He flinched, protecting his face as if prepared to withstand an assault.

"I was just going to say, if we come back here tomorrow that would make me even happier."

"Of course we can come back, love. You didn't really think I would only bring you here once. I know for you, reading a book is like me having a pint."

"Jude, that's a terrible analogy."

"What? I'm just saying I fancy a drink as much as you fancy a book."

"I know what you're saying, but you shouldn't enjoy alcohol that much."

"Why not? It's called nectar for the soul for a reason."

She looked at him half perplexed and half amused.

"When have you ever heard someone say that?"

"People say it all the time, I think it's in the bible or sumthin like that."

"One, that is definitely not in the Bible, and two, you have never heard anyone say that."

He opened his mouth several times attempting to reply, but caught in a lie, the words became imprisoned on the edge of his tongue.

"Well…I haven't personally heard that, but I'm certain they say it somewhere."

"Suuure they do," she said smiling at his stupidity and lack of book knowledge. "You're so cute. Let's leave the books to me okay."

"Agreed, that's a brilliant idea. And you just leave the drinking to me. Speaking of drinking, do you fancy some dinner? I'm starving!"

She didn't want to leave the library, but her empty stomach convinced her otherwise.

He took her to a small restaurant around the corner from the Library, *Angelo's Pizza e Pasta*. The restaurant balanced its petiteness with the elegance of family oriented fine Italian dinning. Due to their late meal there were only twelve other people dinning in the restaurant. They sat at a table a few feet from the fire brick oven, flabbergasted and entertained by the way the chefs tossed the pizza dough through the air like graceful ballerinas all while singing in their tenor Italian voices in perfect harmony. Emily and Jude were going to share a pepperoni pizza, but the waiter had another idea.

"Ah, molto bene! You two are in love, no? Then you get spaghetti, they make specially for you."

Seeing that they didn't have much of a choice they agreed.

They sat gazing across the table at one another, the heat from the brick over inching across their skin in palliative comfort, and despite being in a room littered with people they only had eyes for each other. So much so, they didn't notice the wall beside the entryway coated in photos with people eating spaghetti.

When they finished, the waiter returned to collect their plate and noticed there was still a piece of pasta left.

"NO...NO...you eat all the pasta, no wasting." Jude reached for it with his fingers and the waiter slapped it away.

"NO, you share pasta. Like Disney movie."

"Are you taking the piss, mate?"

The waiter started yelling in what Jude could only make out as nonsense, "FARE QUELLO CHE DICO! E SCIOCCO STRANIERI!"

"Alright, Alright, relax mate. Bloody'ell, you'll pop a vein if you continue on like that." He looked up puzzled at Emily, "Shall we?"

She looked around the room noticing everyone was now staring at their table.

"This is so embarrassing, everyone is staring at us."

"Well, if it shall shut this bloke up then I'm all for it." She still couldn't give in, unsettled by the ridiculousness of the situation.

"Come on, Emily, you know you want to. I reckon it will be quite romantic. You already ice skated with two Disney princesses, why not relive the life of a third." She looked at Jude who flashed a look of encouragement, before seeing the daunting expression that was relayed by the shuffling back and forth of the waiter's robust black mustache.

"Okay, let's get this over with. And for the record, Lady was not a princess, she was just a dog."

They sucked the string of pasta until their lips met in the centre, and the rest of the restaurant began to cheer as if celebrating a birthday. "Bravissimo!" shouted the waiter, snapping a photo with his Polaroid for the restaurant's wall. They both were a tad embarrassed, but still managed a laugh from the situation.

After dinner they headed towards a local canal for a boat ride. They decided since it was getting late and Jude had training in the morning, to make it a short one. He held her close the entire way not really saying much. The stars' reflections sprinkled through the water and the smooth summer air placed them in a state of tranquility where words were not needed. As they pulled up to the dock and prepared to exit the boat, Jude seized the moment,

"I love you, Emily. Do you know that?" He said it with a wholesome sincerity to his voice.

Emily, in fact, did not know that. She had been falling for him ever since their first date, but she was never entirely sure of what to make of her feelings. But with all the things going against them, time, distance, social classes, beliefs; she knew one thing to be true.

"I love you too, Jude."

When they arrived back in their hotel suite, all the wonderful feelings of the night quickly vanished. It's not that she didn't love him or trust him, It's just sleeping with him was a big step, one that scared her. It wouldn't be her first time sleeping next to a boy, as she slept next to Kevin all the time back in college. But she would recall the way Kevin got frustrated at her night terrors and how he always tried to make a move on her, a move that she never felt comfortable receiving or reciprocating. Before she could even convey her concerns Jude walked out of the bathroom wearing nothing but a pair of Manchester United training shorts. She couldn't take her eyes off his solid sculpting abs and the way his tattoos flowed through his creamy white skin.

"What, do I have something in me teeth?" he said, subconsciously running his tongue around his teeth in search for any leftover meat or pasta. She shook her head no and attempted to suppress her hormones.

"Okay, well I'm going to try and get some rest. You can have the bed and I'll take the couch." And with those words it only made her more attracted to him. She walked towards him placing her arms around his chiseled frame, which in returned sent abrupt chills down her spine.

"Thank you. I'm just not ready for that yet."

"No worries, love." Then after a pause he added, "Are you happy?"

"Very!"

"Then that's all the satisfaction I need."

She kissed him before saying goodnight, wishing he would just take her anyway, disregarding her previous comment.

Emily's mother took a bite of the meatloaf that she made for dinner. She reached across the kitchen table passing Emily the warm basket of buttered rolls.

"How was your day, honey?" Emily's face lit up with excitement.

"It was great, mom! Jude took me on a romantic trip to Italy, can you believe it? I saw one of the world's biggest libraries and took a lovely boat ride through the canals."

"That sounds terrific, sweetheart. You two are becoming really close."

"We are. I think I love him."

Her mother smiled just as Emily does with a touch of love and compassion in her eyes.

"Of course you do, sweetheart. I'm so happy for you; you're the best daughter a mother could ask for." Emily was overwhelmed by her mother's praise, looking upon her with such admiration and joy. The telephone rang, interrupting their dinner, "I wonder who that could be? Your father should still be at work, I'll be right back, sweetheart." Emily watched her mother as she left the kitchen, taking several bites of her meatloaf and spinning the spoon through her mashed potatoes, biding time until she returned. The constant ticking from the clock above the refrigerator drowned out all sound, leaving a disturbed feeling in her gut. Five minutes passed; then fifteen, then an hour, until Emily rose from the table and began walking through her house in search of her mother.

"Mom?…Mom?…Where are you?…Mom?" She searched every inch of their one-floor suburban Boston home, but her mother was nowhere to be found. The ticking of the clock got louder and louder. Just as Emily was about to panic, the ticking ceased and she heard chatter coming from the television in the living room. She inquired frightened and unsure, "Mom?" As she stood in doorway of the living room, she saw her father sitting on the couch watching Sports Center and drinking a Budweiser.

"Daddy, where's mom?" He cut off the television. "Daddy?" He placed his beer on the living room table, purposely missing the coaster that her mother had bought from a local thrift store last spring, he crept up to her slowly and she fought to keep her voice steady and unafraid.

"Where's mom?" He didn't take his eyes off her like she was a juicy steak and he hadn't eaten for weeks. Emily backed up slowly making her way into the kitchen, alert to make no sudden movements.

"She's dead, Emily." She shook her head 'no' not believing his words and now crying from fear.

"No...No she's not. I just saw her, you're lying!"

"But she really is, Emily. And you're next if you don't get back in that kitchen." He raised his hand to hit her, the shine from his wedding band glistening through her teary eyes. Just as he was about to connect Emily woke up screaming, "NO!" the tears streaming down her face.

Jude rushed from the couch over to her side, jumping in bed and holding her close.

"Shh...it's alright, love, I'm here. You just had a bad dream, is all." Her body was trembling and wet with sweat. "It's alright, Emily, I'm not going anywhere, I promise." He rocked her gently in his arms while softly stroking her hair, constantly reassuring her that it was going to be all right. Emily whispered, "I'm sorry," before drifting back to sleep. Jude wasn't far behind, falling instantly back to sleep while still coddling her, his body now damp from her sweat.

Around 5 a.m. Emily nudged him awake.

"Jude?"

He turned to her in bed, rubbing his eyes awake.

"Are you alright, love?"

"I'm fine. Thank you for being there last night. You didn't have to stay with me."

"Nonsense, love, I will always be here for you whenever you may need me."

She rolled over on top of him, gazing into his blue eyes and feeling his strong torso between her legs.

"You promise?" she whispered seductively.

"I promise."

She kissed him passionately on his neck and then on his chest.

"Emily…" She ignored his words and continued her kissing assault. He pulled her up from his chest bringing her face back to his.

"Emily, I love you, but you are still emotional from last night. You don't really want to do this—not now." Her look morphed into one of disappointment. "Hey, look at me. I love you."

She forced a smile.

"I love you too."

"Come here." He held open his arm inviting her to rest her head upon his chest, holding her close and kissing her on the forehead.

"Is this going to be our thing? You waking me up at all hours of the night?"

She laughed, "Sorry, I thought you'd be used to girls waking you up in the middle of the night for sex."

"Blimey, that's a bit harsh. And for your information once we shag they don't wake up until lunch the next day, just saying."

"Gee, thanks for that lovely image."

"Well don't inquire if you don't really want to know, but you can feel free to wake me up anytime you'd like. I truly don't mind."

"Thanks, I'll hold you to it."

VII

Emily: A Day in the Life

Before Emily knew it, two days had flown by and it was already the morning of Manchester United's friendly against AC Milan. Jude had to go in early for training, but she didn't mind because it left her with time to head back to the library, which had quickly become her heaven on earth. She spent the entire day there leading up to the match, making her way through every medical book she could get her hands on. She even took several photos of the building and text them to Melissa. Of course she was not as taken by the library as Emily was, texting her back, '*why are you sending me pictures of books when you're in a foreign country. I want to see some half naked Italian men! Come on, Em, priorities!*' she capped off the text with a smiley face as if to hammer home her strong fixation for half naked men.

When dinnertime arrived she grabbed a slice of pizza from Angelo's on her way back to the hotel. She spent thirty minutes packing both her and Jude's things, preparing for their flight back to England directly after the match. Jude lent her one of his training kits to wear so she wouldn't stand out as a clueless tourist taking in a football match. But his idea backfired when she boarded the wives and girlfriend shuttle to the match. She noticed everyone on the shuttle was laced head to toe in some hard to pronounce fashion designer. An exotic Spanish woman with an exquisite figure, bright red lipstick, dark Fendi shades, and a diamond on her finger the size of Emily's mobile phone scooted towards the window, inviting Emily to sit down.

"Hola, I'm Brenda, Fabio's wife."

"Hi, I'm Emily, Jude's girlfriend." It still felt weird saying she's someone's girlfriend.

"Oh, so you're the new guy's girl. He's a handsome one. He must really like you if he bring you to a away match." Her Spanish accent was thick like she had just gotten off the boat, making her challenging to understand.

"I hope so," replied Emily in a joking manner, not taking the conversation too seriously.

"You hope so? Chica, you better hurry and get a ring on that finger before he moves on to the next. So when he cheats at least you get muchos dinero."

"Jude's not like that."

Brenda tipped down her $900 shades to look Emily in the eye.

"Chica, all footballers are like that. They are how we say in Argentina, los ninos pequenos, just little boys with big pockets." Emily contemplated her words briefly, but was still fully convinced Jude was different.

"And uno mas advice, you will never keep him dressing like that. Lose the jeans and t-shirt and get rid of those glasses. Ask to borrow his credit card, no...just take his credit card and take a trip into London, you can find many dresses and cute jewelry there." Emily was beginning to become annoyed now, *who's this lady to comment on my relationship? She doesn't even know me,* she thought to herself.

"Thanks, but I think I'll take my chances."

Brenda shrugged her shoulders while placing back on her shades, methodically turning in her seat to stare out the window as if she had somehow become offended by Emily not adhering to her advice.

"Okay, but I'm telling you, chica, you must look your prettiest all the time or he will get bored."

Emily was relieved when they finally arrived at the stadium. Brenda spent the last ten minutes of the ride pointing out every woman on the coach who had been cheated on. All the talk of cheating and dressing like some starved model was beginning to make her sick. Their seats were directly next to the press box in the centre of the stadium. The green pitch looked immaculate under the floodlights, almost as if it was newly implanted artificial turf. The San Siro was filled to the max with nearly 80,000 people. As the players walked out of the tunnel, the crowd roared and Emily picked out Jude among the players and waved to no avail. When she looked around she noticed just over a dozen girls in her section alone waving just like her. Maybe Brenda was on to something with this whole cheating nonsense? She literally could not hear a word the person sitting next to her was saying. Both sets of supporters were chanting nonstop, pausing only for a millisecond in-between to catch a breath and to let off their continuous bombardment of flares from each section, shining like collapsed red stars.

The game went well for both clubs. Massimo Ambrosini opened up the scoring in the thirty-first minute from a tasty cross from Robinho, and United fired back. On the sixty-fifth minute mark, Jude carried the ball twelve meters passed the midfield line and didn't see an outlet for a pass, so he backtracked and passed it to Patrice who was alert behind him. As Patrice received the ball, a Milan defender slipped, giving United a small window to counter. Jude seized the opportunity to retrieve the ball back from Patrice, and went on a twenty-meter dash, dribbling the ball with exquisite skill while dogging defenders. With his manager's mantra, 'pass the ball' floating through his mind like a banner, he fed a through ball to Van Persie who knocked it back to him in style, leaving Jude one on one with the keeper. He took a solid strike with his right foot, cracking the ball off the crossbar and back into the air. United hit the post three more times in the half before Danny Welbeck equalized in the eighty-eighth minute with a header from a superb Jude cross.

On the flight home, Emily kept to herself, allowing Brenda's words to infiltrate her mind. They left just enough doubt to make her second guess briefly all this relationship stuff. Was she really that naive? Was she only delaying the inevitable? And what would happen to them when the summer ended? She had a lot to think about and knew eventually these were questions that had to be answered. Jude, exceptionally tired from the game, was asleep in the seat next to her, unaware of her building concerns.

For the next few weeks Emily and Jude kept inching closer, but as the summer drew towards an end the nagging doubt still resided in the back of her mind like some catchy song. Every time she raised the question of what their post-summer plans would be, Jude would quickly dismiss her concerns, never really answering the question like some seasoned politician. He just seemed to be so certain that their love would get them through any distance that lay between them, but she was fully aware of the reality and the statistics that summer romances rarely lasted.

As Emily's days remaining in England dwindled, Linda could see the worries beginning to mount on Emily's face. And on a rainy afternoon one week before she was scheduled to return home, she aired her concerns, interrupting Emily's quiet reading session in the foyer.

"Hi, deary, you mind if I sit?"

Emily placed the bookmark on the page before shutting it. "Of course, what's going on?"

"You know you can be honest with me right?"

"Yes." Emily didn't like where this was going.

"Have you enjoyed your summer thus far?"

"Very much so, I can't begin to thank you enough for having me. I've gotten to experience so many things that I never even dreamt of, and of course there's meeting Jude."

Linda smiled at the way Emily's face lit up when saying Jude's name.

"That's lovely to hear. So then what is the matter, dear?"

"Nothing—" Linda saw straight through her lie as if Emily had somehow become transparent.

"Come now, I know these things, a mother's intuition and all of that."

It frustrated her, the way Linda was right. She took a long breath before continuing on in anguish.

"It's Jude."

"Go on..."

"I just don't know what to do. The summer is coming to an end and I worry if I'm too young to try and take on such a long distance relationship. I mean I know Jude is different, but there's still a part of me that thinks he's your typical rich male athlete, and we all know what they like to do. And to make matters worse I just don't think I need any distractions going into my third year of school. I don't know...I'm a mess." Her head sunk into her lap, feeling sorry for herself.

"Oh deary, you are not a mess, you're just in love. I won't lie to you; it's going to be a lot of hard work, but if you truly love each other putting in that work will come easy. You have to develop trust and the knowhow to follow your heart without losing yourself and what makes you special. If you both can do that then I suspect you both shall be fine, no matter the distance."

"You really think we can make it?"

"My dear, I think if he loves you as much as you do him, then you two will be quite all right."

Emily conducted a smile before giving Linda a giant hug.

"Thanks, Linda."

"Anytime, deary—now come downstairs for some tea and biscuits, Charlotte has been requesting your company for a chess match."

VIII

Emily & Jude: Tiffany

E mily began packing for her trip back home the next day. She laid aside the long black dress and matching high heels that Jude had bought her specifically for tonight's football awards banquet. They both would have preferred to spend their last night together in a more intimate setting, but every player that was nominated for an award by the Football Association had to be there, and Jude was up for the young player of the year award. She sat down in front of the mirror running the scorching curling iron through her hair. Her hair was curled and still warm, instantly heating up her back as it made contact. Her cocktail dress adapted to her slender curves flawlessly, but it was still tight enough to make her feel as if doing cartwheels was totally out of the question tonight. The only preparation remaining was to clean her lenses. She placed her spectacles back on and stood looking through the mirror at the beautiful woman she had become. She hardly recognized herself from the person she had known two months ago. If Melissa were here she would fall over at the sight of Emily in high heels. The last time she got this dressed up was her college graduation, and even then she didn't wear heels the whole time.

She noticed Jude would be arriving in a few minutes so she grabbed her purse, another thing she couldn't believe she was wearing, and made her way towards Linda's room.

"Wow, deary, you look beautiful!" said Linda as Emily walked in.

"Thank you. Well, Jude should be here in a few minutes, I'm not sure what time I'll be back but I'll try not to wake anyone when I get in."

"All right, dear. Have fun, and if you happen to run into that handsome David Beckham, tell him as you kids say, he's *hot!*"

Emily laughed, "I will be sure to do that."

"Emily?" She turned back in the doorway.

"Yes?"

"One moment, I have something that will look delightful with that dress." Linda went over to her dresser and began rummaging through a few things. "Ah, here it is." She pulled out an old jewelry box and handed it to Emily.

"Here—put this on."

She opened it and saw a radiant pearl necklace.

"Linda, I can't…"

"Hush up, deary, you most certainly can. I insist. It's doing me no good sitting in that dresser." She held her hair up and Linda placed it around her neck.

"It was my mother's, she told me Princess Diana had one just like it. There, see? Fits like a charm."

Again she stared at her reflection witnessing her complete transformation first hand.

"Thank you, Linda. This is really great."

"My pleasure, deary, you are a part of the family now."

She proceeded outside where Jude was standing in front of a long black limo. He opened the car door for her.

"How is it that every time I see you, you become more beautiful?"

She blushed before staring down at her feet examining the outfit, "You like it?"

He leaned down to kiss her, "You look stunning."

They toasted in the limo, clanging together their respective glasses of champagne and sparkling apple cider. They laughed, joked and shared another glass of their drinks before Emily dropped the mood with a single statement.

"Jude, we have to talk about tomorrow." He just continued sipping his champagne and staring out the window as if he didn't hear her.

"Jude?"…still no answer. "We have to talk about it eventually, preferably before I board the plane."

He spoke in a mixed tone, part patronizing and part upset.

"I know, love, I *heard you*! But can we please just try and enjoy tonight and worry about this later? I promise we can talk after." She held her tongue. "Bloody'ell, can you please just enjoy yourself for once and not always worry about tomorrow?"

They remained silent until they arrived at the banquet. Jude placed his hand on her thigh, stopping her from exiting the limo.

"I love you, Emily, and I'm sorry. I promise we will talk after, yeah."

She removed his hand and planted a kiss on his cheek before exiting.

"It's okay. Sometimes I forget you're a spoiled athlete." He laughed, impressed with her banter and followed her out. They were greeted by a long red carpet and flash bulbs bursting, as the media snapped hundreds of photos dying to get a glimpse of who just stepped out.

"You do know the star is supposed to step out of the limo first?" he whispered to her while waving at the cameras.

"Sorry, I'm new at this." Her cheeks were beginning to hurt from all the strenuous smiling.

"No worries, I actually think they had a laugh when you got out, they had no idea who you were."

"Gee, you sure do know how to make a girl feel special."

"Sorry, I'm just saying it was funny. But I reckon they will know now. We'll be all over the football websites tomorrow." She took his arm and he led her inside through the siege of cameras and journals.

The ballroom was a converted playhouse from the early ninetieth century. Members of the press sat in the balconies overlooking the stage, along with fans who had come to watch their heroes receive awards and give drunken speeches. Thirty-five circular tables draped in white and set with the finest china formed a moat around a hardwood dance floor. The table napkins were exceptionally soft and elegant as if the athletes weren't allowed to wipe their mouths with anything less than what their paychecks consisted of. The room was already beginning to fill with athletes escorting their stunningly beautiful models and actresses. As Emily passed a plethora of superstars she clung to Jude's chaperoning arm, intimidated by the room.

"Jude, over here!"

Jude spotted Michael waving form a table just left of the stage. People were beginning to make their way to their seats so he was easy to spot. The only idiot standing up waving his hand like he's trying to land a plane, Jude thought.

"How are you, mate? You're looking a bit thin—they don't have a weight room in Manchester?"

"Are you havin' a laugh? Because you and I both know I'm the fittest in this room. Besides, I tried not to lift too hard this week; I didn't want to outshine the old blokes like you too much."

Michael laughed, shaking his head as if his previous joke was one-upped.

"Well done. And this must be the lovely Emily. I've heard so much about you. From the looks, you are far too beautiful to be with this tosser."

"Thank you. I keep trying but I can't get rid of him. It's a pleasure to meet you, Michael, I've also heard a lot about you."

"Really? Did he tell you about the time I beat him in sprints at training?"

Jude almost spat his water out, "You did no such thing—you bloody liar!"

Emily looked at Jude with a playful smile.

"No, he forgot to mention that one. But every five minutes he's sure to remind me of how many goals he's scored."

Michael was hysterical.

"I like this one, Jude, that's funny. Get used to it, because he never misses a chance to remind anyone."

"Oi, twenty-five goals is bloody world class!"

Michael looked back at Emily, "see what I mean."

Jude fell into a brief pout, thinking the entire table was somehow against him. Jude's new reluctance to speak made Michael realize how rude he was being.

"My apologies darling, where are my manners? Emily, this is my wife Amy." Amy was a tower compared to Emily; she was six feet with long luscious brown hair and a tight-knit figure. Emily's initial reaction was that she was a model of some sort, but she couldn't pin point for what. She thought if Melissa were here, she would know.

"Hi, Emily, it's a pleasure. You have to forgive these two; they're like brothers constantly fighting over whose better. You and I will have plenty of time tonight to talk about the important things." Her London accent was even stronger than Michael's.

Jude chimed in, "Like what, handbags and shoes?"

"Precisely, amongst other things."

"Good luck getting Emily to hold a conversation about that." Emily's mouth dropped, and she gave him a slight slap on his arm.

"Be quiet! I love fashion."

"Since when?"

She tripped over her words, "Since, um….always….I don't know, I *am* a girl!"

He smiled at her with a sense of surrender.

"Alright, alright, I believe you, don't lose your knickers."

Like a best friend Amy swooped in saving her from further embarrassment.

"Don't pay them any mind, Emily. We are going to take a quick powder break before the festivities begin. If you boys would excuse us?"

As the girls walked away, Jude found his eyes glued to Emily's walk, watching intently the way her hips swayed, hypnotizing him into a state of youthful infatuation. The waiter stopped by, breaking his daze.

"Can I get you sirs anything to drink?"

"I will have a pint of lager and my wife will have a glass of Sauvignon Blanc, please."

"Just two ginger ales for us, mate."

Michael looked at him with a preposterous snarl.

"What...ginger ale?" said Michael, placing his hand across Jude's forehead to check his temperature. "Have you taken ill? You do realize there is no alcohol in that? Jude Macavoy has just ordered ginger ale—I never thought I'd live to see the day."

"Well, Emily doesn't drink and I'm trying to cut back to only a few a day, and I already had me one for breakfast and two on the ride over."

He looked at Jude with astonishment, part proud and part incredulous. "Wow, this girl must really have a hold on you?"

"No, I just need to be fresh for training is all." Of course she had a bear tight grip on him.

"Is this coming from the same Jude that I had to navigate through foreign lands of empty beer bottles and overpaid hookers to drag out of bed for eight a.m. training sessions?"

"I don't know mate, she makes me want to be a better person. It's like, when I am with her I remember that life is alright."

"Bollocks!"

"I'm serious, I love her. It's weird, she's the last thing on me mind before I sleep and the first thing on it when I awake."

"Well, if you ask me it's about bloody time you grew up. If she really is the dog's bollocks, then what is the problem? Because you have that unsure look in your eye, the same one you get before you do something stupid."

"The problem is she loves me back."

The ceremony was fully underway and reaching its peak. Several of Jude's new teammates won awards, Ryan Giggs for a lifetime achievement and Wayne Rooney for player of the year. Jude lost out to a young player from Arsenal, but didn't let the bad news ruin his evening. He still enjoyed spending time with Michael and Emily, and even found it in his heart to have a chat with the media during intermissions to speak up the upcoming season. As the night wore on, everyone became more and more drunk and even Michael began slurring his words.

"Li…lis…listen…Juuude. Doon't…follow…my example tonight…. I….I'm only drinking…because…you're the Padawan and I'm the mas…master…" Before he could finish his long winded speech Amy dragged him back to the dance floor, just as she did Michael Buble's *Haven't Met You Yet* came across the speakers.

"I love this song!" said Emily while slightly mouthing the lyrics.

Jude stood offering his hand, "Shall we?" They proceeded to dance for a few songs until becoming completely deflated by the DJ playing a third horrible techno record in a row. They both took a sip of their now watered- down ginger ales and had a laugh at how bad the drunken people were dancing.

"Blimey, is that how I look when I'm drunk?"

"Please. You make them look like they're on *Dancing With the Stars.*"

Jude felt a soft hand touch his shoulder; his face plummeted to the ground in despair upon seeing her jet-black hair and precisely groomed face, her makeup applied to match the natural glow of her skin.

"You always were a brilliant dancer, Jude." The woman's voice was seductive and confident like an actress in a lingerie commercial. Jude let out an anguish sigh followed by a depressed reply,

"Hello, Tiffany."

Emily studied this new figure. Her dark hair made her blue eyes even more seductive and her perky figure was squeezed into a long white dress that had a long v cut in the front, barely holding in her breasts. She wore a pair of dangling diamond earrings that sparkled off the table's crystal, and Emily noticed her hand had yet to be removed from Jude's shoulder.

"So will you save the next dance for me, superstar?"

Jude didn't take his focus off the glass in front of him. "I'm not sure that would be a good idea." She placed her second hand on his opposing shoulder and began massaging them.

"Relax—you're always so tense at these things. You weren't opposed to the idea of placing your arms all over me the last time we were together."

"Tiffany, don't!" She sat down next to him, finally acknowledging Emily.

"Somebody's grouchy tonight. And who is this? Aren't you going to introduce me to your little friend?"

"Tiffany, this is me girlfriend Emily. Emily, Tiffany." Emily offered to shake her hand but Tiffany did not return the sentiment. Instead she broke out into a bantering laughter.

"*Girlfriend*, are you having a laugh? I'm sorry…I just assumed you were babysitting or something. And I thought you weren't into titles, or at least that's what you told me." He finally looked Tiffany in the eyes; she could see his frustration boiling over.

"That's enough, Tiffany!"

"All right, I don't remember you being so sensitive. So what do you do, love?"

"I currently go to medical school." Emily's American accent further instigated Tiffany's jealousy.

"Bloody hell, Jude, a yank and a doctor? Are you even good enough for her? I'm sorry if my career wasn't prestigious enough to earn me a title from the new millionaire superstar." Jude pulled the glass away from her before she could reach for the little wine that was left.

"I reckon you're drunk, I think it would be best if you pissed off somewhere."

"I have every right to be here. I came with Isaac… he plays for Chelsea you know," she said smugly.

Emily usually got along with everyone, but from the three minutes she'd known Tiffany she knew she didn't care for her.

"Suit yourself. Come on, Emily, let's go." He grabbed her hand and led her away from the table.

"Who is that girl and what does she do?"

"Not now, Emily, let's just get to the limo and get out of here."

Jude slammed the limo door behind him, waking up his driver, Fernando, who was asleep with his chauffeur cap planted firmly over his eyes.

"Drive, Fernando, I don't care where!" He was rubbing his face in stress; ironically his anger worsened despite finally being rid of Tiffany.

"Who was that?"

"Who?" For the first time he saw a frown come across Emily's face.

"Don't play dumb with me, the supermodel Barbie whose breasts were drooped all over you using your shoulders as some sort of breasts rack."

"Don't be dramatic, Emily, she's just an old drunken twat."

"Really, then what does she do for a living? She seemed awfully keen to bring it up."

All Jude could think about was Tiffany winning. She knew what she was doing when she came over. She just wanted to ruin their evening and wind him up, and she succeeded at both brilliantly.

"I don't have time for this."

"What do you mean 'this?' I hate to remind you, Jude, but I don't really have time either." Jude didn't speak, instead his right hand was planted firmly over his mouth as he stared out the window in frustration, all the emotions of the summer and the conversation that he had neglected were erupting like an overdue volcano. Never seeing him this distraught Emily tried to lower her voice.

"We have to talk about it, Jude, I leave tomorrow."

In a last ditch effort to avoid the dreaded conversation yet again, he chose the lesser of two evils,

"She's a whore, or more politically correct a prostitute."

Emily knew Jude was a rebel and liked to drink and go against the grain, but she never expected him to dabble with hookers.

"Did you sleep with her?"

"Jesus, Emily, I thought you went to Yale? Yes I slept with her, she's a bloody prostitute, that's what men do with those, they shag them!"

"And you were going to tell me all of this when?"

"Oh piss off, Emily! What do you want from me, huh, what do you want?" He struck the door with ferocity before continuing. Emily flinched in fear. "What do you want me to say, Emily? I'm a footballer! This is what I do, you knew damn well of me past before you went out with me. I'm not some over wound, uptight, insecure virgin like you. I don't have to answer to you or anybody. If you check me bank account people need *me*, I don't need them."

Emily spoke quietly, disregarding the small tear that was dribbling down her cheek.

"It's nice to finally see what you really think of me. Why wait? Since you don't need me, let's just end it now, save us both the trouble?"

"Yeah, well, maybe we should. It's probably for the best," he said, his breath steadily increasing with each fleeting moment.

Jude took a deep breath still frustrated with the situation at hand, but couldn't bear to see her cry.

"Emily, I'm sorry, that's not what I meant. I'm just trying to sort all this out." He reached to touch her, but she backed away in denial.

"Please don't touch me."

He didn't listen and tried to give her a hug.

"Come on, love, I didn't mean it."

She began crying even more and knocked his hands down turning them bright red in the process.

"Please don't!... Just don't you dare touch me, I just want to go home please."

He sat back in his seat furious and at a loss for words. The situation had escalated far past anything he had ever experienced. Usually he wouldn't care when the girl would go storming off, but this time he actually loved the girl. He motioned to Fernando to turn the limo around,

"Of course. Whatever you want, Emily—I truly don't care anymore. This rubbish is stressing me out and it's not worth it...Take us back to the Bloody inn, Fernando!"

IX

Emily & Jude: Closing Time

Emily's flight back to America was only five hours away and she
still had to get out of her dress from the previous night. Her face
was still salty from her leftover tears and her eyes bloodshot. After
Jude had dropped her off last night, she had run upstairs, not speaking to anyone, and dived head first into her pillow, her tears subsiding
only when she finally fell asleep. She leaned over and grabbed her
phone from the nightstand. There were no missed calls or text messages from Jude, only one from Veronica asking if she was all right.
She must have sent it when she saw her run upstairs crying. Emily
hadn't even heard her phone go off; not that she would have replied
anyway, a heart to heart with Veronica wasn't exactly the comfort that
she longed for.

She really needed to get up. Time was fading and there was still so
much that had to be done, but she just couldn't. Every piece of her
wanted to stay in the bed and cry. Her heart felt crippled and shattered
like someone had rammed a stake through it, and each time she relived
the scene from last night 'I'm not some over wound, uptight, insecure
virgin like you' the stake seemed to plunge deeper. She loved him and
she had fooled herself into believing he loved her, because according
to last night, all they were was a cheap little summer experiment. She
began to cry more just thinking about it.

There was a soft knock on the door; Linda was alert not to startle her in case she wasn't awake.

"Are you all right, darling?"

Emily summoned up what little composure she had left and threw it into her voice.

"I'm fine," replied Emily solemnly.

Linda paused for a moment trying to read Emily's tone as if it were some hidden message in Morse code.

"Okay dear. Well we need to leave within the hour; you mustn't miss your plane."

"I'll be ready, I'm going to jump in the shower and then I'll be down."

The shower wasn't doing much in the area of making her feel better. As the pellets rushed down her body they again reminded her of the tears she had cried last night. Why would he say such things? All she wanted to do was have a mature conversation about where their relationship was headed, a rather simple question she thought, but he had to be immature. If he didn't want a relationship then he should have left her alone. The last thing she wanted was a summer fling, and now she was feeling stupid for breaking her main rule and giving herself to him when all he was doing was stringing her along. She opened up, tried new things, neglected her studies, and even came within an instant of losing her virginity to him. She could hear him now in his stupid accent, 'Yeah, bloody'ell wankers, I shagged the yank' her impression left little to be desired, but the point was clear he didn't care about her and he was probably bragging to his teammates in the locker room as she spoke.

She took her bags downstairs and said goodbye to Charlotte, she attempted to explain how by using the internet they could still play chess, but she may as well have been describing the plot to the *Matrix* films because Charlotte was clueless. In the end she settled on a simple promise to write her. She had one final look at the house, which left a peculiar empty feeling in the pit of her stomach, undeniably coming from the fact that she was missing the house already. For despite how the summer had ended, she had to admit how refreshing it all had been. She got to experience Europe in first class style, eat new foods, break into a football stadium, and fall in love.

"We are going to miss you, Emily. You've been an absolute darling," said Veronica while giving her a hug.

"I'm going to miss all of you too. I had such a good time and I even think I managed to learn a few words, 'taking the piss' is my favorite."

"Just don't use it in America. They will think you actually want to have a wee," joked Veronica.

"But really from the bottom of my heart, thank you all so much for your hospitality and for taking me in. You're like family now."

"Stop…you're going to make me cry," said Veronica, fanning her eyes and rushing in for another hug, "and don't be bothered over Jude. For what it's worth, he was my least favourite signing of the summer." They shared a laugh and Veronica wiped the overly dramatic tears from her eyes.

"Speaking of Jude, can you be sure to give him this letter for me?"

"Of course—I'll see that he gets it. Promise you'll write?"

"I will. How else am I going to find out who won the Premier League?"

"Brilliant! I see I taught you well, down with dreary American sports," said Veronica, laughing and tossing her fist in the air like she was trying to start a revolution. Linda walked through the main door.

"All right deary, I've brought the motor around. Off we go," she said leading Emily out the door.

The gravel flung through the air as Jude's Audi skidded into park in front of the inn. He ran to the front door being greeted by the valet.

"Can I take your keys sir?" asked the valet in the tiny red bellboy hat.

"Piss off!" replied Jude running pass the valet, then shouted back before entering the door, "Sorry mate—didn't mean it; just in a bit of a rush."

He rushed to the foyer in search of Emily hoping he wasn't too late. There was no sign of her, Linda, or Veronica, only Charlotte playing a game of chess with herself.

"Excuse me, Miss Charlotte, have you seen Emily?"

Her face was confused as if he were speaking Spanish.

"Emily... Would you like to play a game of chess?"

"What? No! I'm..." He took a breath, briefly relieving him from his panicked state. "I'm searching for Emily... know what, forget it, I'll just check upstairs. And if I were playing I would say that knight to your rook, checkmate."

She looked down at the board befuddled with amazement:

"Christ on a cracker, the boy's right—he won."

Upstairs Jude sprinted to Emily's room only to discover it was completely vacant. He heard a faint voice come from down the hall and backtracked to the open door where Veronica was sitting on her bed fiddling with her laptop.

"She's already gone."

Jude attempted to catch his breath. He thought, '*I really have to lay off the fags.*'

"What, she's gone?"

"Yep, she left about a half hour ago. She was pretty upset as well. I don't know what happened between you two last night, but you really lost the plot on this one. Here, she told me to give this to you."

"What is it?"

"It's obviously a letter. You footballers are quite dumb aren't you?"

He opened it quickly:

Dear Jude,

This is my first time doing something like this so please bear with me. I love you, I meant those words I said that night on the boat, but after last night it's obvious to me that you can't say the same. With that being said I don't regret our summer together. You showed me many things and allowed me to discover a new adventurous part of me that I never thought possible, and for that I thank you. I promise that I'll never forget the summer under the European stars where I fell in love.

But as we move forward in our lives I think it best if we don't talk anymore. It would only complicate things further and cause more pain than good. So please do not try to contact me. I know how important your job is to you and I respect that, so please understand how important my studies are to me and recognize that I cannot afford any distractions.

I'm sorry things couldn't work out, but perhaps that was for the best. I wish you well in your upcoming season and all your future endeavors.

Best Wishes,

Emily Robertson

Jude's heart jumped to the back of his chest, he felt as if he was going to faint but held strong, up to the task at hand.

"What time did you say they left again?"

"I'm not entirely certain but I think about thirty minutes ago." He folded up the paper placing it in his pocket and headed out the door. "Wait, where are you going?"

"I have to speak with her."

"Just let her be, Jude."

"I can't, it was just a stupid fight… I love her."

"Jude wai…." Before she could finish her statement he was half-way down the stairs.

Jude's mind was frantically racing as he flew down the M56. *'I can't just let her walk out of me life; I have to tell her how I truly feel'* he thought to himself. Every second he would glance away from the road at the clock, hoping he could somehow will it to go in reverse. He knew he would never forgive himself if he let her go on thinking he was some sort of misogynistic pig that didn't really love her. Why did his obnoxious mouth have to get him into so much trouble? He just never knew when to shut up. Again he glanced at the clock—really up against it. He was not only battling time to reach Emily before she took off, but he also had to be back at Old Trafford in two hours to board the team coach to New Castle, a feat which he was quickly coming to realize was virtually impossible.

He made it to the airport in a little less than forty-five minutes, hoping he wasn't too late. He hurried up to the British Airways flight counter cutting the queue and apologizing to everyone along the way *'Sorry, pardon me, excuse me, oops… didn't mean to knock over your magazine.'* One large bald man in line protested like he was at an anti war rally, he would have made a great addition to the sixties:

"OI! This bloke is pushing in!" he said motioning to the officers that were making their way down the escalators enjoying a breakfast biscuit. Jude flared his arms assuring them of no such problem.

"Nothing to see here, I'm not pushing in, I'm just traveling with child and need to make sure her ticket is sorted."

The man didn't buy it for a second.

"Do you take me for a twat? If you're traveling with child then where is she?"

"Um… that's a good question, on both accounts…" He surveyed the terminal looking for an answer until he came across a *Make a Wish Foundation* poster hanging from a wall by the counter; apparently they were running some collaboration with British Airways where two percent of all ticket proceeds go to helping less fortunate children.

"She's in hospital, I just had to rush over and sort her ticket because she's running late and cannot walk. She's proper sick, mate, I'm gutted every time I look at her."

The man sunk his baldhead in embarrassment:

"Well why didn't you say so, mate? I hope you get it sorted."

Jude once again began making his way to the front of the queue, which now seemed to be even longer since his setback. He was stopped again, this time by a man wearing a light blue shirt.

"Hey, aren't you Jude Macavoy?"

"I am, but I really don't have time for an autograph, mate."

"Autograph? Who said anything about an autograph? I'm a Man City fan, United are shite!"

Jude replied sarcastically, more relieved than anything that he didn't have to stop and waste time playing celebrity: "Brilliant, cheers for that, mate."

The teller had been watching him cut the queue and could care less what his excuse was. She ignored him until he moved her current customers, a middle-aged couple dressed in matching khakis and blue and pink flamingo Hawaiian shirts, out the way.

"Excuse me sir, I'm going to have to ask you to wait at the end of the queue like everyone else."

"Me deepest apologies, but I just need to know has flight 122 to Boston departed yet?"

The teller looked at him with a reluctant face before the couple that she was previously helping chimed in.

"It's all right, we can wait." Jude was so grateful he could kiss them, and if it weren't for them being one of the most unattractive couples that he's ever seen he may have.

"Cheers!"

The teller began typing on the computer at what seemed like a thousand words per second and with each keystroke Jude felt the pain that he may have lost Emily forever.

"Well sir, you're in luck. They haven't departed yet but they did just do their final boarding call."

A smile the size of Rhode Island swept across his face.

"That's brilliant!" He turned to run but didn't make it an inch before she stopped him.

"Sir, no one is allowed to the gates without a boarding pass."

"Well how much for a pass?"

She began typing once more; he swore she was the fastest typists alive, like 60 Minutes should do a special on her.

"We are currently fully booked, but there are still tickets available for first class at 3,200 pounds."

"3,200 POUNDS!" he repeated abruptly, "*Bloody'ell*" He pulled out his wallet and placed his Visa Black Card on the counter reluctantly, as if he was parting with a limb. "I guess I'll take it. *Bollocks*, I just got this card… and please put these fine people on me expenses as well and make them first class." He turned looking at the odd couple, "Cheers again mate for allowing me to push in."

The man was ecstatic at Jude's offer.

"Thank you so much!"

"No worries mate, and here, here's a tener, get yourself a new shirt as well because that one makes you look proper bent."

He broke into a full sprint down the terminal corridor, passing gate one then two. Fortunately he had come at the perfect time because the metal detector queue was empty. He could see gate nine in the distance and tapped into his football attributes weaving in and out of incoming traffic until he passed gate seven. He shouted from gate eight, "WAIT, HOLD THE DOOR!" He was more out of breath than he should have been; again thinking *'I need to lay off the fags and pints.'*

"You made it just in time, sir. Once they close the gate doors they don't open until the next plane arrives."

As Jude began walking down the suddenly claustrophobic docking tunnel, he became overwhelmed with nerves like an abrupt ash cloud blocking his brain from the courage that had gotten him this far. His palms were sweaty and his breath was absent, he thought *'this must be what love is.'* The flight attendant took his ticket and urged him to take his seat. As he walked by his first class seat towards coach the captain came on the PA system.

Ding "Good morning ladies and gentlemen, my name is Jonathan Walters and I will be your captain for this nonstop flight to Boston Massachusetts's Logan International airport. At this time we ask all passengers to take their seats and adhere to the seat belt sign located above you. We do seem to be a bit backed up on the runway so we thank you for your patience and we should be departing from the gate in the next ten to fifteen minutes." Jude felt that fate might have finally slipped him a lifeline. He made it to row thirteen when he saw her, her long silky brown hair was tied up securely and her, beautiful, peachy face was buried in a book with her spectacles almost touching the page. He wasn't sure if it were the nerves or facts, but for some reason she looked more beautiful than ever.

"Pardon me, sir; I have a legitimate first class seat, would you fancy a switch?" The gentleman looked up at the same time as Emily.

"Are you kidding? All the little bags of pretzels I can eat, *Hell* yes I'll switch with you!"

Jude let the man out and took his new seat next to Emily. She was so flustered she could feel her cheeks beginning to burn red. She did succeed in finding one silver lining in her predicament, she was glad to be sitting down because her nerves had stolen her legs.

"Jude?" She was as confused as she was flustered.

"I got your letter."

"Good, then you already know how I feel. You didn't have to do all this to reiterate what you want. I know you want this to just be a summer fling. You have a life and I have a life, I get it, and they are a thousand miles apart. Let's just leave it at that."

"No, Emily, you have me all wrong. I was just frightened. I didn't want to lose me freedom, and I feared I would only let you down. I was so concerned with what I'd be losing that I forgot to see what I'd be gaining—you. I love you more than you could possibly imagine. I've only loved two other people more than I do you and both of them died in a motor crash nine years ago, I don't want to lose you as well." A strand of hair fell out of place; Jude tucked it behind her ear and wiped the tear away from beneath her right lens. His voice was soft and reassuring.

"I don't want just a fling with you. I want you and me forever, no matter the cost."

"It'll be impossible with the distance, Jude."

"Perhaps, but we'll never know unless we try. If there's one thing I've learned from me parents, it's that life is short. All I'm asking is for you to take a chance with me. Who knows if we will ever have an opportunity at something like this again?" Her head was pounding and her emotions were racing; she didn't know what to do, a man would only distract her from her goals, the fact that she loved him is irrelevant.

"I just don't…" Cautiousness and tears broke up her words, "I don't know, Jude. I…don't think it's a good idea."

He stared through her lenses into the depths of her soul.

"Listen, Emily, I love you. I wish I had better words than that to describe me feelings, but all I got is I love you. Despite how any of this plays out, the dreadful thought that I will never be able to properly tell you what you mean to me will forever haunt me. Look, I know you're frightened, and look at me, I'm petrified beyond reason, but I believe as long as we have one another everything will be alright. Just have a little faith in fate."

"But why me? I am nothing special," she said, her voice fading into melancholy.

He looked at her, her tears falling and his breath steadying with the assuredness of her beauty in his heart. He saw her—all that she is, like a reoccurring dream that he'd known for a lifetime. With an elegant embrace he placed his hand upon her cheek.

"Special? You don't even know the meaning of the word, Emily. You are so magnificent. No matter how much you fight me, know it will have no effect on me feelings for you. You are the most special person I have ever met."

I love you too. Let's give it a shot. The words were so simple to pronounce but she couldn't bring herself to say them. Why couldn't she say them? Every part of her wanted to give in as if tomorrow would never come, but it felt like an invisible wall was holding her back. They both were silent, Jude running out of things to say and Emily unable to conjure up a coherent sentence.

"Jude…" before she could finish he grabbed her face, their lips intertwining in passion. He could taste the salt from her tears run down her lips as she fell into a calm purgatory. His lips released hers slowly, holding on to every sensation. They sat in peace for a second with their eyes closed and foreheads locked, taking in what had just happened.

"Sooo…we're not breaking up, right?" She shook her head no before going back in for another kiss. Her lips were soft and inviting and he wanted nothing more than to live in them. He stood up electrically, happy, ready, and relieved.

"*Brilliant!* Well, phone me when you land."

"Wait? Where are you going?"

"Yeah about that, I didn't want to mention but I actually have to be in Manchester in…" he looked down at his mobile, "roughly twenty minutes."

"I forgot the season starts tomorrow. Of course I'll call you. But how are you going to get off the plane?"

"Don't worry, love, I'm full of surprises." He shot her a cocky wink and gave her a quick goodbye kiss before walking up to the flight attendant at the end of the aisle. He cleared his throat and put on his best American accent, which strangely came off as a bad southern drawl from all the old west films that he used to watch on BBC 2 at four in the morning when he was returning home from the pubs drunk.

"Excuse me ma'am? I'm one of the Sky Marshals on this here flight and as I'm sure you are fully aware there should only be one. It seems we've been double booked by mistake. That darn Union, they're sure to squeeze every penny out of us. So if you could please get the captain to reopen the gate door I would be much obliged." As he held in his breath, hoping she bought the worst acting job in history, he thought '*GOD that was absolutely rubbish.*'

"Really? I've never seen you on one of our flights before."

He had to think fast, what would John Wayne do?

"Well looky hear, Karen. Can I call you Karen? The thing is it's only my second international flight, so between me and you, I was probably the one who screwed the pooch. So if you could just open that gate I'll be out of your hair and on my way to the two o'clock to Albuquerque."

She hesitated, pondering whether to believe his story. And when she did finally reply, it was in an involuntary tone, siding against her gut feeling.

"Since we haven't left the gate yet I think I can work something out, but in the future make sure you check the schedule. Give me a moment, I'll be right back."

He turned in the aisle giving Emily the thumbs up, feeling a suave sense of accomplishment as if he had just pulled off an epic heist.

Jude called Sir Alex on his way back to Manchester and explained how he would miss the coach due to personal reasons. He caught the train from Manchester to Newcastle and was met by an angry Sir Alex who sat him down in the hotel and gave him the hair dryer treatment for fifty minutes. He scolded him on responsibility, the tradition of the club, and how unless he came up with a more specific reason then he would be fined heavily for missing the team charter. But in spite of the verbal bashing that was raining down upon him there was only one thing on his mind. Emily.

X

Emily: A Trip to Grandmother's

Emily dropped her bags in the middle of the living room before lunging towards the couch in utter exhaustion. She could barely keep her eyes open as she looked upon her small New Haven apartment, which felt vaguely unfamiliar after a summer abroad. She attributed Melissa's bedroom light being out to one last night of clubbing before they began year three on Monday.

She eventually found the motivation to pry herself off the couch and unpack a few of her things. She thought it funny how she left with two bags and returned with four. They were packed with books she had bought in Italy, dresses Veronica helped her pick out in London and Manchester, and souvenirs for her friends and grandmother. When she reached the bottom of Melissa's Juicy Couture bag, she pulled out the jacket that Jude let her keep on their first night together. She recalled how arrogant and annoying she had found him before that night, and could hardly believe she was now in love with that same man. She had already texted him, letting him know she had arrived safely, and she wished she could call him just to hear his voice before she went to bed, but unfortunately she now had to begin coping with the time difference, as it was four in the morning in England.

When she awoke the next morning she noticed a text at 2 a.m. from Jude, *'Good morning love! I hope you have a wonderful day. I'll phone you later.'* She smiled enjoying that he was still beside her in some form when she woke up. She made her way into the living room where she discovered Melissa passed out on the couch, still in the same outfit she wore to the club the night before, her black high heels violently poking the cushions and slight drool creeping down her left cheek. Emily rolled her eyes not even breaking her stride, as it wasn't the first time Melissa was too drunk to make it to her room; to be honest she was impressed that Melissa even made it home. She made a pot of coffee using their ancient 2002 coffee maker and some buttered toast. At the kitchen counter she began sorting through the mail that had been piling up for the last two months. Among the junk mail, grocery store coupons and credit card companies begging for her signature, was a paper copy of her field schedule for the coming year. She was glad to be assigned to Hartford Hospital because the doctors there were extremely pleasant and allowed her to administer treatments when the patient allowed.

As she continued sorting through the mail she stumbled across a letter that had come fairly recent and was address from Manchester, England. She took a bite of toast, sprinkling crumbs across the counter with not the faintest idea of who it could be from. *'I've only been home for ten hours, and the postage says it arrived a week ago,'* she thought to herself.

Dearest Emily,

I know you must be confused since you have just returned home to discover this letter, and if you are then me plan has worked successfully. Please allow me to shed some light on the situation. I am writing you on the week before you return home, and to be completely honest I wish you were staying, but I know you aren't so I shall not dwell on me wishes. It felt like every day throughout the summer you proposed the question to me, 'what will become of us once you return home?' and although I'm sure you already know, I admit I've been avoiding the question. Truthfully I didn't know what to do nor am I 100% sure that this is the right thing to do, hence my neglect for telling you.

You see, we are both young. I am a footballer (and a pretty good one might I add) and you are an aspiring doctor ready to embark on a whole new world. It seems the odds are not in our favour. So a large part of me has been reluctant to commit because I fear that we are doomed from the start. However, after weeks upon weeks of debating the question I have come to a conclusion that I am 100% sure of, and that is I love you. Even if as you read this letter we have chosen not to continue our relationship then at least you will know how I've always loved you. But if we are to continue on then I know we have a daunting task ahead if we are to make this work. So I propose we write one another every day, alongside the mobile and other conversation methods of course. I want to know every detail of your day, all the workings of your heart and mind, how you're managing to save the world one patient at a time. Basically treat these letters like a diary. I want to feel as if you never left, and once I see you again we can trade journals and experience each other's worlds together.

I hope you fancy me idea and your thoughts haven't changed towards me. This whole love thing is rather foreign to me, so please have patience. I hope I speak with you after you read this, and if you do fancy the idea consider this me first journal entry. May it give you something to look forward to.

Love,

Jude

Emily wasn't sure what to make of the letter. Jude had known he wanted to continue their relationship for over a week? Why wouldn't he have said all of this in person? If he had, they both could have avoided that fight and could have avoided almost losing each other forever. But there was one emotion she was sure of, and that was anger. She was furious that he hadn't told her any of this sooner. When they talked later, he was going to have a lot of explaining to do.

She walked back to her room and pulled out a black composition notebook and entitled it 'Letters to Jude,' she then wrote on the first page,

Dear Jude,
You have a lot of explaining to do!

Melissa woke up around two o'clock in the afternoon and, after a much needed shower, she devoured a greasy double cheeseburger, or as she titled it 'the hangover burger,' before sitting down on the couch with Emily to catch up. Emily brought her up to speed with her summer and went through all of her photos from England and Italy thoroughly, as if she were giving a Power Point presentation. Melissa couldn't believe how big the inn was; she had ventured there only once when she was two and didn't remember it looking so enchanting.

"Christ, Emily, if I knew it was going to be that nice I would have gone myself and left you here to intern all summer."

Emily then filled her in on Jude and hers relationship. She made it a point to highlight Jude's being a jerk at times, along with his romantic moments, and how in the end they decided to give it a go.

"It sounds like you're describing some rom-com staring Hugh Grant. I mean you're dating a professional athlete, *that's crazy*, Em! You know he could probably buy Yale. Shoot, come to think of it he could probably buy the entire state with all the money he makes."

Emily laughed at Melissa's exaggeration.

"I highly doubt that. And please don't tell him that. His head doesn't need to get any bigger."

"Wait, so I'm going to get to meet this hunk?"

"Of course you are. He's going to fly up when he gets some days off, but it probably won't be until Christmas."

Melissa perked up on the couch eagerly,

"So let me get this straight, Em. You're going to go five months without seeing your pro athlete, absurdly rich, British, and super hot boyfriend, who I Googled and looks to have abs that were photo shopped on because they're so perfect, and you're not worried about every super model, gold digger, and groupie within a hundred mile radius of him?"

Emily dwelled over her response, remembering the seductive Tiffany and wondering if she was just one of many. True, she was inexperienced in relationships and life in general, but she was wise enough to know that trust is the foundation of every relationship, whether it be love or friendship.

"I guess I am. I trust him—it's the only way this thing is going to work."

Melissa looked at her deranged and with an imprudent sense of pity.

"Okay, Em, I just don't want you to get your heart broken. Because celebrity or not, if he does break your heart then I will do something to him that I'm pretty sure is illegal in every state except maybe Utah and parts of Arizona." Emily didn't have a clue as to what she was referring, and Melissa could tell that by the perplexed look on Emily's face. "Trust me. He'll pay and he won't like it." Emily gave her a hug and could smell the mixture of alcohol and cheese on her breath.

"Thanks. That's why you're my best friend. Now you need to sober up, because we have just two days left before our third year, so let's go out and enjoy them."

"But it's only three o'clock. No one is going to be at the bars except for depressed divorced guys and weirdoes."

"I was referring to the mall or a movie."

Melissa laughed. "Of course you were. I guess Europe didn't change you that much after all."

Emily replied with a taunting tone as she walked back to her bedroom, boasting to Melissa like a fourteen-year-old girl with the hottest new accessory.

"I wouldn't say that. In case you were wondering his abs aren't photo shopped."

"So? A ripped guy took his shirt off in front of you, whoopty-doo."

"Who said 'he' took it off?" replied Emily with a promiscuous swagger.

"Em—you slut! I'm so proud of you. My baby's finally growing up."

Emily walked away grinning and proud that she had for once finished with the upper hand in one of their exchanges.

On her way to her grandmother's house, the subdued swaying of the train kneaded with Emily's jet lag, putting her to sleep almost instantly after departure. The past two and a half months had been the longest she had gone without seeing her grandmother, Audrey Ross, since she had first taken her in. Since her grandmother was only about forty miles away in a rural town in Hartford, Connecticut, she always made it a priority to have dinner with her at least two times a week. Emily also planned trips for them once a month to either the ballet or the opera in Boston. Sometimes she felt bad because her schedule would allow her no time at all to see her grandmother, but even when she couldn't make it up to Hartford, she was always sure to call.

The main attribute that Emily admired about her grandmother was how strong she had been over the years. Despite her age of eighty-four she needed no help navigating through everyday life, and she still cooked her own meals, cleaned every inch of the house, went grocery shopping, and albeit very slowly, managed a walk around the neighborhood every morning. Audrey made Emily vow never to put her in a nursing home as long as she could continue doing those things. It became a motivational tool to keep her fit and eating right. Whenever she went in for a checkup, her doctor would say, "Mrs. Ross, you must really dislike nursing homes because you're as healthy as a fifty-year-old."

The vibrations from Emily's mobile trembled in her pocket irritatingly. She thought twice about not answering and falling back to sleep, but figured since her grandmother's house was only three stops away, she might as well get up. She pulled her mobile out and noticed Jude's name displayed across the front panel, quickly giving her an adulterated feeling of excitement and anger.

"Hello?"

"Hello, love! I see your jet lag has come to pass, I reckoned you would be asleep."

She thought, despite being glad to hear his voice, she wished she was.

"Your call actually woke me up, but since I kind of like you I decided to answer." She quickly adjusted her tone remembering that she was supposed to be angry with him.

"Just sort of? Well then I suppose it's a good thing that I'm mad about you; otherwise this would never work." His charm fused with his accent made it hard for Emily to stay upset with him, but she stood her ground.

"Why did you write that letter?" Her tone was firm and to the point like a seasoned general.

"What's wrong with it? I know it's a tad trite but I truly want to know as much about you as I can. You don't think it's a rather charming idea?"

"It's not that. I think your idea for a letter diary is sweet and I agree with how hectic our schedules are. It will be a nice way to keep informed when we can't get to a phone. But why didn't you tell me all of this in person when you initially wrote it? You just let me go on thinking we were some fling thingy…I don't know what we were, but every time I brought up commitment you had a conniption, and if my memory serves me right, you bit my head off the last time I specifically asked you what you wanted to do." Although she wasn't shouting, he could still hear the anger in her delivery.

"Me sincerest apologies, love. I would never do anything to hurt you and just the thought that you have been upset makes me feel awful. Surely you know I wanted to tell you, but it was all so confusing. When I wrote you that letter, yes I was a little drunk—"

"Just a little?" she added incredulously.

"Okay, a lot drunk. But I was also completely sure I wanted to be with you. But then a day would go by and I would feel differently. I would be timid or feel like I would be missing out on something if I committed, and then I would see you and change me mind again. Me emotions were just so unstable…But that morning when I read your note, and thought that I may never see you again, that's when I knew you were the one thing in life I couldn't be without." He momentarily took the phone away from his ear and began silently bashing his skull with it, as if proclaiming his feelings out loud had finally helped him grasp how foolish he was being all along. "Long story short, Emily, I reckon I sort of already knew I wanted to be with you, I just wasn't sure how or when to say it."

She collected his words and examined them earnestly. A part of her hated the way he possessed the power to put her mind at ease despite whatever emotion she was currently feeling. She couldn't fault his motives too much, because if anyone understood not being able to make up their mind it was her, but still there was a sense of bitterness that resided between them.

"Well, don't let it happen again, because the next time you are confused about whether you love me or not I won't stick around waiting for you to figure it out. But I guess I'll let you make it up to me this time."

He didn't like where the conversation was going.

"Bloody'ell. Go on… what shall my sentence be? Something tells me it's going to be quite expensive."

"You're going to have to wait until you read my first letter."

"I see. That's a rather bold strategy considering I won't see you until possibly Boxing Day."

"Well, I figured you sent your first letter through the mail so it's only fitting that I do the same."

He grinned at the subtle mystery of her words.

"I knew you fancied me idea! You do know you are incapable of hiding anything from me? I see right through you, love."

She struck a sharp smile before returning his playful banter.

"Is that so? Well, did you foresee this?" …A few seconds passed, and her mobile began vibrating again.

"Hello?"

"I can't believe you've just hung up on me!" he said with consternation, secretly impressed with her audacity.

"I guess you can't see through me after all."

"I'm going to get you back. It may come today, it may come tomorrow, it may come three years from now, but rest assured you shall rue the day you hung up on, Jude Macavoy."

They laughed at Jude's extravagant promise and continued talking until she reached her grandmother's stop. One thing they knew was never going to get any easier, was saying goodbye. They prolonged saying the word until it came time for her to exit the train. Every time they were forced to say it, Emily felt a part of the accompaniment of happiness that resided in her heart dwindle, only to return with their next conversation.

The musk smell of mothballs crept up Emily's nostrils as she walked into her grandmother's tiny home on Rider Street. She found it interesting how grandparents' homes had such distinct smells, unlike anything in existence. Her grandmother had owned the house for over forty-seven years. At one point it was home to her grandfather, her mother, and her only pet cat, Sable, who she was told at the age of seven had run away, but she later found out they had to put her down due to age. The walls along with the mantel above the fireplace were occupied with old family photos of her mother as a teenager, of her mother holding Emily on her first trip to the zoo, of Emily's Yale graduation, and her favorite one of her father and mother smiling while they held her two days after her birth. She smiled. 'The Robertson family used to be so happy once,' she thought…'the key word being once.' It's funny how fast everything can change, one minute you're at the zoo smiling and the next your mother's gone and your father has consumed every alcoholic beverage from here to Thailand. It was this very thought that led her to immerse herself in schoolwork in hopes of blotting out the way things had turned out.

Her grandmother was in the kitchen, which was decorated in dull brown wallpaper and bright yellow and pink flowered floor tiles. Every time she entered she felt as if she had arrived in a DeLorean time machine equipped with a flux capacitor set for the fifties. It was half past four in the afternoon, so she was well into cooking dinner. Emily knocked softly on the table before approaching her grandmother from behind, and wrapped her arms around her. Mrs. Ross nearly jumped out of her apron.

"Jimminy crickets, Emily, you nearly scared me half to death. I didn't hear you come in."

She ran her fingers through her short grey hair before giving her granddaughter a hug and a kiss. Emily knew she would have to wipe the lipstick from her cheek when her grandmother wasn't looking.

"Hey, grandma! I missed you." The mixture of mothballs, dinner, and her grandmother's cheap old perfume reminded her just how much she missed her. She held on as tight as she could, feeling like a young girl again, getting excited over a trip to grandma's house. Mrs. Ross stirred the pot a few more times as the steam rose, leaving condensation on her aged skin and retro spectacles.

"Please, sit down…sit down, are you hungry?"

"I could eat. Whatever you're making smells divine!"

"I'm cooking cabbage and your grandfather's famous meatloaf."

Emily sniffed the air again, closing her eyes in ebullience.

"*Mmm*, you know I would never pass up granddad's meatloaf."

Mrs. Ross opened the oven checking the color of her meatloaf, releasing even more succulent aromas into the air.

"So tell me, dear, how was your trip? I didn't even know you were back. I remember the first time I went to Europe, your grandfather took me to France for our honeymoon. It was so romantic. We kissed under the Eiffel Tower and went dancing in *Pointe de Plaisir*—we danced for hours. Although the French weren't too happy with two Americans enjoying their food and drink, being shortly after the war and all, but we didn't care…Oh dear, look at me I'm rambling. Please tell me about your trip." Her grandmother tended to trail off a lot these days. However most of the time it was old stories about her mother or grandfather so Emily took pleasure in re-listening.

"Well, I'm not sure where to start. I stayed at Melissa's aunt's beautiful inn a little outside of Manchester, and grandma, you should have seen it. It was spectacular! You would have just loved it. I got to go shopping in London, took a picture inside one of those red phone booths, and walked outside of Buckingham Palace; which reminds me, the inn used to be one of the Queen's summer homes. How awesome is that? I also went to Italy where I saw a soccer game, had the best spaghetti of my life, and got to browse one of the world's biggest libraries. It was a time I'll never forget, I'm so glad the girls made me go."

Her grandmother beamed with pleasure at seeing how happy Emily was.

"That's great, dear. I always said you were due some blessings in your life. You are always so busy with school and helping me, I don't know how you ever have any time for yourself."

"There is one more thing that happened." She pulled out her mobile and opened up one of the photo albums, showing her grandmother a picture of her and Jude in front of the San Siro stadium.

"I met a boy, his name is Jude. He's really charming once you get to know him. He's a professional soccer player in England."

Mrs. Ross took the mobile and examined every detail of the photo, mimicking one of her favorite television programs Murder She Wrote.

"Oh my, you have been a busy girl. He's very handsome and sounds like a nice young man." Emily was content with her grandmother's approval, feeling more confident about her recent relationship decision.

Halfway through dinner, Emily began her second helping of cabbage. Her grandmother's secret was adding a pinch of brown sugar, making it the perfect blend of sweetness and spice. As she sat there watching the juice from the cabbage run off her spoon in thought, she asked,

"Grandma…what do you think about long distance relationships?"

Mrs. Ross was in mid bite, she placed her fork down and dabbed the corners of her mouth smudging her red lipstick across the napkin.

"Heavens, dear, it's been a long time since I had to think about that." She took a sip of homemade lemonade before continuing. "When your grandfather went off to war I didn't know what I would do. We were so young then, I loved him but I wasn't sure if he would come back, and even if he did whether he would be the same person. So I did what any other seventeen-year-old girl would do, I moved on with my life. I met a new boy named, Thomas Hawkins. His father was a wealthy businessman from the south, and boy was Thomas handsome. Your grandfather would still write all the time and occasionally I would write him back to keep his spirits up, but I saw how distraught other girls in my class were when they received word that their boyfriends had been killed, so it just gave me another excuse to move on. Truth is, I grew quite fond of Thomas. He was very different from your grandfather, and in his own way made me happy. But then, Marvin came home and everyone in town told him about Thomas and me. I was so adamant about no longer being in love with him I practically blew him off when I saw him, but he didn't care. Then one night when Thomas and I were returning from a picture, I think we saw *And Then There Were None*, there was Marvin sitting on my parents' doorstep waiting for me to come home, I tried to explain that I had moved on but nothing I said discouraged him. He asked me to marry him then and there, and the rest is as you'd say history."

"Wow, grandma, you never told me that."

"I don't tell you everything. A woman needs her secrets. But to answer your question, love doesn't care about time, distance, or circumstances, if it's meant to be then that's exactly what it will do—be."

Later that evening they shared a pot of tea by the fireplace, while Emily read passages aloud to her from one of her grandmother's favorite poets, Emily Dickinson. After her grandmother went to bed around seven, she tucked her in and made her way back to the city with a marginally new take on her and Jude's relationship, one that was filled with optimism and a pubescent sense of faith.

XI

Emily & Jude: Becoming Acclimated

The first few weeks of school were brutal, surpassing years one and two in every way. There were twice as many exams, triple the hours of field study, and four times the homework. Melissa was coping even worse with year three. She had already accumulated a $500 Starbucks tab, and had become addicted to energy drinks; so much so, she swore her urine began coming out blue, as if she was a Smurf. However, it wasn't so much the workload that was driving Emily insane, but the fact that she rarely spoke to Jude except through text messages. And the way all the long distance variables added up, placed more weight on her shoulders making it harder to focus, and that's what frightened her. They were constantly missing one another. When he was free, she would have class; when she was free, he'd be training; when training was out, she'd be at field study. No matter how they spun it, their timing was never ideal. Nonetheless, with all the commotion, it made her appreciate Jude's journal idea even more, and by the time she received his second letter she was practically harassing the postman in anticipation.

It arrived on a gloomy Tuesday morning; she must have read it twelve times during her thirty-minute lunch break.

Dearest Emily,

It has been 19 days, 6 hours and 21, 22, 23 seconds since we last saw one another, yet it feels like an eternity. I am so glad we decided on writing these letters. There is nothing I look forward to more than hearing from you, and when I do I get an instant shot of life and energy. But enough about how much I miss you, you already get enough of that whenever we do talk. By the way, you do know you have the power to tell me to shut up if I ever become redundant. Now on to the reason why I'm writing, me, me, me, and of course a little about you (you're so vain, you know that).

Football has been going well. After we last spoke, I had a brilliant match against Sunderland midweek taking us to 4 and 0 on the season. Of course you could have done the math yourself, you did attend bloody Yale. A couple of the lads, okay the entire team, have been taking the piss for falling for a yank who lives across the pond, but I'm always sure to tell them I fell for an angel from heaven, because little do they know you inspire me every day.

We have a massive match this weekend against Everton. I believe it's on ESPN, so if you don't have to go in you can watch it on the telly. I wish I was telling you all of this in person, so I could kiss you and run me fingers through your hair. But besides me going mad missing you, this whole long distance thing isn't that bad. Alright, are you done laughing now? I agree it's bloody awful! I wish the gaffer wasn't a football Nazi and he would give us at least two days off so I could fly and see you. But in due time you will be back in me arms where you belong. Until then know I love you and miss you. Keep revising hard at university (I know I don't have to tell the queen of revising that), and try not to let your flatmate down too many of those energy drinks. A mate of mine at trials in Blackpool used to drink them and he said it turned his piss green like Yoda.

Well, farewell love, I look forward to hearing from you and learning more about your grandmum. She sounds lovely.

Love,

Jude

P.S.

For your next letter send it via email as well, it will go straight to me phone and I can receive it quicker.

Jude couldn't believe how quickly he was adapting to life at Manchester United. In their first three matches he already scored a wonder strike against Newcastle and tallied up two assists. Even though he kept it to himself, he wasn't naive to the fact that everything started looking up once Emily came into his life. He was now less stressed on and off the pitch. Gone from his daily routine were the cases of booze and mornings waking up not knowing how he got there. There was no more hiding away from the world. Everything just felt much simpler, like someone had opened his eyes for the first time. That's not to say he still didn't accompany a few of his teammates down to the pub after matches; he was still British after all. He felt good not having to conjure up some lie as to why whatever female was lying in his bed had to leave, and no longer having to mumble at 6:30 in the morning, 'Just take what you need out of me wallet on the dresser,' to the prostitute for a job well done.

He had been keeping his word and writing to Emily every day. Some days it would be in the journal and others he would send it via email or the post. But no matter how busy his days became, he was always sure to write.

On the team coach to the Everton match, an eerie silence migrated through the coach. They all knew it would be their first true test of the young season and they would do good to come away with at least a point. Their previous three matches were against newly promoted Scunthorpe, Newcastle, and Sunderland, not what you would call elite competition.

Jude sat peering out the window with his music headphones wrapped homely around his ears, like it was twenty below outside. A new record from some American rapper was blaring from his iPod, and despite the overly loud music and the daunting task ahead, his mind was transfixed only on Emily. He wondered if she was taking notes in the back of a hospital room right now, or if she was cleaning her spectacles because it was a humid September day? He bowed under his chair and rummaged up Emily's first letter from his United training bag.

Dear Jude,

~~You have a lot of explaining to do!~~ Sorry, I wrote that before we spoke on the phone. Speaking of which, for the most part you did a good job wiggling your way out of trouble, but next time I see you you'd better be nice to me the whole time. Oh, and you better be carrying the book I wanted so badly from Italy. No, I won't tell you which one. If you can't remember how much I raved on about it over dinner, then you're going right back in the dog house mister.

I'm writing you on my lunch break. I'm halfway through my second day of year three. I have settled in okay but I'm feeling a bit overwhelmed at all the homework. It's not that I can't handle it, but it's a bit time consuming and leaves little time for us as I'm sure you're already aware. But if you think I'm a mess, you should see my roommate Melissa. She's been drinking energy drinks like they're going out of style, all so she can stay awake to get work done. Speaking of Melissa, we were able to catch your first game on TV. I'm so proud of you, you did so well! I love watching you play. It reminds me of when we first met. It's sort of funny, because that day I couldn't wait to get away from you and now it's the complete opposite. And before you begin boasting, it was a very nice pass you made to Wayne Shooney or Looney...whatever his name is, for the first goal. However I'm sure you will still find a way to boast the next time we speak.

I do hope you miss me, Jude, because I would feel like a silly girl for how much I'm missing you. I finally told my grandmother about you and she very much approved, Yay!! To pat myself on the back, I did do a stellar job selling you. Maybe if I fail as a doctor I will become a car sells person. Could you imagine—quiet, shy, nerdy me trying to sell a Mercedes to some forty-year-old with a combover and midlife crisis? Yeah, me either. On a serious note I haven't been sleeping well. I wish you were here to hold me when I wake up distraught in the middle of the night. Sometimes I want to just pick up the phone and call you but then I remember the time difference. It's so hard, Jude, I hope we make it. I suppose we will though since we love each other.

Well, I love you Jude and miss you! Speak to you soon.

Love Always,
Emily xoxo

She always followed her 'XOs' with a smiley face. The smiley face always made him smile. He would picture the way he would call her beautiful and watch as she'd tuck a strand of hair behind her ear and fix her spectacles in embarrassment before looking up at him with those rosy cheeks and soft hazel eyes. He refolded the letter tucking it safely back in his bag. She sprayed some of her perfume on it, making him feel as if she was in the room every time he opened it. The letter eased his pent-up tension and reminded him that no matter the outcome of the match today, he still had someone that was proud and loved him.

The pitch was disturbingly fast due to the way Everton obsessively watered it pre kickoff, but United made due dominating over sixty percent of the procession and creating a number of quality chances throughout the first half. Jude put in another outstanding performance on the right wing, placing pin point crosses all day and playing a tasty little one two on the edge of the box for Hernandez to score his first goal eight minutes into the second half. They went on to withstand several late scares from Everton and win the match one nil.

In the locker room post match, players were either speaking with reporters or getting treatment from the medical staff. Jude managed to sneak out of the locker room unseen; thankfully the media was more interested in the goal scorer Hernandez and the manager. He made his way to the auxiliary hallway, where the boiler room and loading docks were. Despite the boiler sounding like the world's largest vacuum, it was the quietest place in the stadium.

"Hello?"

"Good morning, love!"

Emily's face lit up like fireworks at the sound of his voice.

"Hey Jude!"

"Are you havin' a laugh?" He hated his name, just because his parents were children of the sixties and found *The Beatles* to be nothing less than Godly; he shouldn't have to suffer through the constant bombardment of ill-defined *Hey Jude* puns. "I see you have become quite the little comedian."

"I try—"

"So how are you? Forgive me if I woke you up."

"No, I've actually been up since seven thirty, I even watched the game. One of Melissa's friends at the bar is a big soccer fan, and…"

"For Christ's sake, stop saying SOCCER!"

"Sorry, he is a big *'football'* fan and he gave me a website where I can stream the match. It got a bit choppy at parts so I may have missed a thing or two, but I did see the goal."

"So you saw it then? I can't believe I hit the post on that header, it should have gone in."

Emily's tone was comforting and for a brief second he heard his mother in it.

"Don't beat yourself up over it, you played well. Even the infamous Jude Macavoy has to miss sometimes."

"Perhaps you're right. So what are you doing today, any field work?"

Emily was multitasking, balancing her mobile in one hand and flipping the crisp page of her textbook with the other.

"No, not this Saturday. I've just been sitting here studying mostly. Melissa and I may shoot over to the mall for a few before I head up to my grandma's for dinner."

"Sounds lovely… I miss you, Emily. It's maddening. I didn't think it would be this difficult."

"I know. Me too, December is too far away." Her voice now dejected as if just being told bad news.

"It'll be here before you know it, love. Do you fancy Skype later? We should be back in Manchester in about three or four hours. I could phone you then?"

"That sounds good. Just text me though because we may be at the mall."

"Brilliant, I'll phone you then! But I must go, I still have to shower and address the journals before we head back."

"Okay, I should get back to studying anyway. I shouldn't be letting handsome British boys distract me."

"What about the American ones?"

"Oh they're fine, they can distract me all day if they'd like. It's the British ones I'm worried about."

He laughed, "You really are full of it today aren't you? 'Comedian Emily' has a nice ring to it huh?"

"It kind of does—"

Jude's voice went uncannily silent on the other end of the phone.

"One last thing, Emily—"

"What is it?"

"What are you wearing?" he said provocatively.

"Jude!" she responded embarrassingly.

"Come on, Emily, I'm just curious. Indulge me a little."

She looked down at her dingy Yale sweatpants and her white sweatshirt, which still had a faded imprint of the mustard stain from when Melissa borrowed it junior year for the hot dog eating contest for Taylor Swift tickets. She went on to lose the contest to a robust girl from Harvard who would later appear on the television program, *The Biggest Loser.*

"I don't know. I'm wearing sweatpants and a sweatshirt," she said apprehensively.

Jude sucked his teeth in disappointment.

"Jesus, Emily, you are bloody awful at this. You just had to go and 'Emily' it up didn't you."

"Did you just use my name as a verb?"

"I did, because you did in fact, 'Emily' it up. I'm going to submit the word to Urban Dictionary. *Emily—the act of not having fun or bringing another down so they too don't have fun.*"

"I can't believe you," she said astonished at his intrepidity to coin such a phrase. "Fine…I'm just sitting here at *nine-forty-five in the morning* in a bikini," she replied, hoping that would get him off her case.

"I know you're lying, but still, this is a brilliant start." He closed his eyes, attempting to imagine her sitting there as such. "How are you wearing your hair? It's proper sexy I bet, like that bird from the Whitesnake music video that gets on the hood of the motor."

"Jude, this is stupid. I'm hanging up."

"No, no, come on…don't hang up. I haven't seen you in months Emily and it's driving me mad. Here, I'll show you how it's done." Emily didn't respond, but instead shook her head, smiling, amused at his suppressed hormones. "I'm completely nude, nothing on, and me body is covered in baby oil making me muscles pop." He began rubbing his stomach in imagination.

"And I'm flexing right now and it's turning you on…"

"Mate, what are you *doing*," asked Steven, hysterically laughing in the doorway.

"Does no one believe in knocking anymore? Get out!"

Emily began laughing as well, comfortably curled up on her couch examining a medical textbook.

"Mate, are you trying to have phone sex in the bloody boiler room?" said Steven in-between heavy burst of laughter.

"Will you just piss off somewhere *please*?"

"Alright, but hurry up. The gaffer's looking for you." Steven closed the door and laughed the words "phone sex in the boiler room…what a muppet," as he exited.

"Well love, I reckon we will have to continue this another time. I really must go."

They both fell silent, struggling to hang up.

"I love you," she said softly with sincerity and a hint of despair.

"I love you too, Emily. I'll speak with you soon."

XII

Emily & Jude: A Cold Winter's Night

"So what time does Jude get in tomorrow?" asked Melissa before biting into her still cold in the middle Salisbury steak TV dinner, which she had heated up in the microwave six minutes prior.

"Around four tomorrow afternoon—I can't believe he's actually coming to our apartment."

"And I can't believe you guys have actually lasted five months! The longest relationship I've had was, Steven Walters, in the third grade. He proposed to me at recess and by nap time the next day we were over."

"You had nap time in third grade?"

"Hey, don't mock Mrs. Petersons' teaching methods. She was a teacher among students," replied Melissa smugly, like she had just said something profound.

"What does that even mean? Of course she's a teacher among students."

"See, if you were in Mrs. Peterson's class you would be able to decipher such things."

Emily rolled her eyes before curling both legs on the couch, nestling in with her steaming cup of coffee and her *Biomedical Ethics* course book. She took a sip, feeling the warm caffeine tranquilize her throat as it went down.

"Are you nervous? I almost peed my pants the first time I saw Steven Walters in fourth grade, but then again, my mom was always heavy handed when pouring my apple juice in the mornings."

Emily shrugged her shoulders indifferent to the question.

"I'm more excited than nervous. I already have both our days planned out."

"*Two days? That's it!* I assumed he would at least stay a week—it's Christmas. What, do the Brits not believe in Jesus?"

Emily had come to grips with the two days, but her initial reaction was similar to Melissa's. It wasn't fair. There are millions of people in the world in relationships and they can't stand being next to one another, so why can't she and Jude be granted that much time together?

"I know, but he has a game that Saturday so he has to be back by Friday. It's better than nothing at all."

"Yeah, that's true."

Being in love for the past four months sounded good on paper, but it was austere torture for them both. There were nights when she would be at the hospital until one in the morning while Jude was half way across the world in Russia preparing for a Champions League fixture. They felt constricted by a handicap that no other couple shared. But in spite of the lonely nights longing for each other's touch, they kept their promise of working hard to keep the communication lines open. Jude bought her a new high end mobile with a built in camera so they could video call whenever she was on break at the hospital. They kept a flowing stream of text messages, *'I love you, don't work too hard.'* and *'Good luck today, break a leg'* a saying he often reminded her wasn't appropriate for a football match, he even proposed Skype sex, but Emily shot the idea down hastily saying, "You want me to put my hand where? I'm not touching that!" As for the letters, they kept coming in all shapes and sizes in addition to the ones in their respective journals. One of Emily's favorites was one that Jude FedExed on her birthday in November.

Dearest Emily,

Happy Birthday, love! Today should be the third especially since I paid an extra twenty quid to make sure it arrived promptly on your birthday. I can't believe you are twenty-six now and even more inconceivable is that you are in love with me. I often have to pinch meself to be certain this isn't all a dream. Who would have thought a girl as beautiful, intelligent, kind, and marvelous as you could ever love a bloke like me? I wish I could have sent along 365 presents to thank you for every day that you make me the happiest man in the world, but the post claimed that would cost about 12,000 pounds so I reckon I would send one gift that would suffice. Please go on and open the attached envelope (hopefully you followed the instructions and haven't already done so).

She started rubbing the platinum heart lock pendent incrusted with diamonds that sat around her neck, recalling the chills it gave her when she originally opened the envelope. Her words deserted her leaving her hopeless and breathless, for she had never seen something so captivating and astonishing.

This necklace is a symbol of me heart. Though you have stolen it a long time ago when I first laid eyes on you, I wanted you to be able to have it with you at all times. I do wish I could be there to place it on you, but rest assure I will be there soon enough. So wear this gift love and know you can close your eyes tonight knowing I love you.

Happy Birthday,

Jude

Whenever she would glance down at the pendant it would make her feel apprehensive. She wasn't the one for wearing jewelry, let alone the very expensive kind, but she did find it beautiful and it did succeed in reminding her how much he loved her.

Emily found herself constantly checking the speedometer on Melissa's car. Her anxiety and nerves made her foot heavy, and it was taking every calm cell in her body to keep the meter under a hundred. A part of her believed that the faster she got there the sooner he would arrive. Of course her logic was flawed and moronic, but not seeing your boyfriend in four and half months can drive a girl to believe such things.

Waiting outside the baggage claim, gaping at the automatic doors, Emily found her heart leapt at every man that remotely resembled Jude. It had been so long since she had last seen him in person—she could hardly remember what he looked like without the blurred pixels from her mobile screen. She anxiously fixed her hair in the visor mirror hoping he would still find her agreeable. She had even gone to the length of borrowing one of Melissa's pushup bras from Victoria's Secret to help sway him in case he had lost interest. It was her first time wearing one. She uncomfortably tugged at her left cup, feeling as if something had her breasts in a strangle hold. How Melissa withstood wearing one every time she went out was beyond Emily.

Jude had a brisk pace to his walk as he descended through the terminal. He always got a weird feeling when in an American airport, as if he were behind enemy lines. He felt awkwardly out of place, and knowing he would be seeing Emily in just a few minutes didn't do much to subtract from his frantic state. He couldn't wait to smell her strawberry-scented hair and feel her fluent skin run across his. For months he'd longed for her, and today was finally the day. He had rehearsed his first words to her in his flat earlier that morning and then twice in the plane's lavatory. They would be short and sweet but still with a sense of cool, 'Hello love, did you miss me?' '*Yeah,*' he thought, '*that sounds like something someone cool would say.*' He continued through the revolving doors, sorting through all the people hailing taxis and love ones. His eyes surfed left to right in search of Emily, pausing in the middle as she sprinted towards him. She leapt into his arms, their lips locking instantly like magnets and her legs soundly wrapped around his waist. Their noses rubbed briefly before they opened their eyes peering into each other's windows of love. He still held her firmly and she felt like she was floating in mid air. Emily whispered underneath her brimming smile, "Hey—"

This was it, just play it cool, just like we had rehearsed.

"You're…you're, beautiful…I mean…"

She smiled brighter, finding his nerves attractive and cute.

"Just shut up and kiss me."

He gladly accepted her request and felt her grip around his neck tighten. He couldn't bring his lips to depart from hers so he kissed her more. They both felt it; the moment when life was at its peak.

"What do you say we head back to my place and continue this later?" she whispered seductively.

"Are you certain you're Emily?"

"*Ha-ha,* very funny," she said incredulously, "I don't see you objecting to the idea."

He softly placed her back on the ground and picked up his bag.

"Not at all, lead the way."

For the remainder of the ride home her hand never left his. She didn't even care that it was her first time driving with only one hand on the steering wheel, for much like everything in her life, she did it by the book and the book clearly states, ten and two.

"So how was the flight?"

"Bloody awful! They overbooked first class so since I was the last one to purchase a voucher, I was demoted to coach."

"*No!*" she gasped.

"Mock me all you like, but they don't even offer you a drink until after takeoff. What if I were thirsty? It was all quite unprofessional and rubbish if you ask me."

"Awe, poor baby…" she patronized, smiling at his narcissistic view of air travel.

They came to a red light and Emily looked across at him smiling, her spectacles perched elegantly on the roof of her nose.

"I missed you so much, Jude."

He fumbled over the armrest still holding her hand and kissed her slowly not hiding their affection from the traffic lights.

"I missed you too, love."

Emily was ecstatic at finding a parking spot right outside her apartment building. Usually anytime after noon, Melissa was forced to park two blocks down, but thanks to everyone being away for the holidays, the block was mostly vacant. The half-inch of snow on the ground coated the street and lampposts, as snowflakes continued falling from the sky in abundance and grace. Overall it was a light winter in comparison to Massachusetts's usual standards.

"Well, this is me. Are you ready to go up and meet my crazy roommate Melissa?"

He began rummaging through his knapsack under the glove compartment.

"Not quite. I believe your words were, 'next time you see me you better be carrying' this."

"Oh my God, Jude! You didn't have to, I was joking. I know how expensive this is."

He handed her the first edition Jane Austen *Pride and Prejudice* novel. The smell of the rustic two hundred and one-year-old pages swept through Melissa's tiny Mazda.

"I know, but I saw how much you fancied it."

"I can't accept this, Jude, it's too much."

"I insist. It's the least I can do, you have no idea how much you give me every day. I know you will look after it and cherish it like a baby. You're weird like that," he said smiling at her. She gave him a hug, holding the book high in the air to avoid any physical contact.

"Thank you! This is the best gift ever!"

Melissa was waiting at the front door like an overzealous puppy, as if she could sniff a good-looking man from a mile away. Emily almost ran into her as she opened the door, dropping Jude's knapsack in the process.

"Jesus, Melissa, you scared me! Why are you hovering around the door?"

"Sorry, let me pick that up for you." She looked up from the ground never taking her eyes off Jude, studying him like a Roman sculpture.

"Hi there... I'm Melissa, I've heard a lot about you."

"A pleasure, I'm Jude and I've heard a lot about you as well, '*crazy*' Melissa."

She laughed as if he had told the funniest joke in the world. It was the same laugh she gave guys at the bar in hopes to land free drinks.

"Oh my... that accent, you *are* British aren't you?" For some reason she was breathing deep as if she was somehow turned on by just the sound of it.

"I'm afraid so, have been all me life. I hope that doesn't bother you?"

Melissa's laugh was even louder than her previous one:

"Oh, Jude you're so funny, it's no bother at all. I'll let you in on a little secret; Americans find the accent sexy...What part are you from? My Aunt is British. It sounds like you're from Liverpool?"

"That's a good ear you have. Me parents are from Liverpool so I just took after them, but I was born in Blackpool."

"That's so cool, I love Blackpool! It's only the greatest city in the world."

Emily rolled her eyes in *oh brother* fashion, knowing for a fact that Melissa had never even been to Blackpool. You would think she's never met a multimillionaire, gorgeous celebrity before.

"Yes, yes, we get it. Jude's British and you think he's hot. Come on, Jude, I'll show you around the apartment." She took his hand leading him past Melissa and into the living room, almost tripping over a pair of stilettos that Melissa had left in the middle of the floor like some undetected landmine.

"Okay, well I'll just take his stuff to your room."

"Thanks, and take your shoes too while you're at it. And don't go through his stuff either. You're not selling any of his shirts on Ebay."

They made their way into the kitchen.

"And sadly this is where no magic happens—I'm not a good cook."

"I sort of got that from the no magic happens part. But don't worry love, I've picked up a thing or two on me travels. I can teach you a mean Yorkshire pudding."

She made a gross face at the words *Yorkshire pudding*, recalling a picture she once saw of it in a travel magazine. Not only did it look unappetizing but it looked nothing like pudding. She continued to point out objects in the kitchen until she realized he wasn't listening.

"What? Why are you looking at me like that?"

He was staring at her with a seductive gaze.

"You're just so beautiful. The computer doesn't do you any justice." He walked up to her slowly, Emily stumbling into the refrigerator feeling the cold metal press up against her shoulder blades as they began to kiss.

"Stop, Melissa's in the other room."

"So? I'm certain she's seen you kiss a man before." Little did he know Melissa hadn't. She had never even kissed Kevin in public. Jude's moist lips continued their invasion and attended to her neck. His frizzy five o'clock stubble tickled her skin making her laugh uncontrollably.

"All right, Jude, stop!" She continued laughing, "You're tickling me!"

Melissa called out from her room in artificial concern,

"Is everything okay in there? You do remember that you have your own room, with a bed that is perfect for whatever it is you two are doing in there? And try to keep it Pg-13 for the apples' sakes, they don't need to be subjected to yawls pornography."

They both were breathing heavily, overtook by passion and bliss and ignoring Melissa's words.

"I love you," he whispered.

"I love you too," she replied before irresistibly laughing at another one of his kisses.

"Wait, what time is it?" she asked, suppressing her chuckle.

"Half past six, why?"

"Because we're going to dinner with my friends at seven, I hope that's okay? I want everyone to meet you."

Jude felt the enthusiasm flee from his body, spilling over into disappointment.

"Alright...I just thought it would be you and me since I'm only here for a few days."

"I know, and I promise after I'm all yours. But they'll kill me if I don't take you to meet them."

His expression still read of disappointment and defeat, and straddled the line of anger. '*I flew thousands of miles to spend time with her, not her bloody friends,*' he thought. Emily smiled, trying her best to repel his disappointment.

"Please, for me?" Her hazel eyes grew wide with hope and remorse, officially creating what they call the *puppy dog face.*

"Aw, bullocks, I can't say no to that face."

"Yes! Thank you, I promise it won't be too bad."

"I suppose, I am rather hungry. Which reminds me, did you know they don't serve gourmet meals in coach? Only pretzels and some rubbish they dare call a sandwich. I almost ate me chair I was so hungry."

She handed him an apple from the bowl of fruit above the refrigerator.

"Here, this should hold you over you spoiled brat," she said with a smile.

"Cheers. And I'm not spoiled. I just adhere to high standards. Now do you have any red ones, because I don't fancy the colour green?"

She laughed walking out of the kitchen in glee.

"No we don't, your highness. Now come on. We have to hurry up and get ready. It's already going to take Melissa two hours. You have no idea how long it takes for that girl to accessorize."

He followed her out hurrying to catch up, his words trailing off as he left the kitchen rambling on to no avail.

"It's just that green is an evil colour. Have you ever stopped and really looked at it? It's like it's mocking you..." he wagged his finger, scolding the apple in his palm, "well you don't fool me you diabolical apple, I'm on to you..."

Normally they would walk to Riley's, but flurries overtook the sidewalks and it was twenty-seven degrees cold out, so they crammed into Melissa's two-door *Mazda-RX*. Emily often wondered why Melissa elected to have a car with no four-wheel drive in Massachusetts. It was like bringing a bikini to Antarctica; some decisions are just unnecessarily incompetent. The roads were empty, all to be expected two nights before Christmas, but at the speed at which Melissa was traveling, they may as well been stuck in traffic. Melissa inched forward at snail's pace, cringing with each press of the accelerator.

"I beg your pardon, Melissa, but if you're afraid of driving in the snow, then why not get an auto more capable?" asked Jude, winking at Emily in the passenger seat as if he'd read her mind.

"That's okay, Jude, you can ask me anything," her tone overly inviting, "the dealer threw in a cute MP3 adapter for only forty bucks extra. I couldn't pass that up."

"Ah, I see, very resourceful," he said, in sarcastic fashion.

By the time they reached Riley's, they had broken fifteen MPH only once and were over fifty minutes late. The place was vacant apart from the several people at the bar watching ESPN and Emily's friends occupying the long table by the jukebox that had been out of service for the past seven years. Growing up in England, Jude had become an expert at attending pubs; some would argue too much so, but this was unlike any pub back home. No drunken men stumbling about wanting to pick a fight over anything, no chatting up football to the point where it somehow turned into a fight, and no constant chanting of hometown clubs songs, this place was a Chuck E. Cheese compared to the pubs he's been to. *'Americans don't know how to drink,'* he thought, *'this place isn't at all appealing.'*

As they walked up to the table, everyone stopped mid sentence and began looking at Jude like an animal encaged at the zoo. "Hey everyone!" said Melissa, as she sat down next to Denise at the head of the table. Denise was the only one to reply *hello*; the others were too busy eyeing up this new rich playboy who had won their beloved Emily's heart. Emily was embarrassed with the way their eyes were judging him, giving her a grotesque feeling in the pit of her stomach like they were judging her as well. *'Is it so hard to believe I could land an overly handsome guy?'* she thought. And as she answered her own question in her head she concluded, *'yeah it's hard to believe.'*

"Everybody, this is Jude. Let me introduce you to everyone." They started at the front.

"Jude, this is my friend Lilly. Lilly actually talked me into running for student council sophomore year, but I lost to that goody-two-shoes Jennifer Fefferman."

"Really—Goody-two-shoes, Em? 1962 called, they said they want their saying back," joked Melissa.

"Is that so? Well she was a goody-two-shoes, and 1970 called, they said they want their joke back. So…." Everyone laughed applauding Emily's comeback, making Denise's Margarita spill from her nose. Emily had an almost unfrightened edge about her; an edge that her friends had never seen in her before. Jude took Lilly's hand, kissing it slowly.

"A pleasure. So tell me, Lilly, how long have you been a model?"

Lilly giggled like a schoolgirl and her rosy cheeks became as red as her fiery hair.

"Emily, he really is as charming as you say. I'm no model, but thank you."

"What a shame, I reckon it must have been hard to quit."

Lilly blushed even brighter looking as if she were about to burst.

"Moving along," said Emily, rolling her eyes. "This is my good friend Scott and his fiancée Rachel. I actually set them up."

He shook Rachel's hand.

"That's not entirely true. Emily and I were supposed to be lab partners freshman year, but on the day we were scheduled to choose partners, she decided to get sick, so Professor Lawrence stuck me with Scott and we have been inseparable ever since," said Rachel, happy to reclaim the credit from Emily. Scott stood star-struck.

"Is he alright?" said Jude, waving his hand in front of Scott's face hoping to break him from his celebrity-induced coma.

"Oh...him? He'll be fine. Babe! Babe, Jude is talking to you," snapped Rachel. Scott released his excitement all at once, showering Jude with praise.

"I have to tell you man, I'm a huge fan! I love soccer...I mean football, as you guys call it. Manchester United are my favorite team. I seriously watch every single game! That goal you scored against Sunderland was *sick*! I scored one like that back in college. We we're intramurals champs two years straight."

"Cheers mate, it's refreshing to meet an American that appreciates football. And there's actually a funny story about that goal. You see, I had the football on the wing..." Emily grabbed Jude's arm pulling him away from the conversation, like a mother shepherding a kid through the candy aisle.

"Come along, Jude, there'll be plenty of time for Scott to boost your ego later. And, last but not least, this is Sharron and Denise."

"Ladies," said Jude flirtatiously.

The girls smiled.

"So are you Jude like the Beatles song?" asked Denise, trying to suppress her thoughts of his attractiveness.

"I am. Me mum and dad were massive Beatles supporters so they named me after their favourite record."

"That's really cool!" chimed Lilly, Denise, and Sharron in unison.

"I really like your accent," persisted Denise.

"Thank you. I seem to be getting that a lot around here."

Jude ordered the spaghetti and meatballs. He wanted to try the famous Riley's smothered baby back ribs, but during the season, the team's nutritionist had placed him on a strict diet. He spent the majority of the evening telling Scott about all of his accomplishments and giving him the dirt on fellow footballers like, Steve McCarran, of Arsenal being afraid to shoot outside the box. The girls watched Jude as if he were some mystical creature, smiling and laughing at everything he did. Every time he opened his mouth to speak, they hung on his words as if he were giving some profound speech for freedom. It all made Emily slightly angry; she couldn't believe her friends were so hung up on him. You would have thought she had brought one of the guys from the *Twilight* movies to dinner.

"So how did you two meet?" inquired Lilly.

Jude looked to his right seeking Emily's approval, but she fumbled to give one as she was caught red handed stealing a meatball off of his plate.

"Oi, you little thief. Put back me meatball. Now do you want to tell the story or should I?"

She quivered her bottom lip and batted her luscious black eyelashes at him. Jude sighed and pushed his plate towards her.

"Take the bloody meatball."

She smiled and punctured the meatball with her fork.

"Thank you. And you can tell them. I'm not much of a story teller."

"It's actually a rather funny story. We quite literally ran into one another. She fell right on her ass." They all laughed imagining Emily laid out on the ground like some boxer with a glass jaw.

"How are you still alive? You're like the size of his arm," spat Scott.

"Ah, he's not so tough," said Emily sarcastically as she used his shoulder as leverage to pull herself up from her seat to give him a kiss on the cheek.

"And then when she finally came to, she declared her love for me, and now here we are."

"*OH*, you are so full of it! Tell them the truth," gasped Emily.

"If he would have run into me that's exactly how it would have gone down," said Melissa, taking another sip from her second Strawberry Margarita.

"If any man ran into you, Melissa, he probably would have knocked you down on purpose in hopes to make a clean escape," joked Lilly.

"What can I say? Men are naturally frightened by my beauty. It's in their genes. It's called the *That Dime is Too Fine* syndrome."

"Speaking of which, I've been meaning to ask you, what's the weather like in this fantasy world of yours? Is it partly cloudy with a chance of get real?" teased Lilly from across the table.

"*Ha-ha*, very funny," replied Melissa, incredulously and partly offended.

Jude placed his hands in the air as if about to preach some holy scripture.

"Alright, the truth is she hated me."

"*No!*" gasped the women in harmony.

"Seriously?" asked Scott.

"I did. But trust me, he wasn't always this charming. Within the span of a minute, he managed to knock the wind out of me and ask me to sleep with him."

"So far, minus the first thing, I don't see what the issue was. And depending on how kinky the guy is, the first thing doesn't sound that bad either," argued Melissa.

Denise wasted no time in giving her rebuttal.

"Not everyone is as promiscuous as you, Melissa. I swear maybe Lilly's right? You really are the real life Samantha."

Emily continued, hoping to pre-stop a heated drunken debate.

"But the next time we met, he was charming and thoughtful, and dare I say…the perfect gentleman."

"And on the contrary to me lack of manners in the beginning, she was always an angel in me eyes."

"Awe…" whimpered Rachel while hitting Scott with her napkin. "How come you never say things like that to me?"

"Um, I don't know, maybe because I'm not British. How about, ello govna, is thou more beautiful than a rose? I say'th yes."

"Mate, that was a bloody awful accent! Govna? Say'th? No one says either of those anymore. You do know it's 2013 in England as well?"

The table went back to discussing Melissa's lack of male companionship. Everyone was drunk or on the verge, except for Emily, Jude, and Rachel. Scott's drunken comment about Melissa scaring men away with her Halloween mask, meaning her face, was met with a half eaten jalapeño popper being tossed at his head from across the table. The sober three mingled amongst themselves seizing the opportunity for a less crude conversation.

"It seems you guys are pretty close," asked Rachel. Emily and Jude smiled at one another shaking their heads no playfully. "When will you see each other again?"

"I don't know," replied Jude, "I reckon when she comes back to England in the summer."

"Oh, she hasn't told you?"

"Rachel!" snapped Emily.

"Sorry, I hope I haven't said too much." She took a sip of her margarita acting as if her last statement hadn't come from her mouth.

"I was waiting for the right time to tell you. I'm interning at the Yale-New Haven hospital this summer…sorry."

Jude forced a reassured look, steadying his composure.

"Don't be sorry, love, that's great. I'm very happy for you."

"Really—" said Emily with an optimistic expression on her face.

"Of course, no worries."

She gave him a kiss and he smiled, pretending that all was well.

Emily's bedroom door shut softly behind them and Emily wasted no time getting out of her bar clothes.

"Thank goodness that's over. Thanks again for putting up with all my friends. They can be a bit crazy, especially after a few drinks." Emily was putting on her oversized Yale t-shirt that she had won in a fundraiser during homecoming junior year. They had run out of smalls, but she had accepted it anyway with the idea that it would make a good bedtime uniform. Jude sulked in the old desk chair in the corner, staring at the floor entrapped in his thoughts. She made her way into the bathroom continuing her conversation with herself while brushing her teeth.

"I mean usually Melissa is the worst of the bunch, but Lilly was h-a-m-m-e-r-e-d, I think your model comment went to her head. I hope she got home safe. Usually I'm the one who drives everyone."

She reentered the room bemused at the perturb look on his face. "What's wrong?"

"When were you planning on telling me you weren't coming back to England for the summer?"

She took a deep breath, shaking off her now disheartened look.

"I was just waiting for the right time. I already said I was sorry." Her voice didn't falter, resiliently rested in-between calm and annoyed. "But this is my life. I'm going to be a doctor, you know that."

"I understand that, Emily, but couldn't you get a summer position at a hospital in England? Hell, get one in Wales, for Christ's sake. That's at least a half step up from bloody Connecticut."

She sat down on the edge of the bed hoping she had already fallen asleep and this was all just a dream. It wasn't.

"I can't. Yale only sets up paid internships for their hospital in New Haven and a few others in the Boston area."

"If money is the issue, I have no problem paying for you to come down and stay."

Emily rose from the bed in a ball of frustration and her voice followed suit.

"Jesus, you just don't get it do you? Money can't solve everything. I like what I do and I want to be better at it. This isn't just my education. It's my life...it's my dream. How would you like it if I asked you to play soccer in the states?"

He stood looking her in the eyes matching her tone pitch for pitch.

"For one, you yanks call it soccer, so I think you have answered your own question. And two, what I do is a job. I'm a professional. You're in bloody school—you can revise anywhere. The circumstances are quite different, don't you agree?"

Her tone was now overthrown by a vexation of rage.

"Don't you dare belittle my education! Yale is one of the most prestigious universities in the world, and I've worked my entire life to get here. I'm only a few years away from achieving my dream. I can't just switch hospitals and schools like you switched teams!"

Despite having initiated the argument, he found himself losing. The tension cut through the room as he headed for the door.

"Where are you going?"

"I'm just going to take a walk before I say something I may regret. I'll return in a few."

Contrary to her emotions she did not cry. In an unfamiliar way she found herself more angry than upset. Her mother's words echoed though her head like a persisting mantra, leading to an overwhelming sensation to finish what she had started, not to be derailed by the likes of a man. Lying in bed staring at the ceiling in hopes that it would magically show her the answer; she exhaled, drowning in a frenzy of thoughts. '*How did I get here?*' she pondered, '*Stressed and confused all because I had to go off and fall in love. Fate can be a real jerk.*' For the past twenty years her mind had been securely set on one goal, one dream, and now the main ingredient of her future seemed to point to a man. All of which truly scared her. It was times like these she wished her mother were here to brush her hair and assure her it will all be fine. Just like the time she fell off her tricycle and scrapped her knee.

For the next hour she did not move, trapped in thoughts on her future and where Jude could have run off to. Thinking about him running off only infuriated her more, *'This is the only time we'll see each other this year and he decides to pick a fight and go for some life altering walk.'* Her eyelids became heavy and with the flash of the 4 A.M from her alarm clock she was finding it a struggle to stay awake.

The bedroom door gave an obnoxious creek as it opened. Jude wasn't sure if Emily was awake, so he closed it behind him gently and proceeded to slip under the covers, wrapping his arms around her. He kissed the back of her shoulder and closed his eyes, dozing off comfortably.

"You realize I'm not asleep," said Emily. Her tone scorned.

His eyes shot back open in an instant of nerves.

"I was really hoping you were."

She rolled over meeting his eyes on the pillow, "Well, sorry to disappoint."

"You're not disappointing, I'm glad you're up it gives me a chance to apologise for being such a muppet."

"I guess you kind of are one, huh? Funny thing is that's one trait of yours I can't seem to get used to."

"Alright, I deserved that. But all jokes aside, I'm sorry, Emily. I let me troubles get the better of me. I have no right suggesting you postpone your dream for us. And tragically, the less masculine side of me wouldn't let you go through with it anyway."

Emily's eyes rested upon his. She was finding it harder by the day to read him. It seemed one moment she could be hopelessly in love and the next she could rip her hair out in frustration. Unfortunately she had little experience in the male department. Otherwise she would have known men are just as complicated as women, if not more so.

"Apology accepted. Where did you go anyway?"

"I only walked around the block once and then I realized I didn't have a key to the main door of the building, so I just sat out front and waited for someone to come either in or out. Fortunately a woman had to walk her dog or else I reckon I'd still be out there now freezing me ass off."

She chuckled a little at the sight of him freezing. "Serves you right, being so mean. Have you forgotten my first letter already? You promised to be nice the whole time."

He matched her chuckle with one of his own; sure to not overdo it since her tone led him to believe she was partly serious.

"About that…let's say starting now I'll be nothing but nice, handsome, charming, athletic, handsome, did I already mention handsome?"

She couldn't believe she loved someone who spent more time in the mirror than Melissa.

"You did."

"Well it's worth another mention, handsome and devilishly smart."

"Oh brother, if you look up the word vain in the dictionary, that so-called handsome face would be plastered right next to it." She gave him a tug on his shirt, pulling his lips to hers. His lips were cold from the evening's nipping breath, and as their passion fled from her lips to his they both forgot what they had been cross about.

"So you admit it. I am handsome."

She kissed him again, her lips upset with her for not embracing his longer.

"Maybe a little."

"Well, you're beautiful, love."

He smiled before attempting to nod off again, happy at the outcome of his apology. So much so that he considered the idea that he could talk his way out of anything.

"Hey, I have an idea. Let's read some of our letters now!" Her excited tone made his head hurt, not blending well with his exhaustion.

"It's four-thirty in the morning and you want to read our journals now?"

"Remember the whole be nice thing? That means you have to do what I want."

He shot her a stare that screamed *please reconsider*, and she returned it with one of her own that screamed *you're on thin ice.*

"You're bloody mad. But, alright, give me a tick."

He left the room to return with a black spiral journal. She dove under her bed pulling out a brown shoebox. "I hope that box doesn't smell." She hit him with the pillow as he sat down next to her, almost knocking the journal from his hands. "Hush up. My feet don't smell."

"I know they don't, I'm just havin' a laugh." She pulled out the black and white composition notebook with the words, *Letters to Jude* written on the front, along with the manila envelope that he had sent her necklace in. The room was becoming colder by the second, so they cuddled up beneath the comforter exchanging journals. Jude rested his back against the headboard while Emily rested hers up against his chest.

"Me journal may have a few more pages than yours."

"And why is that?"

"Let's just say I missed you madly, so I may have indulged in two letters a day at some point."

"I won't hold it against you."

They lay there flipping through the pages obsessively, leaving no word unread. Jude admired the smile on her face as she giggled at a joke he had written or the way her heart melted when she read the words *I love you*, which was a recurring theme throughout both journals. The words *I love you* were written more than three hundred times combined, in less than 914 pages—neither complained though. In fact, Jude enjoyed the warm tingling sensation that swept through the pit of his stomach every time he read her words.

Emily held a disparaging look while reading through one of Jude's entries. "You must be joking?" He rubbed up against her shoulder trying to get a better view of the page she was reading.

"Ah, I do recall writing that one. I was in a real tosser of a mood that day. But he did still me goal, that little wanker."

Dearest Emily,

Bollocks!! Forgive me, I know that is a rather odd way to begin a letter, but today was a bloody awful day. Let me paint a picture for you. So there we are in the 81ˢᵗ minute tied one-one on the road at Birmingham. It had been pouring all match and me shoes felt like sponges, squishing and spraying every time I ran. Birmingham wins a free kick and Rio manages to get that massive head of his on the ball and clear it out to Kagawa who starts a pacey counter. Now as you already know, love, I'm the fastest lad on the team. Who are we kidding? I'm the fastest in the world. So I bust me ass up the pitch shouting bloody murder for the ball, and we are now two on one with the last defender. Just as he's about to lay it off to me for an easy tap in, that would surely be the game winner and the easiest goal I would ever score in me life, what does this wanker do? He does a cheeky back heel to Rooney who strikes from about a mile outside of the box. Sure it went in and we won, but let's not lose focus here of what truly happened, HE STOLE ME BLOODY GOAL! Apologies, I had to yell that last bit.

Elsewhere I do hope all is well with you. I miss you and cannot wait to see you. Only a few weeks until Boxing Day!

She lowered the bridge of her spectacles looking him in the eyes, showing him she means business.

"Jude…Jude…Jude? What in all of our time together would give you the idea that I would want to hear about your soccer game exclusively? When instead you should be writing your girlfriend, whom you claim to love so much, letters of love and passion since she's thousands of miles away." She looked down at the page again and then back up at him cross. "And you didn't even sign the bottom with love."

His face held an apologetic expression, one of a dog placing its tail between its legs. He knew what she wanted to hear, so why couldn't he say it? Instead his pride spoke for him.

"I suppose, but you must admit, he did steal me goal?"

She shook her head, climbing back into his warm embrace and placing her eyes back on the pages.

"Sometimes I don't know why I even bother? I'm just glad there aren't any more pages in here dedicated solely to your soccer life."

He bit down on his teeth nervously, delinquently turning his head down towards hers. She took one look up at him and knew instantly. "No—" she said.

"Um, may I see that journal for just a moment? I need to get one thing." He proceeded to rip out several pages, balling them up and tossing them in the waste bin under her nightstand. "There, that should sort it. The rest are all letters to me lovely, beautiful, immaculate, ravishing..."

"Yeah, yeah, keep it coming. It's going to take a lot more than that to get you out of the dog house, again," she smiled, hastily taking the journal back.

In contempt of his mistake they both went back to reading again. Emily was deep in thought over an entry:

"Emily?"

"Yes," she replied half listening, still entrenched in the current entry she was reading. His voice was quiet but earnest,

"He did steal me goal though."

"You're unbelievable! If I admitted it then will you drop it?"

"I reckon I might."

"Then yes, he stole your damn goal."

His mouth sprung open in surprise, looking as if she had asked for his hand in marriage.

"Why, Emily Robertson, do you kiss your grandmum with that mouth? I never thought I would live to see the day I could bring you to swear. But I do appreciate your honesty on the situation, it was bloody highway robbery," he said in a teasing manner. Jude waited several minutes before whispering to her again,

"Hey, Emily?"

"...Yes, Jude," her tone now fully agitated.

"I love you."

"I love you too," she replied softly under her breath while making a last ditch effort to dive back into his journal.

Their eyes traveled back and forth between the lines as the room again fell silent. With each entry he read he discovered further how much Emily loved and missed him, mirroring his affections towards her. Her letters made him feel bad for having to go back to England and spurred the question, how long could they keep this up? The whole not seeing each other thing was a novelty that grew old fast. And the time apart and distance was developing into a determined nemesis, slowly draining them of any satisfaction they hoped to receive from their necessary phone conversations and video chats.

"Well, you'll be happy to know that in spite the schtick I get from the lads, I always keep the second letter you sent with me. I must have read it a thousand times now. But after reading some of these, it may have some competition. These are brilliant, Emily! Like this one…" he continued out loud:

Dear Jude,

It's about two in the morning and I just got home, Ah!! The hospital really kicked my butt today. Granted, I'm not exactly performing heart surgery or transplants yet, but you would be surprised at the millions of other task there are to do. I have to collect the doctors' medical forms, help deliver babies, administer shots, restock gloves in E.R., do coffee runs for breakfast, lunch, and dinner, drop off food for patients in the left and right wing, the list goes on and on. But while I stumble through my front door like a mindless zombie I quickly forget all the struggles of the day, and instead have a smile on my face, and it's all because of you. You make me so happy, and between you and me, I haven't felt this way in a long time.

Although you may think you're tough, you're the sweetest guy I know and also the most vain. I'm so thankful I ran into you that day on the street. I've become more confident and far more outgoing since you've come into my life. In fact, just the other day I ordered a venti instead of a tall at Starbucks; I'm really living on the edge aren't I? Also, every time I see my grandma the first thing she says is, "You're glowing. That boy must really be doing a number on you." But don't get a big head because she says that about all the boys.

Well, I know you're probably sick of listening to me babble on about girly love stuff, so I'll say goodnight or good morning. I'm not entirely sure which; it's 2:30 a.m. here so you figure it out. And before I forget, thanks again for the flowers every week; you really don't have to do that. I'm seriously running out of places to put all of them. But they're all very beautiful and lilies are my favorite. It's nice to know you do listen to me sometimes. Anyways thanks for treating me so special and acting like I'm the only girl in the world. Promise to never stop?

Love always,
Emily

Jude wiped away a fake tear from his eye as he finished reading, "awe…I think I may have a cry."

"Whatever—Mr. Macho. Don't make fun of my letters."

"I'm not, love. Seriously, I love them and I love you." He rolled her over in his arms, her body now lying horizontal to his. He took off her spectacles and placed them next to the pillow before bringing her breath close and kissing her slowly.

"I love you too. Even though you throw spoiled temper tantrums like a petulant child—" she was half joking but mainly serious.

"Well aren't you the dog's bollocks. That's the love of me life everyone!" He stared through her eyes thinking, *'and there's no place I rather be than right here with her.'*

XIII

Emily & Jude: Just Jump

Jude watched the road as the yellow traffic lines raced by. The roads were more abandoned than yesterday, all to be expected on the morning of Christmas Eve. The freshly-fallen snow rested peacefully on the side of the road, reminding all of its arrival the night before. He had passed the state of exhaustion hours ago, leaving his sanity and consciousness back in bed. On the road at seven in the morning wasn't his preferred wakeup time, primarily because he had fallen asleep only two hours ago. Recalling the last time he had been up this early only made him more exasperated. It was for a punishment last season following his red card against Everton. His manager had him come in and run the stairs. Even more baffling was how awake Emily was, considering she had awakened even earlier than Jude to drop Melissa off at the train station to ride back to New York for the holidays.

Part of Jude's silence during the ride to her grandmother's house was, yes; due to his punctuate state of tiredness, but also the lingering thought that a day from now, he would be stuck in the grey area, not knowing when he would see Emily again. They had agreed to shelve the discussion on the matter until after he'd return to England, but not withstanding, every bone in his body wanted to bring it up now.

"Should I put on some music? I feel like I can hear your thoughts from over here."

His vision didn't break from the yellow lines.

"Jude?" asserted Emily from the driver's seat.

"Sorry, love, did you say something?"

She eyed him suspiciously.

"I was just asking if you want me to put on some music. Are you okay?"

"I reckon I'm just tired. But sure, music would be fine."

She turned the dial to 100.7 FM, a classic rock station out of Boston, which was playing David Bowie's *Suffragette City*.

"Ah, I love this record. If you ask me Bowie is a bit overrated, and I blame me people for that, but I don't mind a good Bowie record from time to time."

"I tend to gravitate more towards the classic genre, but Melissa loves this station. It's either this or one of her Taylor Swift CDs."

Jude made a face as if he had just sucked on a soured lemon.

"Taylor Swift? That sounds like something that should be sold at a hardware store, not a musician."

Emily laughed: "Don't tell Melissa that. She worships Taylor. I think she finds the way she bashes her exes appealing."

They drove for ten more minutes listening to a Rolling Stones and a Nirvana song before turning down her grandmother's street. The tiny street had yet to be paved, making Emily steer carefully as she made her way down, hearing the crunching of the snow with each tire rotation.

"Do you think she'll rate me?" inquired Jude timidly.

"Of course she'll like you. Wait…don't tell me the macho Jude Macavoy is frightened of a little eighty-four-year-old woman?"

"Are you mental? Jude Macavoy isn't afraid of any woman, young or old. I just know how much she means to you, so I don't know—I just want her to fancy me is all."

She wanted to look at him but was afraid to look away from the snowy road in front of her.

"Don't worry. If I like you, then so will she. Just try not to be yourself and you'll be fine."

Her joke did little to ease his tension, instead backfiring and making him more certain that she wouldn't like him.

Mrs. Ross answered the door with an elated smile on her face, the same one she always greeted Emily with. She was still dressed in her light pink robe and matching puffy slippers, resembling two pink cotton balls on her feet. Jude was already beginning to tremble with nerves as the musty scent of mothballs filled his nostrils. He played in front of thousands of people, walked the red carpet, and was constantly in the public's eye, but nothing he had done previously could prepare him for meeting his girlfriend's family. Come to think of it, he had never had a relationship that lasted longer than four weeks, so he never had to.

"Emily! Come here dear, it's so nice to see you!" She shuffled forward slowly, giving Emily a hug, scratching the soles of her slippers along the hardwood floor. "Oh, and what's this?"

Emily handed her the bag she was carrying with a small box wrapped in Christmas tree wrapping paper.

"This is for you—Merry Christmas, grandma!"

"Thank you, Emily. You're always so thoughtful."

Jude stood next to Emily in the doorway shivering, happy to see Emily smile, but freezing and desperate to get inside despite the smell.

"Grandma, I'd like you to meet Jude. Jude, this is my grandma, Audrey Ross."

"How do you do madam? It is a pleasure to make your acquaintance." He took her hand and proceeded to give it a little kiss.

"You didn't tell me he was so charming, Emily. I haven't been greeted like that since Paris 1947." Emily noticed that rolling her eyes at him was becoming much more an instinct than a habit, but she couldn't help it. Knowing Jude's true personality it was always funny to see the way he over-exaggerated his elegance.

"Yes, he's quite the charmer isn't he," she replied sardonically.

Jude reached into his coat pocket extracting a Christmas card, "and this is for you—Merry Christmas."

"Why thank you, you didn't have to."

"Nonsense, it was no trouble at-tall."

She stood aside in the doorway, welcoming them in.

"Well, come in you two. If you stand outside, you'll catch cold. Have a seat in the living room and I'll grab us some refreshments."

"Would you like me to help, grandma?" It was more of a rhetorical question, as Emily already began making her way towards the kitchen.

"No, I will have none of that, Emily. You're my guest today. Have a seat, I can manage."

As they sat on the vintage couch smelling of old leather and Bengay, Emily gave him a morbid look.

"What," said Jude, unsure from her look if he was in trouble or not.

"Uh, kissing her hand? And when did you get her a card? You didn't tell me you were going to get her something."

He regally fixed the white collar under his navy sweater, sitting up straight as if above her.

"Well, believe it or not, many people find me to be quite charming and irresistible."

"Okay, Brad Pitt. But really, thank you. That meant a lot to her. The card that is, not your nasty lips on her hand."

"No worries, love. I told you, I know how important she is to you and if it's important to you than it's important to me."

Audrey reentered the room carrying a silver tray full of refreshments. "Here we are," she said placing the tray on the table. "I poured you a cup of coffee, Emily, and I thought you would prefer tea, Jude, being it's the drink of the Queen."

"You're quite right madam, tea would be wonderful. Thank you."

"Speaking of the Queen, have I ever told you, Emily, about the time I ran into the Queen in the middle of a hotel in London, back in the spring of sixty-eight?"

Of course Emily had heard this story a hundred times before, but she thought about the future and how her grandchildren would have to endure her crazy European adventures, like the time she fell in love with a professional soccer player, so she played along.

"I don't believe so."

"I beg your pardon. You've met the Queen...our Queen, the Queen of England?"

Audrey nearly spat out her mouth full of coffee. "Met her? Heavens no, I literally ran into her, knocked the wind out of her I did."

Jude gave a resounding laugh, "That's brilliant! So what happened?"

"I had just received a telegram from Emily's grandfather Marvin about his plane being delayed from New York. Marvin was a great pilot and he looked so handsome in his Pan Am uniform. I flew out the previous day to meet him in London for our sixteen-year wedding anniversary. Thanks to his status at Pan Am, we were able to book the nicest hotel in London. Anyway, I was walking back to the elevator reading the telegram and she was coming the opposite way in a hurry, leaving some media conference or something, and the next thing I knew I was laying on top of the Queen. I was so frightened because she couldn't catch her breath, and then her guards pulled me off of her before I could apologize."

"Brilliant! You're a proper pioneer. I once saw Paul McCartney at a fundraiser in Blackpool, but that's as close as I've come to royalty."

The remainder of the morning ensued with continuous embarrassment of Emily, as Audrey took out photo album after photo album filled with baby photos and elementary school Christmas pageants. She even showed Jude Emily's least favorite photo, when Emily had just gotten her braces put on in fifth grade. By lunchtime Audrey had run out of albums and reverted to telling stories about herself, like the time she backpacked through Europe and shared a taxi with Sean Connery. Emily loved the look on her grandmother's face when she would tell these stories. You would think she was on *60 Minutes* with her level of detail and concentration. They capped the afternoon off with a late lunch around four o'clock. Audrey prepared tuna sandwiches and potato chips, and poured Jude a sixth cup of tea.

Overall, the visit was a success. Audrey got to experience firsthand how much Jude loved her granddaughter, and she found him charming and caring. But in deference to her newly formed opinion of him, she noticed a heavy glimmer of pain and suffering in his eyes, the same gaze that once resided in Emily's eyes long ago when she had first told her all the horrible things her father had done.

After they left Audrey's, they wasted a few more hours in Boston sightseeing. Emily showed Jude different landmarks, including Fenway Park, which did little to impress him. "Is that it? It's the size of me locker at Old Trafford," he said. She pointed out all the best pubs according to the impeccable alcohol stylings of Melissa Hall. They grabbed a quick bite from a McDonalds in New Haven, neither particularly liking their meal but made do with the only thing open on Christmas Eve. For their final stop of the night, Emily showed off Yale's main campus.

The campus illuminated the night's sky as the cloak of snow beamed off the moon's smile. The campus was deserted, not even a public safety officer insight. Emily showed Jude the science building where she had taken chemistry her freshman year, the cafeteria which she made a point to avoid at all cost, and the track where she ran in the mornings before her 8:15 econ class. He felt the warmth of her hand as Emily wrapped herself up tightly around his arm, taking every measure to keep warm. Enjoying the evening's walk back to the car and the university's romantic charm, Jude spotted the athletic center next to the parking lot.

"Is that a pool inside?" asked Jude, stopping to admire the complex.

"It is. I've actually never been in there. Melissa almost joined the swim team sophomore year, but then she found out they practice at five-thirty in the morning so she joined the newspaper instead."

He trotted over towards the large old building, mindful of the snow and black ice.

"Where are you going?" her voice at a whisper, fearful that they were doing something frowned upon.

"Let's have a look inside. You said yourself you've never been in," he replied shouting, now several feet in front of her.

"Jude, I don't think this is a good idea. We're not even supposed to be on campus. Besides, all the doors are locked for break."

The main door was locked and he peered inside in search of any life forms. He discovered a maintenance door twelve yards down the backside of the building, twisting the cold silver handle it clicked open.

"You were saying?" he said arrogantly, not afraid to rub in his tinny triumph.

She finally caught back up to him, her pant bottoms covered in snow.

"Come on, Jude—let's just go back to the apartment. This is a bad idea. I'm sure it's pitch black in there for a reason."

"And why not, we're in America. Everyone keeps telling me it's the land of the free, so let's exercise our freedom and have a little look around. We're not hurting anyone."

She stood behind him in the doorway crossing her arms in frustration, fending off the cold and her gut feeling.

"Come on…" she proclaimed, unenthusiastically leading him into the building, "I hate you by the way."

He laughed, "I love you too."

The only presence of light was issued from the two red glowing exit signs in the opposing corners of the room and the transparent blue water. Apart for the smell of chlorine, the ambiance was exceptionally peaceful. The water was swaying but silent and only the buzzing from the exit signs provided any sound.

"Okay, we've seen it. It's blue, dark, and wet, now let's go." …… "What are you doing, Jude?" she asked in an irritated whisper.

He began untying his shoelaces and making his way to his belt buckle.

"Okay, that's it. I knew it was only a matter of time, but you have officially gone off the deep end, no pun intended. Granted I didn't think it would happen so soon—" she kept rambling on nervously as Jude was now naked and cannon-balling into the pool. "I have to put my foot down, this is the dumbest idea that you've ever had, and I mean you've had some real dumb ones…"

"Emily…*Emily*!" he shouted. "Stop and look at me for just a moment. I love you, but bloody'ell, shuttup and get your ass in this bloody pool. Haven't you always fancied swimming in the winter?"

Emily stood still contemplating her next move. She took off her spectacles and placed them on the bench beside the window, followed by her coat and shirt.

"You know, I'm beginning to think you're a bad influence on me."

"That's funny, because I always thought I was the best thing to ever happen to you."

Her bra and jeans shortly followed and she held her breasts securely in her hands out of embarrassment. He whistled, "Take it off. You're gorgeous!" She could feel her cheeks turning rosy red and all of her morals flying out the window. Letting out a deafening scream, she plunged into the crystal blue water. She emerged with her long brown hair dripping down her back.

"I can't believe I'm actually skinny dipping, and in the Yale pool no less. *Ahh… this is crazy*!"

His eyes gazed upon her like a fine painting, studying every curve of her body.

"You are truly immaculate, Emily, you know that?"

She swam into him slowly, now face to face.

"Prove it." She leaned in to kiss him and as she closed her eyes he splashed water in her face laughing as if he had just pulled off some lucrative prank.

"Cheeky aren't we?"

"I can't believe you," she said wiping the water from her eyes. "Well, two can play it that game."

They began trading splashes, protecting their faces when possible. She managed to jump on his back attempting to dunk his head under water, but he squeezed from under her placing himself again face to face, holding her close with no space between them.

"I don't want to go a year without seeing you," he said earnestly, wishing he could live in her arms.

"Neither do I," she replied, bringing her lips forward to meet his. She felt an unfamiliar sensation sweep across her body, making her short of breath, as he kissed her neck slowly, gradually reaching her left breast. Unable to control herself, she closed her eyes falling into a rapturous abyss, her nipples hardening like two soft pellets.

"Jude?" Her voice was winded and unconvincing.

"Yes, love?" his kisses continued, her body trembling in bliss.

"Let's get out of here..."

Both their breaths were heavy with temptation on their tongues.

"Alright," he replied, wanting her with all of his being.

They reached Emily's apartment still kissing profusely. Emily struggled to open the door, not bothering to open her eyes to view the lock. He kicked the door shut behind them as Emily tossed her shirt to the floor and Jude quickly following suit. Trails of damped clothes lead from the front door to her bedroom. He laid her gently on the mattress, quickly admiring her breasts and soft stomach, still matching her kiss for kiss. Her hands ran down the grooves of the muscles on his back, every kiss and every touch coinciding with the beat of her heart, sending her senses soaring past their peaks. He touched her as if he were touching a cloud, gracefully and attentively.

Her breasts brushed up against his smooth muscular skin, transferring all of his body heat to her in a rush of ecstasy. A soft whimper built up in her throat as he squeezed her right breast gently, gliding his tongue up and down past her navel. She could feel the moistness left over from his kisses as his lips explored every inch of her body. He positioned his body on top of her, his muscles expanding from his exertion. Her breath was heavy and with a wince of pain, she pulled him closer, letting out a pleasurable moan as their lips latched on to one another's again.

As he gently went deeper inside her, her nails drove into the valleys of his back, leaving his skin with passionate red marks. She could feel every part of him, controlling her from the inside out, strong and fierce like an ox, making her body tingle from head to toe in a mystic sensation. She wanted him, needed him, and yearned for him, unlike anything she had ever known.

Her body shook as he rhythmically thrust above her, running his heart back and forth across her breasts. She kissed him on the shoulder and then the chin, feeling the sweat drip from his forehead as it landed on hers in a showering of love. She opened her eyes for a brief moment, staring into his, as he entered her again slowly. Her lips trembled and she bit down on her bottom lip in a pleasure of pain, letting out a cry in heavenly satisfaction as her body continually accepted his, and he whispered,

"I love you."

But she couldn't speak. Her lips quivered in ecstasy and her thighs sizzled in pleasure, slowly becoming jelly. They gazed into each other's eyes, at one with the other's movements, knowing that for this single moment in time they were the only two people on the planet.

They made love three more times that night before Jude fell asleep holding her safely in his arms. Emily, however, was wide-awake, overwhelmed with a new understanding of love, life, pleasure, and fear. Her body was satisfied and at peace with the magic that had just occurred, but her mind was fragile and scared, not knowing the next time she would be in his arms again, if ever.

XIV

Emily & Jude: A Change in the Weather

Time bled on, winter turned to spring then spring to summer and before Emily realized it, she was entering her final year of medical school. As predetermined, neither Jude nor Emily had time to see one another. Jude was training every day and spent the bulk of his summer with the club on their annual Asia summer tour. But there wasn't a moment when he wasn't thinking of her in some way. He text messaged her at every opportunity, and sometimes felt her absence consume him. He continued writing her, many of the letters were kept exclusively to his journal while others he had made an effort to mail out. The last letter he had received from Emily was two months ago, well, on July 3, 2014, approximately sixty-three days, five hours, and seven seconds, but only he was counting. The time ticked away in his head like a cuckoo clock ready to explode at the question of, 'what could she possibly be doing that was so important, that she couldn't reply to any of his twelve letters, five phone calls, and twenty-two text messages he's sent her in the past fourteen days?'

Lying in his bed, his eyes were transfixed on the white ceiling of his upper Manchester flat. His stubble, which was a rough five o'clock shadow seventy-two hours ago, had developed into a scruffy rug covering the lower half of his face. His hand flopped along the side of his mattress scrounging the floor in search of the half empty bottle of whiskey that he had begun drinking a half hour ago. A large part of him knew he shouldn't be drinking. The *Community Shield* was tomorrow against Chelsea commencing the 2014/2015 season, and he could practically see Michael scolding him like some futuristic hologram from *Star Wars*, for drinking less than twenty-four hours before a match. But he kept drinking anyway because he missed her and because it depressed him how easy it was for him to relapse. His hand found the bottle. He took a substantial gulp and placed it back down beside the bed spilling a few drops in the process. Checking his mobile for the six hundredth time in less than forty-five minutes, there were still no missed calls, text messages, or emails from Emily, *'no missed calls for fourteen days!'* kept running through his head like breaking news on CNN. *'What could possibly warrant such an exile of communications?'* he thought out loud. Was it something he did? The last time they spoke on the phone their conversation was peppered with their usual inquires over their days and the weather—nothing out of the ordinary. He carried on opening his text log on his mobile only to see it filled with outgoing messages, *'Hey, phone me., Where have you been?, I hope everything is alright give me a ring., Alright, love, I have officially crossed into stalker territory I miss you give me a ring., So I saw Melissa's Facebook status today 'excited for me and my roommate's last year at school' so unless she's gotten a new flatmate in which case have her phone me.'* Upon reading them he became further depressed at how pathetic he had become. *'I'm bloody Jude Macavoy...'* he thought out loud to himself again, creepily turning his thoughts into a full blown conversation, *'I make 38 million pounds a year, so you Emily Robertson can piss off!'* Maybe he was overreacting? It had only been fourteen days, and maybe she was just really busy, that's not beyond the realm of probability. But in defiance of his optimism, he'd been around the block enough to know better. No one besides the President of the United States could be this busy. This was precisely what he did to girls he no longer wanted to talk to, the old *'fade out'* move, as he called it. He would slowly start to miss calls and not reply to text messages, until the other person just gives up on the relationship. It was one of his favorite break up strategies because it saved him giving the *'it's not you, it's me'* speech.

Scrambling again for his bottle he noticed the tiny black waste bin by his nightstand with a crumpled up piece of paper in it. He unraveled Emily's last note reading it again as if it had somehow changed since throwing it away.

Dear Jude,

I'm glad to hear your tour is going well. Things are great here, my internship is going better than I could ever have imagined. I've met so many people and have made so many contacts. I hope they offer me residency once I graduate, but we'll see.

Take care,
Emily

He crumbled it back up and threw in ferociously against the wall continuing his conversation with himself, *'Really Emily? That's all you could muster up to write? This is no letter, it's a bloody Tweet. You may as well have done it in Morse Code!'* He reached again for his bottle, but found it empty and the room no longer at a standstill. He passed out moments later with his hand still attached to the bottle, mumbling the words, *"You didn't even write I love you..."*

Jude's face collapsed in his hands, as he could not bring himself to make eye contact with his manager or his teammates. "That was bloody awful," he said, unaware that he had done so out loud.

"No shit," replied Steven Frye from the locker across from Jude's.

Jude still in a daze could barely grasp what had just occurred. Part of him wanted to blame Emily for making him resort to his old ways. But if he was being honest with himself, he was always subconsciously searching for a reason to shut the world out again and return to the drink. He wasn't even four days ignored by Emily before he began drowning his sorrows in alcohol.

"I'm sorry, mate…I just…I was….did I really get substituted in the fifteenth minute?"

Just having to ask the question proved how pitiful and tragic he had become, and if it were indeed true then he could do with a high ledge to jump off of. *'What footballer gets substituted in the fifteenth… THE FIFTEENTH MINUTE of the first half?'* he thought. To put it into perspective, a footballer getting substituted within the first fifteen minutes of a match due to lack of performance is the equivalent to a math professor being fired on the first day of school because he couldn't add two plus two.

"Yeah, you were. You were completely rubbish, mate," answered Steven in a disgusted tone. "If the Gaffer didn't take you off, one of the supporters would have come on the pitch and had a go at you."

"That poor?" ask Jude humiliated.

"Mate, would you like me to recall your numbers for the fifteen minutes you were on the pitch?"

"You know them?"

"Everyone who watched the bloody match knows them. Your pass completion percentage was a big zero! You literally passed the ball to the other team every time you came into possession. I reckoned you just bet a tenner against us and were assuring your pay."

Jude's head plummeted back into his palms in agony, "bollocks." Steven leaned in close so no one else could hear their conversation.

"Really, what's going on with you, mate? For the past two weeks you've been out of it. Like alien outer space out of it."

"I don't know…" of course he did, Emily was the perpetrator of his recent demise, "I'm fine."

"Well whatever it is you better get it together, because if you keep this form up you won't just be substituted, you won't be in the squad."

Jude finished getting dressed and went over the checklist for the worst day ever in his head. *'Play the worst football match ever? Check. Get*

Charles A. Bush

hung out by the Gaffer in front of the entire team? Check. Not hear from Emily in fifteen days? Check. Deal with the media bashing?...Bollocks! He had forgotten he still had to attend the post game press conference. For there are certain moments in one's life that are predetermined and unavoidable, and the media slaughtering him for today's performance was one of those moments.

Walking down the long red and black Old Trafford hallway, the walls covered with old photos of past great Manchester United players and squads, Jude's pace was unsettled and lethargic. Feeling a nervous wreck, he found it peculiar that all of the sudden he was alone in the hallway, leading him to believe that beyond that press room door lay a storm waiting to erupt. This wasn't the first time he had to handle the media when he was in less than good favor with them, but the difference was this time he hadn't performed well on the pitch so his charm and charisma won't be able to talk him out of it. In defiance of being ten seconds from walking into a media execution, all he could think about was Emily, and just when he thought matters couldn't get any worse he heard his manager's thick Scottish accent yelling at him from the opposing end of the hall. The first thing to run through his mind was, *'bloody'ell, this day can't get any worse!'*

"Jude a moment please," said Sir Alex, summoning him forward with his finger like he was being sentenced.

"Yes, boss?" his voice was guilty and bashful.

"Do you know how old I am?"

Jude's face was baffled to say the least.

"Not quite sure, boss, I would guess forty-five? Which reminds me, have you been working out? You look brilliant."

"Don't be a wise arse. That's part of your problem, you think everything is this elaborate joke that only you're in on." His eyes were locked on Sir Alex's now, intent on listening. "I am seventy-three-years-old and that was by far the worst display of football I have ever seen from an individual. You have succeeded in taking the entire game of football back thirty years." A bit harsh, Jude thought. "However, despite that

164

wretched shite you dare call playing football that you displayed today, I'm still going to be of some assistance. I want you to go home and pull your head out of your arse." Again, a bit harsh he thought. Not entirely sure where this conversation was going Jude debated whether to speak at all, but he looked at the big, upset, grey haired Scotsman and thought *what's the worst that could happen?*

"What about the press conference?"

"I'll handle it. I'll say you had a knock and against my better judgment I played you anyway, and that's why I pulled you off after fifteen minutes. Now get out of here before I change my mind."

He could kiss him he was so relieved, but he understood this was a punishment not a reward, plus Sir Alex wasn't his type, far too old and bossy.

"Thanks, boss!"

"Don't thank me just yet. I'll be seeing you at five a.m. tomorrow."

He knew he shouldn't have spoken. He should have just left when he had the chance.

"For what? You said we only have weight lifting in the afternoon because we won."

"I did, but now you will be running sprints for me as well. And when I say me I'm referring to the groundskeeper who I gave a few extra pounds to look over you. I didn't play like shite today, so I won't be waking up early."

"Bollocks!" snapped Jude while sucking his teeth in defiance.

"I'm not punishing you because I enjoy it. I'm punishing you because you're a good lad and it's time to grow up and start acting like it. If you think I can't smell the alcohol on your breath then you're having a laugh. I know you think the world is against you but whatever it is you are going through I promise that's not why it's happening. The world is constantly going to knock you down on your arse, but it's not the way you puff out your chest to embrace the hit, it's the way you take it on the chin and persevere." Like any big shot being read the riot act, Jude didn't want to hear it, but considering how poorly he had just preformed, he made the wise decision of soaking in his manager's words, at least for the time being.

"Wow, Em, another A! I'm beginning to think you're cheating off me," joked Melissa, peering over Emily's shoulder stealing a peek of her most recent cardiac exam.

Emily laughed,

"You wish."

"Seriously, Em, if you keep this up you're definitely going to be in the running for valedictorian come May."

They continued walking down the aged Yale hallway that smelled of rich mahogany and $65,000 worth of tuition. It was already September 13th, and Emily had aced both exams she had taken. Placing her exam in her knapsack, she couldn't help but feel an overwhelming sense of gratification and exhaustion. In the past two weeks alone she had racked up over seventy hours at the hospital in field training, another twenty-eight studying, and ten hours of classes. She couldn't even recall the last time she had a full night's sleep.

"I hope so, but there's still two semesters left. How'd you do?" She knew Melissa ignored her advice to not go out the night before the exam. Instead Melissa attended a Yale Frat party. She showed up ten minutes before the exam smelling of beer and cheap Axe body spray, dressed in the same low cut jeans and high heels from the night before. The only piece of clothing that was new to the day was a sweatshirt from her 'walk of shame kit,' which was the name of a box with a sweater and toothbrush that she had always kept in her trunk for occasions such as this.

"I got a C. I swear Bartlett has it out for me. If he weren't so old I would consider sleeping with him for an A. That whole beard and elbow patches look is kind of hot."

"That's gross!"

"Well obviously we wouldn't tell his wife." Emily couldn't believe Melissa. Even for Melissa this was low, and even though she knew she was joking, the thought of Melissa using her sex appeal to get something she wanted wasn't beyond the realm of reason. "Just one A, that's all I want. Is that too much to ask?"

"You know there are these things called books? Which when read translate into an ancient human ritual called studying. I'm no rocket scientist but couldn't that help you get your infamous *A* without having to seduce a sixty-four-year-old man, probably giving him a heart attack in the process?"

"Very funny, but sarcasm isn't your strong suit, Em. Besides if I studied, then that would make me like you and unlike you I enjoy having fun. And my way I have another excuse to wear that sexy new bra I just got."

They shared a laugh as they passed through the school to the courtyard. The leaves on the large oak trees had already begun metamorphosing into a brown and yellow blend in anticipation of the fall. Students were sprawled out under the trees, gawking at their iPads and typing on their laptops. One guy almost ran into Emily while tossing a Frisbee around with some fellow students.

"Speaking of sexy bras how's Jude?"

"How on earth do you get Jude from sexy bras?"

"Have you seen his body?" Emily could see Melissa imagining him in her mind. "If I were you, every time I saw him I would be wearing something sexy in hopes he would rip it off me."

Emily hated when Melissa fantasized about Jude.

"Jesus, you really have to stop Googling photos of him."

"Well this is what you get when you date a celebrity. Trust me, I'm not the only girl to Google *Jude Macavoy shirt off.*"

"To answer your question though, he's fine." That was a lie. Her stomach swirled knowing that she hadn't spoken to him for three weeks now.

"Really? Scott's been telling me he's playing really bad. How did he put it? Oh, 'it's like he switched bodies with the most uncoordinated person in the world.' So in other words he switched bodies with Scott. Why do I feel like you're not telling me something, Em?"

Continuing down the New Haven street, Emily focused on the cars passing as if they could somehow drown out what Melissa was saying.

"Like, when was the last time you two spoke?"

"A few days ago I guess." That was another lie. Her stomach trembled even more—she wasn't cut out from this lying thing.

"You know… he's busy with the team and I'm busy with school and the hospital. I guess we really haven't had that much time to talk." Not a complete lie, her stomach felt a fraction better.

"You don't have *time*?" exploded Melissa, "You have a boyfriend who is super hot, has the sexiest British accent, and is worth over thirty million dollars. If it were me, I would have nothing but time. Wait, listen to this…" Melissa reached into her handbag and pulled out her mobile phone. "This was his Facebook status last night, which I just happened to notice when I signed on." Emily glared at her not believing she *happened* to stumble across it. "What? Okay so I don't just use Google for pictures of him, sue me. But here take a look."

'I'm downing these shots like there's no tomorrow. Gutted I have training in the morning, oh well.'

"He posted that at 11:42 last night. Take it from a drinking pro, I don't think he's referring to the shots they yell goal after."

Emily acted surprised and upset like she hadn't seen it, but indeed she had when she had checked her Facebook on her dinner break last night.

"I'll talk to him about it."

"Look, Em, Whatever's going on between you two is you guys' business. But don't forget he's a celebrity and with that comes a lot of baggage; just be sure you're ready to carry it. And I know it's our final year of school and you're working hard, but we sent you to England last year to open up and try new things, not to just focus on school and work exclusively. You're my best friend and roommate; I want to see you more than just in class."

Emily hated when Melissa made sense, it was one of those rare things in life that made her speechless.

"Well my car's over there, you sure you don't want a ride to the hospital?"

"Yeah I'm fine. I could use a good walk. I'm doing the three to twelve shift, so don't wait up for me."

"I never do. I'll leave some Chinese for you on the counter. Eat it, Em! Even world-saving doctors have to eat."

She chuckled, "I will."

"Okay I'll see you tomorrow. And, Em—"

"Yeah..."

"Think about what I said."

The hospital was exceptionally busy for a Tuesday afternoon. The waiting room filled with patients begrudgingly waiting for a nurse to call their name, some in more pain than others. Usually around dinner time it calmed down, like no one wants to get sick on an empty stomach, but today everyone seem to be more fixated on seeing the doctor than a meal.

Emily had just finished putting one of the senior doctor's patients through a round of chemotherapy. She carried the test results under her arm in a folder, passing through the west wing in-between the fraternity ward and rehabilitation, when she ran into Doctor Landry at the end of the hall by the level B elevators.

"Hello, Ms. Robertson."

"Hello Doctor, I was just on my way to your office to drop off Mr. Adams's chart."

He smiled at her, making her feel important.

"What a coincidence, I was just on my way to see you. Let's go back to my office so we can talk."

Dr. Brad Landry was a brilliant and kind man. He was punctual at work, made every nurse and patient feel as though they were more important than the doctors, and possessed cheek bones that when paired with his smile made every female in the break room salivate. He was 6'3, wealthy, young, and handsome, or as Melissa would say, 'the complete package.' As Emily stared across the desk at what she hoped would someday be her future employer, she couldn't help but think he resembled a young better looking George Clooney, if such a thing even existed. He began writing on the folder transferring in his own words, notes she had written on the patient. She studied his hair. No gel and maybe a single comb brushed through it, but yet it was perfectly groomed and suited him flawlessly.

"So, Ms. Robertson, I take it Mr. Adams's treatments are going well? Since you're looking at me with a smile and not a look that says I need to make a phone call to the family."

Emily blushed, almost forgetting she was asked a question.

"Oh…yes, sorry Dr. Landry. Mr. Adams seems to be taking very well to chemo. Here—" she said, reaching over his desk pointing at the left side of the folder, "If you look at page two of his chart you can see he's extremely close to declaring remission."

"I see—that's fantastic! Great work, as usual, Ms. Robertson. And we've been over this. Please call me Brad." She was determined to remain professional and not blush, but did so anyway. "You know, Ms. Robertson, sometimes I wish you were coming to my office just to speak with me and not for business issues." She gave off a little smile. "But I'm glad you're here nonetheless. Now let's get down to business. I called you in here to talk about your future. As you know I got my first position unprecedentedly only two years after graduating from Penn Medical four years ago, and the funny thing is I wasn't half as bright as you. What I'm getting at is all the staff love having you, patients are obviously satisfied with your work, and I have no doubt you will make a great M.D. someday. So if you're interested, I would like to offer you a full-time paid residency spot here after graduation, with the pre-option of filling the vacant hospitalist position in two years. The way I looked at it is you're already putting in full-time hours so you may as well get paid for it."

Emily was flabbergasted at his proposal. Her jaw practically spattered on the floor like she had just hit the lottery.

"I don't know what to say."

"Of course you don't have to give us your answer now." His handsome smile was making it harder for her to collect her thoughts.

"I know... it's just... well, it's always been a dream of mine to become a doctor. I just can't believe it's all finally happening. I would love the position."

Brad laughed, "Well here's the contract. It's a good thing I took the liberty of making sure they offered you a salary well worth your talents, because you're not a very good negotiator."

"Sorry, I know I should have read it first, I'm just so excited."

"I can't wait for you to officially be part of the team. If you're up for it, maybe we could grab some dinner one night to celebrate?"

Within a second all the joy was sucked from her. And looking at his perfectly chiseled chin was making it hard to answer with anything but a 'yes.'

"Oh, Dr. Landry..." He gave her a correcting look, "I mean Brad. Thank you so much for the offer, but I'm sort of dating someone right now and I wouldn't feel comfortable."

"Say no more. The offer stands should you ever change your mind. He's a lucky guy."

Part of her wished he was less understanding, his compassion and maturity only made him that more appealing. They both stood and Brad put out his hand shaking hers firmly.

"Well, soon-to-be Doctor Robertson, I am proud of you and you deserve all the good fortunes that are coming your way. I look forward to working closer with you."

After the meeting, Emily text messaged Melissa, '*I just got offered a paid residency and hospitalist position after graduation.*' Melissa was ecstatic for her, but the last words of her text message left Emily deflated and joyless in spite of her good news, '*have you told Jude?*'

XV

Emily & Jude: The Talk

I t was October first, a full month since Jude and Emily last spoke. Since their hiatus Jude has found himself benched for lack of form and drunk five nights out of the week. The papers were constantly hammering him for his rediscovered nightlife presence, labeling him, *The Bust That Likes to Party*. Just a year ago, they were praising him for helping Manchester win their twenty-first league trophy and the FA cup, '*how did things get so bad?*' he thought. He knew the answer but refused to admit it. Instead resorting to blaming Emily, who did play a part, but being blown off by your girlfriend was no excuse for his actions. Nights consisted of drunk dials to Emily's mobile, some cursing her name while others pleading his love, more alcohol then he could handle, and night clubs where he was made VIP instantly. The things he loved most appeared to be slipping through his hands like grains of sand and he didn't know what to do about it.

Emily continued excelling in her final year of medical school. She was laying superb groundwork to succeed in her residency post graduation, and was even succeeding in warding off the infrequent advances from Dr. Landry. For as much as she could see herself with him she was still officially with Jude and would never consider betraying him in that way. The only aspect of her life that she wasn't excelling in was keeping contact with her now yearlong boyfriend. She knew they needed to talk and she felt awful for not returning his calls or text messages, but her busy schedule and lack of conviction about their relationship all got the better of her. And as much as she fought to admit it, she let things spiral out of control to the point where each day it became a further daunting task to call him. In the grand scheme of things, she knew he probably hated her, and she wouldn't blame him for doing so, but when considering the only outcome to their inevitable conversation, her heart imploded, knowing he would only come to despise her more.

Emily had her first day off from school and the hospital in over a month, and felt it was as good of a time as any to finally address the elephant in the room. Who was she kidding; at this point the elephant was a fully-grown blue whale. She had spoken to her grandmother several days prior and with her help, was now more assured than ever that the situation wasn't fair to either her or Jude. She paced her room for over fifteen minutes, rehearsing what she would say, but as Jude's mobile rang all of her words disintegrated.

Jude laid spread out across his bed with the pillow entrapped over his head sealing in the stench of alcohol on his breath. His mobile rang persistently, the sound amplified by his massive hangover making him feel as if he were sleeping next to a church bell. His hands hunted through the comforter until locating the maddening source.

"Oi! This had better be good, it's like four in the morning," he mumbled, still half asleep and hoping he was talking into the correct end of the phone.

"Hey…" her voice nervous and soft.

His eyes shot open sobering up spiritedly.

"Emily?" he questioned, unsure if the alcohol was playing tricks on him.

"Hi stranger—sorry we haven't spoken in a while."

"Sorry? You're bloody sorry? You haven't returned one of me calls, letters, or text in over a month. As far as I'm concerned you can keep your sorry! What the hell is going on with you? With us?"

Emily wished she could remember what she had rehearsed, but unfortunately her mind was a blank canvas: "I...I don't know."

"Oh come off it, Emily. You haven't bothered to phone your so-called boyfriend for over a bloody month...a BLOODY MONTH! And all you can say for yourself is 'I don't know'? Are you havin' a laugh?...Well, *are you*!"

She tried her best to remain composed and stick to the script that she had now forgotten.

"Look, Jude, I didn't call to argue. I just called to talk about us."

"Brilliant! Ladies and gentlemen, me girlfriend has finally decided that she wants to talk about us. Aren't I the luckiest muppet in the world! And just so you know I shouted that out of me window, just so all of Manchester can see how much a bloody tosser me girlfriend is."

"Can you please not raise your voice to me right now? You haven't exactly been a saint either."

"Emily, you haven't spoken a word to me in over a month. Can you not comprehend how absurd that is when you are quote unquote in a relationship, especially a long distance one? I think I earned the right to raise me voice."

In a last-ditch effort to defend herself, she began recalling some of the reasons why she hadn't phoned sooner. But as she said them out loud she discovered her excuses were few and far between.

"You have every right to be upset. Recently I've been a horrible girlfriend. But I've just been so busy with school and work, I just lost track of time."

His volume rose immensely in a tornado of anger at her reasoning, or lack thereof.

"Oh *piss off*! I'm so sick of hearing you fall back on your school and work for all your little problems. You went to bloody Yale for Christ's sakes and are revising to become a doctor. Your life isn't exactly filled with hardships and trials. And one more thing, you *don't* have a job. You assist at hospital for university credit. The last I checked, someone who has a job gets paid for their services. So spare me the whole work rubbish yeah."

"Are you kidding me? I spend more time at the hospital than you do at you're precious pub, and that's a lot of time. Or are you too drunk to remember how long you spend there?"

For a brief moment she felt bad for attacking him, but her human reflexes were kicking in and when you're in a fight you must fight.

"What I do with me free time is me own damn business."

"Well then stop tweeting it for the whole world to see."

"So you do acknowledge me existence for the last month? I wasn't sure if you were ignoring the social media world as well, but since you've had time to read me tweets it's clear only I received the honour of being ignored." His sarcasm was laid on thick, only infuriating her more and pushing her past the point of sarcasm. She never felt herself get so angry.

"YES, JUDE, I'm sorry I didn't call, but we both knew the difficulties of this relationship going in, we were QUITE clear about that! And like I said, I've been busy with school and work, yes WORK, I actually got offered a position the other day after graduation, jerk!"

"Well, stop the bloody presses," he said, laying the sarcasm on so thick he was practically mocking her, "you got a job, good for you. So what now, you spend even more time at the hospital? Leaving even less time for us and practically rendering the possibility of us ever seeing one another."

They finally took a moment to catch their breath. Emily was proud of herself for holding back the tears this long and when she again built up the courage to address him her voice was soft with little distortion.

"Look, I really don't want to spend this entire conversation shouting at each other."

He matched her tone lowering his voice.

"Then what do you wish to spend it on? Because you obviously didn't phone to say you miss me."

Her heart crumbled in her chest as she refocused on the real reason for her call. She took off her spectacles, rubbing the bridge of her nose in anxiety and wishing she were doing anything else besides talking to him.

"It's not that simple, Jude."

"Sure it is, just spit it out."

She took a deep breath in hopes to piece together her thoughts.

"I don't know. I guess when we talked last Christmas about not seeing each other until who knows when, really bothered me. And the crazy thing is I seriously considered quitting my internship so I could spend the summer with you again, and the fact that I would consider hurting my chances of becoming a doctor all because I was in love with you tormented me for months, and I felt awful because of it. But then I realized I can't see you when I want, I can't call you without thinking of the time difference, we can't go to the movies on a whim, I guess I just finally realized it's impossible to be a couple with us being so far apart."

He was silent, attempting the process all that she was saying.

"I love you, Jude, but look at my life and all that I hope to accomplish and look at yours and all the things you've already accomplished. Our lives are just moving in different directions." She began to cry now, finally subsiding to her emotions. "I love you, Jude...I really do. I'm so happy when we're together but we're so different and so far apart...I'm so confused."

"I know, don't cry, love, I love you as well."

"I just think it would be best if we go our separate..." A faint background voice interrupted her sentence. Emily tried to decipher it from the opposite end of the receiver. It sounded like, 'What are you doing? It's four in the morning.' Jude smacked his face in disbelief of his companion's stupidity. "Excuse me for a second, Emily—hold that thought." Emily pressed her ear firmly against the receiver trying to overhear his conversation.

"Bloody'ell, what are you doing in here? Bollocks, don't answer that, just go back in me room, now is not the time." He placed the phone back to his ear. "Okay, Emily, sorry about that please continue."

Her tears turned to rage and envy.

"Who was that?"

"Oh that? That was me mate from the team, I reckon he slept here last night after the pub. He was just asking if I fancied a sandwich, what a nutter huh? It's like, 'hello? It's five in the bloody morning no I don't want a sandwich' he's such a muppet."

"Jude seriously, who was that?"

"Love, it's me mate. Honest."

She managed to tame her voice, steadying it to the point of authority.

"You promised me you would never lie to me."

"And you promised we would always be together, yet here we are having this conversation."

"Don't try and change the subject. Just answer me this, is that Tiffany?"

The silence in his voice seemed to go on forever, as if someone pressed the pause button on his vocal chords. His voice sounding defeated as he finally broke the silence.

"I swear, love, I don't think anything happened."

"You don't think!" She exploded back at him, punching his tone in the face.

"What did you expect? I 'm a footballer who hasn't heard from his girlfriend in over a month, so yeah I drank a few pints!"

"You know what, Jude? So what we haven't spoken in over a month. The fact is you reverted back to your old ways in less than a week of us not talking, which shows me who you really are, and that Jude Macavoy disgusts me—the drinking, the women, the drugs. I'll stop beating around the bush, you're not the man I fell in love with and I can't do this long distance thing, so I think we should go our separate ways. I hope you can grow to love yourself."

He pleaded with her desperately.

"I know you're upset—"

"No, Jude. It's clear; whatever we are isn't going to work."

It was a fight he was losing and with no other cards to play he went for broke.

"Alright! I shagged her. Is that what you want to hear?"

She steadied her voice, certain to mask her pain in her words.

"Take care of yourself, Jude."

"Emily wait! Let's just talk for a moment?" Silence echoed over the receiver. "...Emily!"

As the end call flashed across his mobile he knew within an instant of truth she was gone forever.

XVI

Emily & Jude: Wake-up Call

Jude stroked his scruffy beard looking out of the window of the team's charter traveling from Norwich to Manchester. Effectively sobering up enough to gain a bit of form, he made his way back to the substitutes bench, even getting a good thirty minutes of playing time this week. Since the breakup, a phrase he tried to avoid saying at all cost, he discovered the pitch was the only real place he could achieve any peace of mind. He took out his mobile, as he often did, typing '*I miss you*' in the text box under Emily's name, before erasing it and placing it back in his pocket out of harm's way. Out of the past six months that they had been separated, he had only broken down and called her once, drunk off his mind in a strip club bathroom in Wigan. Still to this day he had no idea how he ended up in Wigan of all places, but of course Emily didn't answer so he left a rather long and excruciating voicemail where he stumbled over his words as if about to go into cardiac arrest, saying how much he missed her and a little bit on how strippers are the ballerinas of the night.

Jude staggered through his flat's door. Knowing they didn't have training tomorrow due to the match today, he took the liberty of indulging in several extra pints at the pub. He could have sworn he was throwing a party tonight, but since no one was present and it was already 10:30 p.m. he figured he had rescheduled. In reality, he was far too drunk to realize it was actually only 5:30 p.m. He didn't even make it to the bedroom before having one final glance at his mobile and blacking out across the arm of the couch.

The sun creaked through the blinds reflecting off Jude's living room table, where he somehow found himself lying beneath, still drunk and unconscious. The living room, reminiscent of old, was littered with bras and knickers from women coming and going, empty beer bottles, fag ashes, and crisp crumbs scattered across his Persian rug. The flat smelled of fags and booze with a faint scent of worn gym socks. To close your eyes would transport you to a rundown brothel in Yorkshire.

"Jude, get up!"

Jude's hand motioned towards the kitchen counter while the rest of his body lay still, remaining asleep.

"Just leave your number over there, love," he said in an exhausted mumble.

"Seriously, mate, get up! I'm not one of your bloody hookers."

His plea for Jude to get up only acted as a catalyst to send him into further slumber. The sink's faucet ran only for a few seconds before a bowl of cold water was discharged in Jude's face.

"Wanker!" shouted Jude. He leaned over and grabbed a loose bra from under the couch, wiping his face dry of the excess water. "Michael?" asked Jude, regaining his vision. "How'd you get in? I don't remember you being here last night."

"Your door was wide open. Speaking of which, I'm fairly certain someone nicked your Blu-Ray player, mate."

Jude took in a deep breath yawing in an effort to wake up. He lay there in nothing but a pair of briefs and the crisp crumbs that resided in his beard.

"What are you doing here? And where is everyone—" he asked mid yawn.

"I kicked everyone out, and a better question is what are you doing? I mean you're passed out under a bloody coffee table for Christ's sake."

Jude made his way from under the table to the couch, dusting off the fag ashes before he sat.

"Yeah, I'm not entirely sure how that happened."

"Look at yourself, mate. I'm worried about you. You never come round anymore to visit Amy and me, you've succumbed to shagging anything that moves, and you've obviously gone back to drinking like it's your job." Michael picked up a bottle from the floor to prove a point, smelling it intently. "Bloody'ell, what sort of beer is this? It's bloody rank!"

"Oh, that, mate, would be piss—didn't quite make it to the loo last night."

"Aw!" Michael dropped the bottle instantly, spilling it on the rug just adding to the abysmal smell. "You see, this is precisely what I'm talking about. You're living like you're bloody Charlie Sheen, except from what I hear he actually uses the loo. All the alcohol and birds, you're like my brother, I can't keep watching you throw your life and career away. What happened? When you were with Emily you were doing so well."

"That was six months ago. That bitch crushed me heart. She was right from the start, long distance is rubbish...here, you fancy some breakfast?"

Michael ripped the liquor bottle from Jude's hand.

"Would you give me that! You're not drowning your sorrows in vodka for breakfast. And yeah, she left you, so bloody what! She left you because you don't talk to her for a week and you resort to acting like an alcoholic petulant child. No woman wants to deal with that. Stop crying about it and man up! You guys being together isn't what made you clean up your act. It's the message that she finally got you to see."

"And what message is that?" replied Jude, cupping his mouth as a little vomit came rising up his throat, as if his body was reminding him that he should have passed on that twenty-fifth shot of whiskey that he drank from in-between some girl's breasts last night.

"For starters, she finally got through to you that you were a good person. You always have been. You're the one who visited my dad when he was in hospital; you're the one who drove all the way to Sheffield just to get Amy her favourite ice cream when she was pregnant, and you're the same bloke that knows every single person at Blackpool's name and birthday. You remember when you bought that janitor and his family season tickets to Arsenal because they couldn't afford it? That made his year."

Jude gave a faint smile recalling all the good in his life that he had done.

"Well, Richard was a brilliant janitor. He always made sure me favourite stall had T.P."

"Honestly, Jude, besides your sudden lack of hygiene, the obsessive drinking, and the high probability you have an STD, you have the biggest heart I know."

"Gee…thanks. And I don't have an STD, it's just dry skin," he replied, rubbing his crouch region.

"And finally she showed you what I've been telling you for years, that in order to receive love you must first learn to love yourself. And by the look of that beard you clearly don't right now."

Jude sat there feeling as if he had just been scolded by a teacher for not applying himself. He again stroked his heavy beard slowly in thought, sprinkling some of the remaining crumbs in it onto his lap.

"…I don't know? I miss her madly."

"And I'm certain she feels the same. But do you think she's out there shagging every bloke she sees and letting people nick her Blu-Ray player?"

"Um…I really don't want to picture her shagging blokes, but cheers for that image."

Michael gave him a smile, seeing his words were beginning to sink in.

"Well, the answer is no, wanker. She's getting on with her life trying to fulfill her goals and dreams and you should be doing the same. It's what your parents would have wanted."

Jude began growing even more frustrated, because if there was anything worse than being scolded by Michael it was when he made sense when doing so.

"Ugh…" said Jude in disgust, "Why are you here? Can't a man wake up from a crazy party he doesn't remember in peace?"

"Nope, I'm not leaving until you admit I'm right and promise me you'll get your act together for good."

"Fine, you're right. I promise to lay off the shagging…a little." Jude shrugged at *a little*.

"Seriously, Jude, until I get a serious promise I'm not going anywhere. Do I need to sing you a certain song?" Michael opened his mouth to sing and Jude looked at him as if a bomb were about to go off.

"Please don't, I already have a massive headache."

"*Hey Jude…don't let me down…*" Jude tossed a pillow at him in surrender.

"Alright…you bloody win, just don't sing! You're right, I need to stop acting like a wanker and get me act together. I promise starting tomorrow—"

"Jude!"

"Alright, starting today, I'll try to shape up."

Michael stood to his feet satisfied with Jude's promise, even if he didn't fully believe he would shape up without Emily's assistance.

"Good! Well, my work here is done, I'ma head out. Because unlike you overpaid buffoons at United, some of us still have to train the day after a match." He made his way past the mountains of booze and knickers to the front door. "Oh, and Jude?"

"What now?" he replied, fed up with their conversation.

"Shave that God awful beard, you look like you have a newborn Wookie on your face."

Emily Robertson was nestled comfortably in the Yale library finishing up her dissertation. Although it wasn't due until the final week of classes several weeks from now, she felt it could do with some extra editing. She was forced to cut back her hours at the hospital to just twenty-six to have more time to study, but the majority of the extra time was spent thinking about Jude. She tried to convince herself that it was perfectly natural to reminisce after you've been truly in love with someone for as long as she had. People were always saying that you need the same amount of time that you were in the relationship to fully get over it. However, despite how much she may miss him, she understood she could never go back. Because he clearly wasn't the man she had originally fallen in love with, the DWI he had picked up three months ago that was all over TMZ and the drunken messages about strippers being ballerinas proved that. But more importantly she was 'focused,' just weeks away from achieving her dream, and nothing was going to deter her from fulfilling her lifelong promise.

She was retyping her final paragraph when Melissa showed up.

"Hey slut—" *Hey slut* was a new phrase Melissa had picked up from one of the hundred woeful reality television shows about real house-wives and an STD infested beach shore that she watched regularly.

"Hey. And please stop calling all your friends sluts."

"Why? The Kardashians call each other that all the time, or is that what Snookie says? I don't remember I get those shows confused."

"Well it's degrading and dumb, so please don't call me that."

"Okay, okay, grumpy. I'll say 'what up bitch' instead."

Emily cracked a smile, not immune to Melissa's crude sense of humor. Upon doing so, she realized it was the first time she had smiled in weeks.

"You're ridiculous. What are you doing here anyway? You know this place is filled with books?"

"*Ha-ha*, very funny," replied Melissa sarcastically, removing her laptop from her knapsack and placing it down beside Emily. "I'm doing the same thing you are."

"What? Finishing up your dissertation?"

"Holy shit, you're finished? I'm just getting started."

Emily stopped typing for a second, taking the time to turn her body to face Melissa, who was firmly planted in the chair beside her ready to work.

"Melissa, that's horrible even for you. We're three weeks from graduating and our dissertation is due in two."

Melissa raised her hand to Emily as if trying to calm her down. "Now in my defense, BC has been throwing some pretty sweet parties recently." Emily shot her a scalding glare. "Don't worry I'm going to get it done. But let's get down to the juicy stuff. Come on, don't leave me hanging." Melissa was now retuning Emily's glare with one of mischief and scandal.

"What juicy stuff? And why are you looking at me like that? You look like the Grinch after he stole Christmas."

"How did your date go last night?"

"What? It wasn't a date. We just went out for some coffee."

"This is the fourth time you and doctor handsome went out for coffee after work. On this little planet called earth we refer to these as dates… You see, Em, it's all a part of the male playbook."

Emily's head fell on the desk shaking *no* profusely. Melissa read one little article in *Glamour* about how men pick up women and now all of the sudden she was acting like she had her doctorate in pickup lines. She had even started her own Facebook group called the Male Playbook where she quotes "educates women" on the male mind. It was all a bit ludicrous and bogus for Emily's liking.

"Oh…here we go," said Emily, preparing her mind for the nonsense to come.

Melissa began her explanation like a world-class professor addressing her class.

"As I told you before, the male playbook is a very vital tool in the male arsenal. As foretold by the female playbook entitled *Glamour.*" Emily couldn't believe Melissa was actually about to recite for the third time in less than two weeks this article. The first time was two weeks ago when a guy kindly asked for the time and she swore he was trying to seduce her. The second was when Jim from Human Anatomy class dropped his pencil and asked Melissa to pick it up, apparently that means he really wants to get you in bed.

"You see, Em, a man will ask you to coffee because he knows caffeine will keep you awake and talking about yourself. So while you babble on about work and your nephew's tenth birthday party, he acts like he's listening, making you believe he's a very caring and noble guy for listening to your problems. But then knowing you're now wide awake from all the caffeine, he offers to take you to a nice Italian restaurant down the street where he heard from a friend it was really good. Turns out the restaurant is really only an Olive Garden but he acts like he's unaware it's a chain, but of course by this point in the evening you're three cups of coffee in and exhausted from work so you jump at the chance for food. But what's waiting for you at the Olive Garden? Wine! He suggests the waiter bring over a bottle even though you say you'll just have water. But as he drinks a glass, you can't help but indulge, because again you were exhausted from work. Then one glass leads to another and before you know it, you wake up in a BC dorm room with no recollection of the night before and photos of you doing a keg stand in your bra on Facebook."

Emily smiled trying not to laugh out loud at how absurd Melissa's story was.

"I couldn't help noticing something vaguely familiar about the end of your little lesson. So to be clear, Jim uploaded those pictures of you from last Friday at BC on Facebook?"

Melissa sighed, followed by a brief pause as if she had been caught red-handed on the jury stand.

"Yeah..." she sighed deflated, "but they did get sixty-four likes and the first part of the lesson is really from the male playbook."

"And there's just one flaw in your excerpt from your female bible. I had green tea all four times."

"That's not the point..." said Melissa, now partly forgetting what her point was, "the point is he thinks they're dates."

Emily actually found herself believing Mellissa, only for a moment.

"No you're wrong. It's just two colleagues having tea and coffee, that's all."

"Okay, but don't say I didn't warn you."

Emily rose from her chair grabbing her laptop and knapsack.

"Now if you excuse me, I'm going back to the apartment to finish this paragraph and actually get a full night's sleep."

Melissa was perplexed by the unusual way Emily insisted on leaving the library. In fact, she had never wanted to leave the library before. In a perfect world Emily would live here. Melissa's thoughts began wondering, and sensed an act of foul play.

"You're meeting him again tonight aren't you?"

Emily's shoulders fell and her face cocked to the side staring into space as if she were dreaming about him.

"Yeah, he's just so dreamy…"

"Aha! I knew it."

Emily began laughing and zipped her knapsack up to the top.

"I'm only kidding. I'm going back to my room and finishing this assignment, just like you should be doing. Besides, I already told you, I don't have time for boys."

"You won't be saying that when you're single with twenty-two cats with names like Mr. Snuggles and Mrs. Mittens."

They both shared a laugh before Emily headed home.

Emily spent only twenty minutes touching up her final paragraph and after she did, she quickly threw on some comfortable clothes and jumped into bed prepared for her first eight-hour sleep in over nine months. In anticipation of her full rest, she went to set her alarm clock, only to remember she had the morning shift, which meant she had to be at the hospital by 6:30 a.m. So despite her excitement, she would have to settle for six hours of sleep, which was two up on her previous four hours from last night, so she didn't complain too much.

Melissa's words rested skeptically in Emily's thoughts, *what if he really did think it was a date?* She knew she didn't want a boyfriend now, if ever, but she could not deny that she found her coffee partner to be handsome and sweet, and unlike Jude, he was in the same country and understood her passion for medicine. As she dozed off, the more she thought of him, the more he sounded like an idea worth exploring.

XVII

Emily: Graduation

"Get a move on, Emily!" Melissa shouted from the doorway fully dressed in her cap and gown. Emily was in her room finishing up getting dressed, which was a tad bizarre, because Melissa was already finished, leading Emily to the only conclusion that Melissa wasn't wearing anything at all under her gown. She decided to select the snug black dress that she had purchased for Melissa's sister's wedding three years ago. The black lace straps rested on her thin shoulders revealing the four petite brown freckles below her left shoulder blade. The dress fit as if it had been tailored for her body, accentuating her curves like an old country road. She straightened her hair so that it lay flat on her neck, peeking just below her triceps. The rich texture of her free-flowing hair accented her peachy face perfectly, as she put on only a little blush and mascara. She grabbed her spectacles and placed them on before placing her cap and gown in her handbag.

"Of all people I cannot believe you're so eager to attend a school event," said Emily, while Melissa rushed past her walking out the front door like a dog anticipating a walk.

"Are you kidding me? I want to hurry up and receive that M.D. before they change their minds about that seventy they gave me on my dissertation. Oh…and before I forget, my mom texted me about an hour ago. She said they already picked up your grandma, so they're probably there already."

Melissa placed the key in the ignition before having one last look at her hair in the rearview mirror.

"Well, we should get there with plenty of time to spare," said Emily, fearful for her life. "So don't drive a hundred miles over the speed limit. I would actually like to walk across the stage today."

It was a perfect summer day for a graduation, the forecast eighty-seven and sunny. The heat was rising off the Yale football field with precise warmth, making Emily glad she had chosen the dress she did. At her undergrad graduation, she had worn an ankle-length dress that had her legs sweating like a sauna by the time the Dean wrapped up the opening ceremonies. The stage was set up on top of the Yale bulldog logo on the fifty-yard line in the center of the field. Above every gate's entrance fitted large banners, *Congratulations Yale M.Ds. of 2015.*

Emily was in the middle of the pack among the rest of the Rs on the twenty-five yard line. She turned towards the stands and attempted to wave at her grandmother, who was sitting next to Melissa's family. But Emily could barely see her, so she was certain her grandmother couldn't make her out among the sea of other graduates; for her eyesight was far worse than Emily's.

The opening ceremony lasted about an hour, consisting of the Yale president and the dean making speeches that sounded all too similar to the ones they had made four years ago. By the time the Dean called for the valedictorian, Emily Robertson, to give her speech, most of the crowd was dozing off and ready to fast forward to the cap throwing part. Emily wasn't nervous. This was mostly due to the fact that she had gotten all of her nerves out when she gave her undergrad valedictorian speech. During which, she had most gracefully tripped when walking to the podium and had accidentally substituted the word breast for best when referring to her large-chested pre-med professor Mrs. Strickland. It was safe to say the all too familiar advice of picturing everyone naked had backfired. But Emily's newly found composure for public speaking along, with her reserved demeanor, made for a perfect speech on the day. It lasted all of two minutes and thirty seconds. She even achieved roaring laughter for her joke on the weather: "Thank goodness it's a beautiful day. I was worried that my speech along with Dean Prichard's toupee would fly away if it was windy." Surprisingly the dean laughed as hard as the audience, no doubt his sense of humor heightened because his star pupil was saying it. Emily then shot a wink at Melissa because as Melissa had said when she suggested the joke, "Everyone will love it, because everyone loves you."

The ceremony's guest speaker was Dr. Thomas Cumberbach, a neurosurgeon who had graduated from Oxford with what seemed like the class of 1902. He went on and on about how the economy is in the toilet and how unlikely it is that any of the graduates would find a position in the coming months; it was so depressing that if someone were to have studied the faces of all the graduates that had to endure the speech they would assume they were attending a funeral.

The names of the M.Ds. where called. Melissa made the rock 'n' roll symbol to the crowd as she accepted her diploma, striking her tongue out in the process like some female member of *Kiss*. Emily, on the other hand, was far less rebellious. She walked across the stage in tears wishing her mother was there. She flashed back to her mother's final days in the hospital, when the cancer was at its worst. She had leaned over the medical bed, resting her head on her mother's weak lap, soaking her hospital gown in tears. As any nine-year-old would do, she made a promise she was unaware was impossible to keep. She promised her mother that she would become a doctor so she could save her. And then three days later with her mother's last words she said, "I'm so proud of you, Emily. You're so beautiful and smart, I know you're going to make a great doctor and save many lives someday. I love you sweetie. Remember to follow your dreams and know I'm always here with you."

As hundreds of caps and gowns went soaring through the air in true Mary Tyler Moore fashion, the reality of their becoming real doctors was finally cemented in the graduates' brains. Emily had finally done it. The promise she had made to her mother, all those years ago, had molded her life and guided her to this day. All that was left to fulfill her mother's vision was to save lives. The thought of being graduated was one of excitement and relief, as she was eager to tackle the next phase in her life head on without any regret or remorse.

Emily proceeded to shake a lot of hands and take even more pictures with fellow graduates, some of which she hadn't even met until today. Melissa was snapping a photo of Emily and her grandmother in front of the end zone, when Melissa slowly submerged the camera from her face and motioned to Emily with a series of eyebrow pointing. "Em, look…" Emily turned around now facing the stage and ninety-nine yards of field. She instantly froze while her nerves flickered like a loose light bulb, making the hairs on her neck stand at attention. Melissa intervened and politely took Mrs. Ross's hand, "Mrs. Ross, let's let Em and her friend talk. We can go try to steal us some of those little sandwiches from the reception that you like so much."

Emily motioned to her grandma. "It's okay, grandma, I'll be fine."

Hundreds of people surrounded them in Yale blue gowns, laughing and celebrating with their families and friends. But in the midst of all the commotion, all Emily could see was Jude standing twenty yards in front of her, dressed in a fashionably sharp suit with a light blue handkerchief tucked in his left blazer pocket and an identical tie that matched his sky blue eyes. His dark blond hair was styled and gelled, mimicking a young successful businessman from the sixties. As he walked up to her he smiled as if looking upon her for the first time.

"Congratulations, Doctor Robertson. These are for you." Jude handed her the bouquet of fresh violet and yellow carnations with daisy poms.

"Thank you," said Emily, still unsure if her nerves would ever regain consciousness. She could barely speak as her tongue fumbled over her words, "Wha…what…are you doing here?"

Jude was both confident and clean, his charisma oozing out of his cool suit, acting like he didn't have a care in the world and they had never separated.

"Now you didn't honestly think I would miss your graduation from university did you?"

She smiled, her nerves now working on seventy-five percent capacity.

"But what about soccer—don't you have a game or another obligation today?"

He returned her smile with one of his own, as all his feelings for her began to overthrow his face.

"Don't worry about that. Today, everything stops for you."

They both fell silent as neither one could look past the other as if they had suddenly found themselves locked away in an empty room.

"You look beautiful by the way. I swear you become lovelier with each passing moment."

Emily took a deep breath, sucking in the memories of their love before she spoke.

"Thank you. You don't look half bad yourself."

"I'd better; it took me over an hour to get me hair proper. I had to stop in some place called CVS to get some more gel on me way here."

Emily smiled, remembering how vain he could be. She lunged her hands at his hair attempting to mess it up. Jude leaned back laughing while fighting off her assault, desperate to protect his well-groomed hair.

"Oi! I haven't spoken to you in seven months and you're already trying to mess up any photos I may take today. This hair is a national landmark, you know, knighted by the Queen."

She smiled again, finding herself surprisingly happy to see him. After he fixed the few strands of hair she managed to shake out of place, he stood surveying the hundred-yard field.

"So this is what you would call a 'football' field yeah? Why are there so many numbers on it? It looks like a bloody Sudoku puzzle."

"You have to get ten yards to get a first down, so it's how they measure."

"That may be the dumbest thing I've ever heard—you yanks and your silly games," he joked.

An awkward silence then fell over them, both clearly with more on their minds than leading on. Emily jumped first, ready to let out her true intentions.

"Listen, Jude, I'm happy to see you and I'm so glad to see that you're doing well, you really look like you've gotten your act together and I'm so happy for you. But I have to tell you…" he cut her off before she could finish.

"No, let me go first. I didn't just come here to say congratulations and tell you American football is a redundant sport."

"I know but…" again he cut in.

"Just hear me out, Emily. I've traveled a long way and waited many nights to tell you this."

She exhaled patiently, reluctantly giving in. "Okay, go ahead."

"Alright, well…um…bollocks! You'd think I would have rehearsed this better, especially after that whole 'I've come a long way' bit. Well I reckon the best way to begin is by apologizing. I am truly sorry, Emily. I was a selfish wanker and had no excuse to expect all your time to be devoted exclusively to me. You didn't deserve to be treated that way. I've been through a lot in me life and I've been in a dark place for the past ten years. I relied too much on booze to drown me sorrows and managed to push everyone who has ever loved me away, especially you. I will be sorry for that the rest of me life." His voice was weary as if he wanted to cry, but his masculine genes would have none of it. "But you know what? I can't be fully sorry because every poor decision I've made in me life has somehow led me to you. And for that I will never apologize. All I kept thinking was that I rather have my heart broken everyday by you than having never loved you. You were the best thing to ever happen to me, Emily. With every smile you gave, every kiss, every touch, I became more certain that I loved you…and I still do.

For even if you don't ever want to speak with me again, just to have met you has been the greatest gift that I have ever received, and one that I will cherish for the rest of me life." He paused briefly again, trying to collect his words and making sure he left nothing unsaid. "I love you, Emily Robertson. I have since the first time I ran into you on that Manchester street. And I know now that there is not another second that I wish to spend not by your side…Please…" He swallowed his word, feeling the lump in his throat spurring on the tears. "…Please, if you no longer love me as I do you, then tell me and you will silence me where I stand."

Emily looked up aimlessly into the sky breaking eye contact in hopes to halt her oncoming tears that had already begun spilling out. Her voice was just above a whisper and filled with tears, "I do still love you, it's just…." He stopped her, coming face to face and intertwining his hands with hers.

"That's all I needed to hear, love. I know we both love one another and I know the long distance won't work. So that's why I signed a transfer to the New England Revolution this morning."

"Jude!" she gasped, "But what about your dream of playing in England and for Manchester? I couldn't ask you to do that…I can't believe you did that! What were you thinking?"

"Love, me dream is you now. I love you and will do until forever has come and gone. I want to do this right this time." He looked her in the eyes, seeing she was mad at his decision, but disregarded it. "Emily…marry me."

Her lungs struggled for air as if her mind found breathing to be insignificant in her current situation. Her head shaking left to right in a monsoon of tears, leaving her speechless at the question. Her body was trembling and her palms sweaty. Just as she was about to attempt to give an answer, Dr. Landry intercepted the moment. Emily quickly wiped her tears, hiding them at all cost. Brad leaned in placing his hands on the smalls of her back and kissing her softly on the cheek.

"Hey, sorry I'm late. I was on call until two. Who's your friend?"

Charles A. Bush

Jude's heart sank into his rib cage. He didn't know whether to punch the guy or be happy for Emily, he considered doing both.

"Brad, this is an old friend of mine, Jude. Jude this is my boyfriend Doctor Brad Landry."

Brad placed his hand out in truce.

"Pleased to meet you, Jude—"

Jude didn't take his eyes off Emily, inconsolably looking at her with disappointment and dejection. He took the high ground and shook Brad's hand, but didn't bother addressing him while doing so.

"I truly regret now not letting you go first—" said Jude, trying to make a joke out of the situation.

"I'm so sorry, I tried to tell you." Her face was distraught and heavy with imprisoned tears.

"No worries, love. I think I'm going to go now anyway, still a bit jet lagged from the flight you know. And Doogie Howser over here seems to have everything under control."

"You don't have to go," said Emily, her voice lacking conviction. Brad smirked trying not to take offense and instead took Jude's comment as a compliment, happy to discover people still view him as young.

"No, I reckon I should. Again congratulations, Emily, I'm very happy for you. I always knew you would do it. I promise you, your mum is so proud of you right now," he gave her a hug, embracing her far longer than he should and doing all he could to mold her touch and scent into his brain. "Cheers, love." He turned and didn't look back until he reached the exit gate, smiling upon her, no longer resentful, remembering the time they shared under the summer's watch learning from each other and falling in love. It was a moment that would remain forever etched in his soul and a story he would tell his grandchildren when he is old and grey. He would speak of love as a mythical creature and assure them he encountered it once, changing his life for better and defying the universe and all of its forlorn rules.

Jude stopped at the crosswalk across the street from his hotel waiting for the walking symbol to grant him passage. He walked the last six blocks from the Yale stadium in tears, having not cried this much since the Lancashire police phoned him and said his parents where in a motor accident. His breath was strangely heavy, but he concluded this was due to his tears and the partial panic attack he had just encountered. A voice off in the distance was calling his name and still upset from having to say farewell to the love of his life fifteen minutes ago, the last thing he wanted to do is deal with a fan. The walking symbol flashed a fluorescent yellow and he began his descent across the street. He broke his stride and looked back when the distant voice finally caught up to him.

Emily was running in her dress and gown, with her heels in her left hand and her diploma in her right.

"Did I forget me wallet?" asked Jude, not happy he was going to have to withstand another goodbye. Emily smiled at him through her tears from the opposite sidewalk. He retraced his steps to the sidewalk, meeting her face to face. She shrugged her shoulders, bowing out of all her past reserve. She shouted over the ongoing traffic, her voice fully overwhelmed by the moment, "Yes…My answer's yes!"

"So…I did forget me wallet?" he asked, now thoroughly confused.

"No. Yes, I'll marry you! I love you…I don't know what else to say."

He seized her face quickly, bringing her to his lips and profoundly kissing her, tasting the nectarous salt from her tears. All their history and suppressed feelings came flowing out in a monsoon of love, disintegrating the past seven months and leaving them with only one thought, that they loved each other. People walking by began to cheer, followed by the passing drivers honking their horns in approval. Emily embraced the passion that rushed through her body like a tidal wave, jumping in his arms and plunging her legs around his torso.

She could feel his enduring touch as his left hand held her up from the small of her back, and his right remained firmly planted on the back of her head keeping her kiss in place. Nothing that they have ever done had felt so pure and true, both feeling they discovered the meaning of life in that moment. She slowly pulled away resting her forehead upon his in a moment of perfection.

"I promise if you hurt me and sleep around, I will have Melissa kill you in your sleep."

He smiled, hopelessly in love with her, wiping the tear from her left eye.

"Never again, love."

"Promise?" whispered Emily before stealing another kiss.

He chuckled shaking his head yes, not daring to look away for a second from her heavenly hazel eyes. "I promise."

XVIII

Emily & Jude: This Very Moment

It was all so surreal. Only two weeks ago, Emily had agreed to marry him. Since then, Jude had switched teams taking far less money, moved half way across the world, and now he's in their new flat in uptown Boston waking up next to his fiancé, a term that he often repeated to remind himself it was actually true. Emily still spent most nights at her and Melissa's apartment in New Haven to remain close to the hospital. Also, she figured since there were still a couple of months remaining on their lease she may as well put it to good use. But on the rare days she didn't have to take a morning shift, like days such as this one, she stayed with Jude in the city.

Neither wanted to admit it, but it was a bit exciting coming to terms with the fact that they could now see each other as often as they wished—being relatively in the same state, not to mention the same continent, helped immensely. They often forgot there was no time difference and even that they lived together until walking through the door and seeing the other on the couch or in the study. But, all in all, they were adapting well to their new lives. In fact, Jude woke up every day overjoyed as if his parents were alive and next to him. There was something in the way Emily made him feel that provided him with a sense of contentment and stability. For the first time in his life, he could honestly say that he's never been happier.

The hospitable orange sunrise stabbed through the long white designer blinds, slightly brightening the room and reflecting momentarily off Emily's naked back. Jude scooted over under the sheets placing his pelvis against her butt and gently wrapping his arms around her. Emily, still partly asleep, smiled as he kissed the back of her neck. His soft skin felt cold as his chest pressed up against her freckled shoulders. As they lay there transfixed in passion and comfort, Emily realized that she too had never been happier than she was now. She had finally received what she believed to be her fairytale ending. She had the man she loved, the perfect residency, her grandmother's health, and to top it off, she hadn't had a night terror since agreeing to marry him. Her only selfish thought was a wish that it were night again so she could continue lying here with Jude.

"Good morning, love." He tucked a strand of her brown hair behind her ear and kissed her tenderly on the cheek.

"Good morning. I think I may be starting to get spoiled waking up next to you all the time."

"Well, it's just one of the many advantages that come with being me fiancé. I can also do this…"

He entangled himself in her, repeatedly kissing her neck passionately and making a trail down to her breasts. His head disappeared under the covers sweeping her skin with kisses, going lower and lower, and running his firm hand up and down her inner thigh.

She let out a soft gasp, "Jude…stop," she said flirtatiously.

"What? You don't fancy it?"

"No, I like it…I like it a lot," she said, taking a breath to regain her composure and cool back down her body. "But it's already ten and you still have to pack for your first game with the team. It's one of my new duties as your fiancé, keeping you in line."

He paid her no mind, continuing his kisses, blatantly disregarding her concerns.

"Who cares? They can wait. I'd much rather be lying here with you, love. By your side is where I belong."

She pulled his head from under the covers bringing his eyes to meet hers in a no nonsense fashion.

"No, you have to make a good first impression. You don't want to show up late for your first game. That's unprofessional, not to mention inappropriate."

He sighed bitterly, rolling off of her and falling back into his pillow with his pouting face now fixed on the ceiling.

"Alright, mum. Is this what the rest of our life is going to consist of—you sucking the fun out of everything?"

Emily leaned over as to kiss him, but before meeting his lips she bailed out and twisted his exposed nipple.

"*Ow*! Bloody'ell, Emily—that hurt!"

She smiled in self-accomplishment, feeling as though she had taught him a lesson.

"Well, don't be mean then. I only want what's best for you, because we all know your childish mind can't look after itself."

"Bollocks, I don't have a child's mind," his tone sounding like a spoiled child, proving Emily's point.

"Oh no?"

"No, not at-tall—"

"Okay—big boy Macavoy. How about this? You start packing, I'll make us some breakfast, and if you're fast enough you may, and I reiterate '*may*,' get lucky in the shower. So what would you like?"

"Ooh…some scrambled eggs and toast with jam. And don't forget to cut off the crust and make them into tiny triforces."

She rolled over on top of him on her way out of the bed, planting a kiss on his lips, "I rest my case."

She put on his dress shirt from the previous night and headed towards the kitchen. Jude shouted from the bed as she faded out of sight, "I'm not childish! The crust is bad for you, it's a fact! And the triangle patterns allow for better digestion…Google it, madam reads-a-lot!"

Both felt completed and alive, as if the other's touch was the missing puzzle piece that held their worlds together, making their struggle to get out of bed a reoccurring theme. Jude packed his bag quickly with the gear he needed for the game and joined his beautiful fiancé in their newly renovated kitchen. Emily was hunched over the stove scrambling the eggs with a spatula. As she extended her right arm forward to scrape the excess egg from the frying pan, Jude watched as his dress shirt rode up her thighs, accentuating her enticing figure and briefly exposing her panties. He paused to admire her perfection, knowing that he was the luckiest person to have ever lived. What did he do in life to deserve her? If his life before her had been a résumé for the position of becoming her husband, he was certain it would have been declined solely based on his early twenties. But who he was before her made no difference. He now had her and she had him, and one thing was certain, he wasn't going to mess it up this time.

Unaware that Jude was watching her, Emily began humming an upbeat melody in joy as the eggs finished cooking. Waking up next to Jude, cooking breakfast, and going to work at a prestigious hospital—this is what life is supposed to be. Jude interrupted her moment of inner bliss, as he crept up behind her placing his arms around her waist, smelling the leftover cologne that resided on the collar of his shirt that she was wearing. She leaned her head back resting it on his shoulder, happy with life's decision to give her Jude.

"Did you pack your things?"

"I did, mum." She smiled at his joke, "Now how about that shower? A deal's a deal—"

"You would like that wouldn't you?" she replied, her tone on the verge of being seductive.

"Is that meant to be rhetorical?"

"After. You need to eat something first. I may not be an athlete but I am a doctor, and I know you need fuel for your body. Now go sit down and I'll bring you your food."

"Yes ma'am," he said flirtatiously, grabbing her butt as he walked past her, following orders. She giggled as if it tickled.

They had breakfast on their terrace overlooking the Boston skyline. The morning was still young and only the birds and the sun's welcoming glow were awake with them. Neither bothered to get dressed, Emily still wearing only her panties and his shirt, while Jude was clothed in only his white boxer-briefs. Jude took a sip of his orange juice, studying Emily's beautiful face as she stared off into the morning sky. Her hair stirred in the subtle breeze, making her look as if she were posing for an album cover.

"Love—" he called to her passionately.

She turned her attention away from the city skyline and looked at him.

"Mhm..." she answered, chewing on a piece of buttered toast.

"I have been meaning to ask you. Have you thought about us possibly starting a family?"

She prolonged the swallowing of the piece of toast in her mouth, hoping for an extra few seconds to formulate an answer. She had never really thought about kids. A part of her knew her biological clock was continually ticking and a woman only had a certain time frame for these things. But she had only just wrapped her head around being engaged. For the past seventeen years she had thought of only one thing—becoming a doctor. And now that she had finally accepted Jude into her life, did she really want the stress of accepting a child? Not to mention, Jude, was only recently removed from acting like one himself. *'For heaven's sakes,'* she thought, *'He just watched Star Wars for the thousandth time last week.'* But glancing across the steel patio table at her husband to be, she saw the change in his eyes and knew if anyone would make a perfect father it would be him.

"Why, do you want kids?" she replied, trying to judge his level of enthusiasm before giving her answer.

"You know, I never really thought about it. For the longest time I reckoned they would cramp me style. But come to find out, they actually can help you pick up birds."

Emily playfully tossed a piece of her toast at him, hitting him in the forehead.

"You're horrible," she laughed, "But seriously, Jude."

"In all honesty, love, there's nothing I would rather prefer than to begin a family with you."

She was touched and partly shocked by his enthusiasm.

"Do you think we could handle it?" she asked skeptically.

He pushed back his chair, inviting her over to join him. She glided across the terrace towards him, her bare-feet cold from its chilling marble surface. She sat down on his lap resting in his arms as if they were a cradle. He kissed her on the head, getting a whiff of her passion fruit scented shampoo.

"I think as long as we're together, we can handle anything."

She angled her head in his chest to meet his eyes.

"You really think so?"

"Emily…I know so."

She kissed him slowly, accepting his words, knowing them to be absolute truth. Happy is a word that was now insufficient to describe her life, it was much more than that. It was an infinite ocean of love and contentment, as if heaven had somehow become her reality.

"Then I would love to start a family with you." She kissed him again slowly. "But after I finish my residency and get the position."

"Of course, love. I would have it no other way."

They lay in each other's arms quiet for the next few minutes, imagining the beautiful child their love could create. Would she be beautiful like Emily? Would he be athletic like Jude? Or would their child be a perfect combination of either his or her multitalented parents?

"What would we name him or her?" Jude thought out loud for a second. "I know…Luke or Leia of course." He shook his head *duh,* as if the answer was clear all along.

"No, Jude—we are not naming our kids after *Star Wars* characters," she protested.

But he ignored her and continued, "Or how about Padmè or Kenobi?!"

She smiled at him, concluding there was no getting through to him when he was like this. She planted a parting kiss on his cheek before getting up and returning inside.

"Well, you keep thinking of names. I'm going to get dressed and you should too. You have to be at the field in twenty minutes."

"Emily…" he called out to her, as she was about to shut the sliding glass door to the terrace. She turned to listen. "Quick shower?" he questioned, practically pleading for her answer to be yes.

She motioned her head towards the bedroom.

"Come on. We have to make this quick though."

He leapt from his seat with glee and followed her inside, hopelessly in love with both her and his life.

Jude felt the butterflies flying rabidly in his stomach. He finally understood every cliché in the book, mainly the weight of the world being on his shoulders. For tonight would mark the first time in history where a world class European footballer in his prime would play in Major League Soccer. There have been many before him, including his idol David Beckham, but none were in the twilight of their careers like Jude was. ESPN had been running stories on him all week leading up to today's match, and Adidas also created an ad campaign where Jude stood in the middle of the pitch surrounded by the stadium's flood lights and screaming fans, with a picture of his new boots flashing and the word *savior* under it.

He stood behind his new teammate, Kyle Rowe, in the Gillette Stadium tunnel prepared to walk out and warm up. This is usually the time in the movies where someone would ironically say *'no pressure,'* he thought. An onslaught of cameras flashed as both teams took the pitch, but every camera was aimed at Jude. It was a brisk summer's evening with the temperature serene and the grass perfectly moist from the pregame watering. The PA announcer went over the starting eleven and Jude jogged to his position at the top of center circle in attacking midfield. In attempts to downplay the situation for the sake of his nerves, he began talking to himself under the cool breeze.

"Okay Jude, don't be nervous. You're the best footballer on this pitch. Michael's playing a friendly against Chelsea today, one of the best clubs in the world, while you're here up against the Seattle Sounders? This should be rather easy. I mean what is a Sounder anyway? Some sort of flounder with the hearing quality of a Beagle? And why do Americans always find it necessary to create a mascot for everything? There are even mascots on breakfast boxes and motor insurance commercials." By the time he finished rambling on in his head about the ugliest mascots the game was well under way and he no longer felt the nerves or pressures of a nation.

It took him sixty-five minutes to find the rhythm of the match. The English game had far more pace and was distinctively more physical. He had already been booked once for a tackle that wouldn't even have been considered a foul in Europe. He managed to string together a few passes with his new teammates and struck the left post during the seventy-first minute from a few yards outside the box.

It was now the eighty-fifth minute and Seattle had a corner. This would surely be Seattle's best chance to break the deadlock and secure all three points. The cross seemed to hang in the air forever before meeting a New England defender's head and clearing it twelve yards to New England Striker, Larry Mile's, right foot. Larry instinctively turned and placed a phenomenal chip over the midfield clearing Seattle's back line, providing Jude with over twenty-five yards of free space to go one on one with the keeper if he could catch up to the ball. Jude pumped his arms profusely, with his legs working overtime in a full out sprint to hunt down the traveling ball. And then it all happened so fast. Like a shooting star, gone before it arrived, he hadn't a second to grasp it. First his right leg went, buckling as if it had been shot. Then, before hitting the ground and rolling seven feet, his right arm went numb as if it were asleep for days and his cry of 'shit' was inaudible due to his slurred speech. The moist grass did little to soften his fall, as he felt the turf burn his only working side. The lights went black and the world's existence muted. It didn't hurt and he wasn't scared, he had little time to ponder such things. The only thought he could form with his final moment of consciousness was, '*Emily.*'

"Thank you, Dr. Robertson, I've been feeling much better since our last visit. I think the meds are really helping," said the seventy-year-old man taking off his shirt to be examined.

"I'm glad, that's their job. You know, Mr. Harrison, you won't be calling me Dr. Robertson much longer. I got engaged two weeks ago."

Emily smiled at him before placing the cold stethoscope on his chest.

"I heard. Nurse Jenny was telling me when I signed in. Congratulations! He's a lucky man."

"Yeah, he is isn't he?" she winked at him. "Now take a deep breath for me."

As he inhaled, the door creaked open and Dr. Landry poked his head inside.

"Excuse me for interrupting. Emily, can I please see you in the hallway?"

She removed her stethoscope and placed it besides Mr. Harrison's chart on her rolling stool.

"Of course, Excuse me, Mr. Harrison."

Richard closed the door behind her, with a troubling look on his face.

"Emily, there's been an accident."

Emily was mystified with caution.

"I don't understand…"

"We just received word from a paramedic unit at Gillette stadium. It looks like Jude had a severe heart attack on the field. It was out of our jurisdiction so he's in transit to Massachusetts General right now."

The shock felt like an uppercut to her skull, leaving her on the verge of fainting. Her voice was almost at a whisper as her fear and tears seeped through.

"How severe?"

He shook his head, trying to escape the question.

"Emily..." he answered nervously, "...I"

Her voice erupted, startling all in the hallway and her tears no longer subtle. "How severe?"

"The last I heard he wasn't breathing...I'm sorry, Emily."

Emily began racing frantically down the hallways of the hospital, accidentally knocking over a nurse in the process. Her mind addled with thoughts, but at the same time absent in fear. She hailed a taxi as soon as she reached the main entrance.

"Where to Ms.?" The taxi driver's eyes caught Emily's in the rearview mirror, "Holy shit...you okay, lady?"

"Just drive! Massachusetts General, and don't stop for anything."

Massachusetts General was a media circus. Every news van in the city was parked out front, scrapping for any information they could conjure up on the situation. As Emily exited the taxi a young female reporter from Channel 6 shouted "Hey! That's Macavoy's fiancé." The reporters collapsed on her like a black hole, shoving countless microphones and tape recorders in her face as if trying to persuade her to have a bite. *'Ms. Robertson? Any word on Jude's condition?'...'Why weren't you at the game?'...'Did stress at home cause this?'...'Is he alive?*

The taxi driver summoned up the courage to politely escort Emily through the wave of reporters to the E.R. entrance.

She rushed to the middle age nurse manning the front desk, "Excuse me! What room is my fiancé Jude Macavoy in?...Is he all right?" she demanded.

"Calm down ma'am. The doctors took him in about two hours ago. If you'd please have a seat in our waiting area, the doctor will be with you as soon as he can."

"Is he all right?"

"I'm sorry, ma'am, I don't know. I only know what patients are where."

Emily's emotions were racing a hundred miles a second, so much so she was asking questions that she already knew the answer to like, 'Is he all right?' Every doctor knows you don't inform the receptionist of a patient's status before family. One second she would be sobbing uncontrollably, thinking he was dead, and then the next she would catch her breath from the anxiety and assure herself he was okay. She eventually dozed off momentarily in reaction to the exhaustion of her tears. Fifteen minutes after Emily had dozed off, Melissa came racing through the sliding doors to her side, giving her a big and overdue hug.

"Oh my God, Em! I got here as fast as I could, is he all right?"

Emily's face was now firmly planted on Melissa's shoulder.

"I don't know. The doctors have been working on him for over three hours."

They sat back down in the waiting chairs. Melissa reached in her handbag and passed Emily a tissue to help soak up her tears.

"What do you think it is?"

"From the little information I know, I would say something's clogging one of his valves, so they're most likely trying to regain flow to his ventricles."

"Like the Johnson case study sophomore year?"

"Yeah, from what I know that's what I think it is anyways."

"Well, that's good, right? I remember that surgery being a success," asked Melissa, fairly certain the surgery was indeed a success, since it was the only case study she had ever gotten higher than a C on.

"It was, but these things are never a sure thing, you know that."

"Well, he's a strong guy, Em. I'm sure he'll be fine.

"I hope so…"

Seconds turned to minutes and minutes to hours as they waited impatiently through the night. The waiting room fluctuated throughout with people coming and going for all kinds of trauma, some more serious than the next. It was now 2:25 in the morning and the only people that remained were Emily, Melissa, and the homeless guy in the corner hording the free coffee with his face buried in the television watching a marathon of *Cheaters*. Melissa was passed out in the seat next to Emily, partially drooling on the armrest. Emily's eyes were bloodshot and heavy from all the tears and frustration over the past eight hours and her stomach nagging from hunger. But despite her sleep deprivation, her body was keeping her awake through adrenaline on the off chance that Jude would come walking through the doors perfectly healthy and smiling like it were all one big prank. What scared her more than anything was knowing that if her rough diagnosis was correct then he shouldn't have been in surgery this long.

"Ms. Robertson?"

Emily heard her name from across the room and stood, accidentally waking Melissa in the process, whose face was fast asleep on Emily's shoulder in mid drool.

"Yes, I'm Emily Robertson. *Please* tell me Jude's okay?"

"How do you do, Ms. Robertson, sorry to be meeting under such circumstances, I'm Dr. Bates. If you'd follow me I can fill you in on his situation."

Situation was not the word she wanted to hear, situation was doctor for *complications*.

He led her down the hall of the intensive care unit, stopping directly in front of room 909B. She could smell the stray traces of latex and peroxide on him, also noticing the blood stain on his scrubs just below his scruffy grey beard. The door to the room was closed and Dr. Bates grabbed the chart that was lying inside the container under the room number.

"Please, Dr. Bates—tell me he's okay…"

"He's lucky to be alive. When our paramedics brought him in he had no pulse and according to them that had been the case for several minutes prior. Thankfully we were able to revive him fairly quickly."

Emily's face had a glimmer of glee. "But I'm afraid it's not all good news, there were some complications."

Just when her emotions thought they could shed a slight sigh of relief, they relapsed into panic mode with an extra dose of panic.

"I'm a doctor too..." she said pointing at her medical coat that she had no time to change out of, "so don't beat around the bush, what are we looking at?" He gave her a reluctant look as if to say, *'okay, but you asked for it.'*

"Well, originally we felt it was just an ordinary cardiac arrest that was preventing proper blood flow from his atrias to his ventricles, which calls for a fairly routine procedure as I'm sure you are already aware of being a physician yourself. However, upon opening the sternum to drain the fluid from the open mitral and tricuspid valves, we encountered a far more severe problem. It seems a large tumor has grown over the right coronary artery, massively cutting the circulation to the heart. Normally if we catch such a tumor during the early stages of its growth we could cut it down and attempt to treat it with chemo and so on. But this particular tumor is already in the later stages of its development, there's no telling how long it's been growing. If I had to guess I would say two to four years at least."

Her expression was ghostly pale and her breath depleted from the news. She already knew the answer to her next question, but elected to ask it anyways as if hearing it come from him made it less true.

"So how long does he have?"

"At the rate the tumor is growing and the late stage it's already in, I fear he doesn't have long. He could have anywhere from two months to a year, you can never be a hundred percent on these things; it's mainly up to the patient at this point...I'm sorry."

As he finished his words Emily's mind slipped back to when she was a little girl and her dad sat her on the end of her pink Sleeping Beauty bed handing her Mr. Kite, her favorite teddy bear. She remembered being petrified because she had never seen her dad cry until then.

Charles A. Bush

He then articulated the best a grown man could to a nine-year-old that her mother had died. He told her that her mother was extremely sick and had to go away to a better place where she is happy and safe.

She felt Dr. Bates's hand on her shoulder, awaking her from her trance.

"Ms. Robertson, again I'm sorry…I know this must be difficult. But do you recall him having any trouble breathing or keeping his wind? For no one to have caught this for so long is an astonishing case."

She thought briefly but drew a blank.

"No, not to my knowledge, he's been his normal self."

"Hmm…interesting," he said stroking his beard in thought, "that's the same thing he said. See if you can get anything out of him because I think he knows more than he's leading on. If you'd like to go in and speak with him, he's conscious. However he has lost a lot of blood and needs to regain his strength."

Emily attempted to clean up her face before entering the room. She dried the tear residue from her cheeks with a loose Wendy's napkin she had in her coat pocket from lunch. She always told her patients loved ones to be strong, and in her current predicament she felt it wise to take her own advice. She regained her composure while letting out an enormous breath and opened the door slowly. The initial devastation of seeing Jude so helpless nearly crushed her soul. The shades had been drawn, letting in no light from the moon, and the bedside lamp basked him in an uncomforting glow. He lay there disturbingly still. His complexion was as white as snow from all the lost of blood and IVs were running from his arms like little plastic tentacles. She took a subtle step inside, thinking him to be asleep, but the closing of the door behind her woke him. His voice was shallow and hoarse like a frog had become entangled in his vocal cords.

"Emily…" his voice struggled.

She walked over beside the bed, pulling over a chair from the corner to sit down. She faintly ran her fingers through his still stylish hair: "I'm right here, Jude."

He cocked his head to the left side of the pillow managing to open his eyes beyond a squint. He smiled at her with all of the remaining strength in his jaw muscles, studying her like an artist examining his masterpiece.

"What—" said Emily confused and embarrassed.

"You're so beautiful. Have I..." he choked, "...ever told you that?"

She smiled, knowing with every part of her being that she loved him, "you may have mentioned it once or twice, but a girl never gets tired of hearing it. Thank you."

"Well, it's true. I could look at you all day and never grow tired of doing so."

"That would be nice."

He attempted to get up to kiss her but his chest gave way, sending a sharp pain to the top of his left shoulder blade. Emily overpowered him and held him down in place.

"Easy there, Romeo, you need to rest. You lost a lot of blood."

He laid back down wincing in pain.

"Bloody'ell...it feels like an elephant is sitting on me chest. What... happened?"

Emily took his hand and began softly stroking it in comfort.

"You had a bad heart attack during your game."

He was still wincing in pain, but made sure Emily could hear the serious intention of his voice.

"A heart attack? Bollocks! You've seen me abs. I'm the fittest bloke around."

"I'm a hundred percent sure that your absurdly ripped abs have nothing to do with your heart's condition. Speaking of which, have you been experiencing any lost in breath or struggles to get your wind back quickly?"

"That's the same rubbish the doctor asked me. I'm a professional footballer for Christ's sakes; I'm..." his voice once again lost the strength to form the words. He continued after a breath, "I'm fit as a fiddle."

"Okay, I was just asking. Try and relax it's not good for you to get all worked up. But if you did know of anytime that you've lost your breath, we really should know, Jude. The doctors are here to help."

Jude pouted briefly, not being able to stay upset too long since his chest was thriving in pain. He looked up at Emily with apologetic eyes. "It started a few years ago." Emily didn't interrupt, letting him go on. "Right before I joined United. I would just be doing the most mundane task and I would lose me breath. Some days I could run for hours and nothing, and others I would be short of breath in warm ups. But it always came back. I just reckoned it was all the partying. But I'm fine, Emily, I promise. It's no big deal, I've given up the fags and booze—you know that."

She was proud of him for telling her, but found his naivety troubling. "Did the doctor tell you anything?" she asked, hoping his answer was yes.

"What? There's more besides a heart attack? What are you going on about?"

Her face evolved into a crushing look and her eyes dropped to the floor in despair.

"Emily…what are you not telling me?" She remained silent and still, staring off into space trying to conjure up the right words, but not having the courage to do so. "Well…go on, out with it." She could hear the emotions rising in his voice. Even though he was hoarse, it still held some authority. Tears began running down her cheeks again, replacing the ones she had wiped away minutes ago. She laid her head on his shoulder, careful not to hurt him.

"It's alright, love, please don't cry. I'm a big lad. I can handle it."

After a prolonged pause filled with grief she spoke solemnly: "They found a tumor on your coronary artery."

He barely made her words out from her mumblings through his hospital robe. "Are you saying I have cancer?"

She pulled away sucking in through her nose and wiping her face. Her spectacle now completely fogged.

"Yes…"

"Fuckin'ell! There must be some sort of mistake. I'm twenty-seven, I can't have cancer, I'm fit—I play football every day."

"The tumor's there, Jude. They said it's been growing for at least several years. How they never caught this with all the physicals you go through each year is beyond me."

"Because those physicals are rubbish. They just grab your balls a few times and ask you to cough. Then they check to make sure you can walk and talk at the same time, and then, presto, you're declared fit."

"Well it's fully developed, placing you in the later stages of the disease. It's amazing that it hasn't affected your body beyond your heart. He said you only have…" she trailed off, swallowing her breath in sudden horror.

"Have what?" He wiped away her tears with his unsteady hands, trying to urge her to continue.

"That you have anywhere between two months to a year to live."

Everything she was saying was beyond comprehension. He thought, *'I'm fit, I'm fast, really fast, and I'm young. This is all some prank.'* His mind was in overdrive trying to piece together this horrific nightmare, which he could not seem to wake up from.

"So…cancer?" A single tear fell from his left eye; he didn't bother to wipe it, not caring that she saw his fear. "Ah, it could be worse I reckon. That American bicycling bloke had cancer like a thousand times and he's still alive and pedaling." Emily chuckled through her tears. "Don't cry love, it's going to be alright. Come here—" He wiped away his tear before sliding over in the tiny bed to make room for her. She nestled under his arm, alert to avoid the IVs.

"We'll be fine. Our love can get us through anything. It got us through your awful dressing phase didn't it? Remember when you used to wear all those old university sweatshirts all the time?"

"Jude, I love you, but this isn't a movie. You're dying. This is serious…"

"I know it is, but you just have to have a little faith it'll all work itself out."

She replied softly, her voice still pessimistic and defeated, "how's it going to work itself out?"

He kissed her on the forehead, "I don't know…but it will love, it must."

They lay there for several minutes, neither saying a word. Jude's left hand brushing up and down her arm gently as she held him tight. Her eyelids were exceptionally heavy as if they were filled with water, she wished she could fall asleep and wake up to none of this having ever happened. Emily glanced up at the generic black and white clock on the wall and noted that she would have been awake twenty-four hours straight in only two hours. Her eyes became even heavier at the thought, fluttering abruptly before closing, as the sound of his heartbeat played her to sleep.

Jude whispered softly in her ear, fixing the edge of her spectacles that were pinching his shoulder, "Emily?"

She answered. Her arms still draped around him and her eyes still shut prepared for sleep. He could hear the tiredness in her voice. "Yeah…are you okay? I'm not hurting you am I?"

"Not at-tall. I'm still a bit sore, but I'll be alright. I've just been lying here thinking." Emily struggled to open her eyes.

"Sorry, I didn't mean to fall asleep on you. How long have I been out?"

"Not long, just forty-five, fifty minute's maybe."

"Oh, well go ahead I'm awake now. What were you thinking about?"

"I'm just not certain what to make of all this. It's not every day someone tells you, you have cancer, especially since I felt relatively fine a fortnight ago. But then out of nowhere it hit me. One moment I'm watching you sleep thinking why me, and the next I'm having a bit of an epiphany; it all felt a bit Sherlock Holmes."

Emily was curiously optimistic at his new upbeat attitude towards the situation. Because despite how Jude played down the news earlier, she could see it in his eyes that he was frightened and heartbroken, and

Emily completely understood that. For not only was his life ending before his very eyes, he was being stripped of the one thing he could do well, and that was playing football, and equally for her, she was losing the best thing to ever happen to her and her best friend.

"Well, what is it, Sherlock?"

Jude struggled to turn his body, now meeting her face to face on the tight-knit hospital bed.

"I thought what if someone came to you and said today would be your last? What would you do? What would you eat? Who would you call? And the more I thought about it the more pissed off I became because I may soon be faced with that exact question… until I came to the realization that it doesn't matter. I don't care what tomorrow brings. Let it bring death. Let it bring suffering. Let it bring the end of the world for all I care. For as long as you are by me side, Emily, I can handle anything. So if what the doctor says is true, and any day could be me last, the one thing I know to be certain is I want to spend every remaining second with you. I wish to never part from your side again."

She stared into his blue eyes, falling in love with him all over again.

"What are you saying?"

"I'm saying I want a life with you, and in spite of all that's happened tonight I still believe it's not too late to give you that life. Let us spend whatever time I have left doing what you will forever do in me mind, living. Let's get married, travel, let's take on the world just you and me like we always planned. So when me heart finally does stop working, I can look upon you and smile knowing I gave you the life you deserve."

Emily lay still, as if someone had stolen her tongue. Every ounce of medical knowledge, common sense, and brain cells within her were telling her this was a horrible idea. He was sick and by all accounts belonged in the hospital where he could get the proper care; those were the honest hard facts. Scaling pyramids and seeing the Grand Canyon would do nothing to improve his health. If anything it would only hinder his condition. These, along with an encyclopedia of reasons why it was a ridiculous suggestion, all ran through her mind. But still, with a trusting look on her face, she said: "Let's do it."

His eyes lit up like a kid on Christmas opening the perfect gift.

"You're serious? I was half taking the piss. I know you could never get that much time off from your new job."

He was right. The odds of her marching into Brad's office just several weeks into her residency and requesting a disclosed leave of absence and actually being granted it were slim to none. In fact, she would consider that exchange a success if they didn't laugh her out of the building for asking. The waiting list for her residency spot alone is filled with over five thousand students eager to fill it. Life is full of choices, which define and mold us into the final product that we will one day become; leaving no room for redoes and remorse. Emily knew this was one of those choices. There was always the part of her that prioritized her schoolwork and personal success, but on the opposite side of the spectrum, she was fully aware of how much Jude had already sacrificed for them to be together. She wished there were a clear answer, like one of the many exams she had taken over the years. Those were easy, there was a right and wrong, a black and white, but when it came to a relationship everything became so uncertain. But it wasn't hard to see he had changed her, he had discovered her heart and encouraged her to live. Without him she would still be that shy, timid girl, and now as she reflected on her life with him she saw a strong, confident, successful woman, who has the love of her life.

"Well, if they don't, then I'll quit."

Jude raised his lip in disgust at her notion. "Piss off, Emily, I could never ask you to do that. You love your job and have worked your entire life for this residency. Just forget I even said anything, we'll think of another way to spend our remaining time together."

"No, Jude! I want to do it. I love you and I want to marry you… you're right, we deserve a life. We are two young and good people who deserve to be happy…even if it is just for a little while."

He smiled and took her hand knowing he never loved anything more, and with his remaining strength struggled to raise it to his mouth and placed a kiss on it.

"You never cease to amaze me, Emily. I love you so much."

"I love you too. It's like you said, you are my dream now."

He winked at her before closing his eyes for some much needed rest, "and I'm so happy to be spending the rest of me life with mine."

The next morning was spent pleading with Dr. Bates, who spat out his cup of coffee in laughter at their plan, only to realize they were dead serious. He explained, in a reproaching manner, that Jude's condition will only worsen from lack of care, the words, 'you're a doctor, you should know better, Ms. Robertson,' had come out of his mouth several times. After a blitz of statistics that frowned upon their request, he subscribed nine medications and signed off on Jude's release.

"I cannot believe I'm agreeing to this, but you both are adults and technically I cannot keep you here against your will if you are still able to somewhat function in society. But knowing Ms. Robertson will always be by your side makes me feel a smidge better," said Dr. Bates grudgingly.

"Cheers doc, we really appreciate this…it means an awful lot to the both of us."

Besides the excruciating pain in his chest and the incision under his left breast, Jude regained the bulk of his strength overnight. And with the assistance of a cane and multiple drugs, was standing next to Emily on his two feet. He thought to himself, '*the first thing I'm doing when I leave this place, is tossing this rubbish thing in the bin.*'

"You're both welcome and I wish you the best, Jude. Just know you're lucky your situation appeals to the romantic in me, otherwise you'd be staying here where you can be monitored and receive proper treatment. I blame my wife for all the years she forced me to watch all those sappy movies. Alright, well off you two go before I change my mind. Remember, when the medication no longer relieves his pain or keeps his lungs breathing at a regular rate, you are to come straight back here immediately. And under no circumstances are you allowed to do any strenuous activity. That means no heavy lifting, no alcohol, no hanky panky, and absolutely no *soccer*! Do I make myself clear?"

"I got it, doc. No bench pressing, only Shirley Temples, let Emily be on top, and no playing whatever this thing called soccer is. Consider it done!"

Dr. Bates was unimpressed by Jude's word play and stared him down in parental fashion as they left his office.

Truth be told, Jude had no intention on following any of Dr. Bates rules. He had lived life to the fullest and would continue to do so until his last breath, and who knows, maybe a little longer after that depending on the nightlife in heaven. I mean did he really expect them to stop making love? There was no way he would be taking sex advice from someone who referred to it as 'the hanky panky.' *'Who says that nowadays anyway, was he going to reference the soda parlor next?'* Jude thought. Now the drinking rule was going to be much harder to defy, because he knew Emily would actually see to it that he followed up on that promise. Nonetheless he had already begun plotting ways to sneak in a drink here and there. Like replacing some Sprite with a little vodka, and an elaborate plan to replace a Capri sun with some Guinness, but that would entail a laser pointer and a box of silver painted plastic sheets, both of which he was too lazy to obtain.

Jude had one last private meeting with Dr. Bates before taking off for an indefinite amount of time with Emily. In the end, he accepted that leaving to travel was a suicide mission, but he wanted to go out the same way he lived, with a bang and with Emily by his side.

XIX

Emily & Jude: Two Months and Fifteen Days Later

J ude was finally asleep. He had been coughing up blood since 7 p.m. and didn't even have enough strength to lean over the side of his hospital bed to vomit up all the meds that his body had been reject- ing. Emily was sat beside him. Her bottom half covered with the grey wool blanket the nurse had given her. She slowly sipped on what was her fourth cup of coffee, attempting to settle her nerves. Her insides were battered and bruised from seeing Jude in such agony. She was his wife and that was a wife's job, take care of your husband, a task she felt she was clearly failing. But the doctor side of her knew it was now completely out of anyone's hands.

It has been a week since Jude had been readmitted to Massachusetts General; sixteen hours after his heart gave out while in the middle of their lunch at *L'Aprège* in Paris. Emily noticed his condition worsen- ing in the days prior, when he became out of breath from just walk- ing to the bathroom in their suite or clutching his chest in pain when laughing. And in-between a bite of shrimp risotto and listening to her ramble on about how fragile the pubic bone is, he lost sensation in his right side and fainted, thus marking the end of their two month trip.

Or as Melissa referred to it, 'It sounds more like a bucket list than a vacation to me.'

Recently she had begun thinking maybe her boring medical stories had caused his heart to fail that day, but Jude constantly insisted that he honestly enjoyed watching the way her face lit up when going on about surgery and symptoms. Two nights, pre shrimp risotto, they caught an episode of *Grey's Anatomy* while lying in bed in their French suite, during which Emily diagnosed every patient in the episode; Jude had stared at her in awe with a huge grin on his face.

"I'm sorry, I'm rambling aren't I? I'm becoming more like my grandma every day, I'll shut up."

"No, it's not that. I actually quite enjoy watching you when you talk all your medical mumbo jumbo. It's quite cute and you look genuinely happy. I know I say it often, but you're just so beautiful."

As she thought back on that morning in Paris, she pondered where the time had gone and replayed the last two months in her head.

It seemed like just yesterday she was being escorted down the aisle by her grandmother, with her stomach tied in pretzels from her nervousness. The wedding ceremony took place just three days after Jude's release from Massachusetts General. They secured an old quaint church in New Haven whose claim to fame is having sheltered thirty-five Redcoats during the Revolutionary war, a church, Jude constantly reminded her, they overpaid drastically to reserve on short notice. It was a tiny, lovely, and intimate wedding, one that most would argue lack the bells and whistles of a typical celebrity wedding. It was attended only by Emily's close friends, her grandmother, and Michael and Amy. The wedding was just the right size as far as Emily was concerned, but even so she still considered it a miracle they were able to keep it a secret. The media had been heavy on Jude's heels in light of his illness, and they became even more persistent once Jude announced his retirement from football because of it. His phone continually rang off the hook with reporters doing their best Scooby-Doo detective agency impersonation trying to get the inside scoop, thus leading him to change his mobile number and stay away from his and Emily's flat uptown, only returning once to pack a bag of their belongings.

The church was no bigger than half a basketball court. The pews, trimmed and meshed with rich brown maple, were chipped and faded from the years, resembling a place that Benjamin Franklin would have once sat. Stained glass windows beamed from both sides of the church, filling the room with ancient rainbows. The windows themselves depicted the Virgin Mary, fallen angels, and saints that neither Jude nor Emily could name. The centerpiece of the building was the altar. The ancient, once-red carpet, led through the aisles and pews like a cranberry canal directly to the cherry wood altar beneath a crucifix that overlooked the congregation in judgment. Despite Jude's religious tattoos covering the majority of his arms, which he would claim were mainly for decoration, neither he nor Emily were particularly religious, especially Jude. He often found church to be among the most depressing places in the world. He always thought, '*where else could one go to see a dead man resembling Tarzan hanging from a tree trunk?*' But for a mere second when he was standing beside Michael at the altar, watching Emily walk towards him as if she were floating, he believed. In that instant he knew, that God must have spent a little more time on her.

Emily's long, elegant, and fully laced-back rippled wedding gown hugged her body flawlessly, almost melting into her soft vanilla skin. The one-shouldered bodice featured an aristocratic soft chiffon ruching that twinkled over her left shoulder. Her faceless veil rested upon her curled hair that resembled miniature brunette waves, which flowed down past her shoulders. To complete her fairytale ensemble, she wore the perfect white pearl graduated teardrop necklace with matching earrings that Jude had surprised her with earlier that morning straight from *Tiffany's*. The end product of the outfit made her look like an immaculate diamond lying in a field of snow.

As Jude stood at the altar with his perfectly styled hair, in his satin finished shawl collared two piece night black tuxedo, which he had imported overnight from Italy for two thousand pounds, he took her hand and muttered the first thing that came to his mind, "until this moment I have never see true beauty." The priest was instructed to stick to the short version since they had a flight to catch to Egypt. He meandered through words like *dearly beloved* and *holy matrimony*, for a lack of better words, the *Cliff Notes* version of the ceremony.

"Now as I understand you both have chosen to compose your own vows. We will start with the bride first—" said the priest, motioning the bible in his hand at her to begin. Melissa reached into her bra retrieving the six-by-nine sheet of loose-leaf paper and passed it to Emily. Emily shook her head frivolously in disbelief. "Gees, Melissa, you never cease to amaze."

Melissa's face was one of innocence and righteousness:

"What? You asked me to hold your vows, and this dress doesn't exactly have pockets…I'm not sweating or anything. Besides, I did you a favor. Now your vows smell like *Bath and Body Works*."

Emily ignored Melissa's erotic hiding place and continued on with her vows. She took a deep breath before beginning, suddenly overtaken by nerves and wondering if someone had turned up the heat.

"Here goes nothing…" she said, smiling at Jude for support. "When I was nine-years-old my mom passed. It was the most difficult thing in my life to endure. She was my best friend and my hero. The last thing I told my mom was, 'I promise to become a doctor to save you.' Well, that didn't happen. But I was still determined to keep my promise, so I swore to myself that I wouldn't let anyone or anything stand in my way of becoming a doctor in hopes to make my mother proud. So when I met you, I knew it wouldn't last, because the last thing I wanted was a boyfriend taking me away from my promise. But for some reason I slowly let my guard down and as time passed I found myself stumbling into love. You've made me break all of my rules…and I mean all of them. But you also showed me love and introduced me to a world I never knew existed. You held me when I couldn't sleep…" The priest fired a disparaging look at her at the hint of their sharing a bed before wedlock, but she continued. "Laughed at me when I wasn't funny, called me beautiful when I didn't feel like it, and had faith in us when I didn't believe. But as you know I'm stubborn and promised to let nothing deter me, so when times got hard, I found it easy to runaway and hide myself behind the promise I once made. But here we are. I'm about to be your wife and you're going to be my husband. So I give up. You win. I am unconditionally in love with you and surrender all. I know now that you are the loophole to my promise, the one exception. So I promise you the same way I promised my mom all those years ago, I promise to love you the rest of my life and to not let anything or anyone deter me from doing so."

Jude looked at her with such admiration, not being able for a second to take his eyes off hers. She returned his look with an enchanting smile, feeling his love deluge over her.

"That was brilliant, love. I know this is frowned upon at this point in the proceedings, but what the hell…." He surged forward clasping her head, frailly bringing his lip to hers, an avalanche of passion and love transferring between them like a power line of bliss.

"Me apologies for that Father, but I couldn't help meself."

The priest was less impressed with the gesture, giving him a look as to say *why I oughta…* The rest of the attendees smiled at the kiss. Melissa went as far to whistle like a *Loony Tunes* character and yell, "Take his shirt off!" Emily's grandmother was not too pleased at the comment.

"No, no, it's okay. We'll just pretend God, who is omnipotent, wasn't looking. As we gather in his glorious home, under his holy cross. We'll just pretend he wasn't watching." His sarcasm thick, like an unimpressed headmaster scolding a student. "Now if you would please proceed with the reading of the vows, *Mr. Macavoy.*"

Jude cleared his throat several times as if a cough drop had become logged in it. He straightened his posture doing his best Prime Minister impersonation.

"Yes of course, Father. Sorry about the delay, but boys will be boys, yeah."

Emily was staring into his blue eyes prepared to hang onto his next word.

"Well, I'll try me best to make this brief, since I've recently been forewarned that I haven't got long." An awkward silence fell deafly over the church, tempting Emily to reach over and slap him at his horrible sadistic joke.

"What?" he asked after a long awkward pause, "...Too soon?" Emily's furious look answered his question. "Yeah, I can tell, too soon. Come on you lot, lighten up I'm only havin' a laugh. See? Father gets it, don't you ol' chap?" asked Jude, giving the priest a soft punch on the shoulder, channeling his inner 1950s dad, which was usually followed by words like 'sport' and 'champ.'

"Alright, Alright...I know, on with the vows," he protested definitively, as if he could read the priest's mind. He cleared his throat again in preparation, this time earnestly.

"Emily, as I stand in front of you today looking upon me angel, I see all that you are. I see your beauty; that is unmatched by any other, I see your smile; that lights up me day every time; and I see your love and know instantly that this world is better because you are in it. Me point is, in me eyes you are perfect, and you deserve a man that is truly worthy of you. I vow to do all in me power to be that man. For I know I'm not perfect, but I swear I'm perfect for you.

I wish I could also promise only good times, but I cannot lie, we will undoubtedly share hard times and we'll have to work at this, but I'm willing to work every day for your love because I love you. I have always loved you and promise to do so until forever has come and gone. You have bewitched me, Emily, consuming all that I am. I am a better man for having met you, and lived the happiest life for having loved you. It will be both an honour and a dream to call you me wife, I love you, Emily Robertson."

Emily was on the verge of tears and mouthed the words '*I love you too*' back at him. For there comes a time in a one's life when everything falls perfectly into place, when the cosmos align and love and bliss intertwine, and you know with all your heart that you will never experience a moment superior. For Emily Robertson, this was her moment.

"Alright, Father, bring us home, mate."

"With the power invested in me from the state of Connecticut, I now pronounce you husband and wife. *NOW*…you may kiss the bride."

Their lips locked onto one another as if meant to be one, framing them in a moment in time where they could always visit true love.

She took another sip of her coffee doing her best to prolong the cup. Her eyes slowly gravitated towards the hospital bed where she realized he was just a shell of the man that once stood in front of her on that altar. Physically he hardly resembled her husband. He was excessively thin now, having lost fifty pounds this week alone from his meds, which allowed him to keep little to nothing down. The color of his skin was rapidly fading rendering him cadaverous. But if she learned anything from the past two months it was that he loved her, and that would never change.

She swiftly recalled their two-night stay in Egypt to reassure her of his love.

Just fourteen hours after being wed, they found themselves on a G5 jet overlooking the Atlantic Ocean, sipping ginger ale in celebration. During their stay in Egypt, they experienced the pyramids and spent time in the hotel's bedroom, ignoring Dr. Bate's *Hanky Panky* request. Jude even talked Emily into trying snake at the hotel restaurant one evening for dinner. Oddly enough, while not finding it to be among the best things she'd ever tasted, she didn't rate it among the worst either. Overall she found it to be acceptable, a word often used by Michael and Jude when describing the *Star Wars* prequels. For their final night in Egypt, Jude surprised her with a nighttime picnic on the roof of the hotel. They lay under the Egyptian stars encased in each other's arms like a force field, neither bothering to say much, instead using their mouths for the majority of the evening to make-out, while the remainder of the night they were perfectly content to just lie back and bask in the city's beauty and drink in the moment. The hotel, resided in the heart of the city, and looking out from their prospective view of the skyline, seemed to be never ending. The elegant landscape was immaculate and resembled what could be a futuristic scene from *Aladdin*. The frigid summer's breath made for a perfect excuse to hold her through the night. They made love once before she fell asleep in his arms under the vibrant moon, which bounced off the pyramids and illuminated them like a spotlight.

Their next stop took them to Jamaica where they stayed for two weeks, a week longer than they had planned, but they genuinely enjoyed it so they extended their stay. They rented a charming beach house, fully equipped with two hammocks, that was twenty-five yards away from the transparent blue ocean. The house wasn't very large; in fact it may be better described as a hut. There was only one bathroom which was a snug tighter than a phone booth, a pathetic kitchen consisting of two burner stove tops, a refrigerator that barely outsized one found in a college dorm room, wretched brown and green floor tiles, a wardrobe that was being passed off as a pantry, and what Jude insisted to be the first microwave ever invented. Ceiling fans were planted throughout the hut like traffic lights, including a big one in the living room/kitchen above the tacky old dusty brown sofa. The single bedroom had one dresser and a king size bed encompassed by one very large bug net. Besides Jude's vendetta against the ancient microwave, neither of them cared, because they spent the majority of their time on the sublime beach.

However, much to Emily's dismay, Jamaica posed to be a perfect catalyst for Jude to break the most rules. He was able to sneak in several drinks, including showing up one day on the beach with a clear plastic cup filled with a strawberry margarita that was far more tequila than margarita, convincing Emily it was a smoothie from the resort bar up the road. She later discovered the resort didn't serve anyone who didn't have a room there. He even succeeded in what he considered his biggest triumph of their travels, breaking Dr. Bates number one rule, 'no soccer!'

They were taking in a nice afternoon at the beach, soaking up the tropics. Emily was spread out across her yellow and gold beach towel with her back eyeing the sun. She was putting forth her best effort of obtaining a tan but no matter how long the Jamaican sun pounded, her skin never turned any color but pale. She wore a pair of cheap sunglasses that she had purchased from a thrift store in New Haven, her head deep in a Boston Medical procedure book that she was reading for work and not pleasure. Hating the feeling of contacts she wanted nothing more than to rush through it, but knew it was important to take her time and study the procedures attentively because Brad and the hospital agreed to give her a leave of absents to attend to Jude. She was so relieved when Brad told her, 'I would be a fool to let your talents go to another hospital.'

Jude was resting in his beach chair diving in and out of sleep as the sun and meds cooperatively drained his energy, when out of the corner of his eye, he spotted a group of islander kids playing five aside beach football fifty-yards up the beach. A light bulb went off in his head and if not for Emily being so deeply enthralled in her book she would have seen it flash.

"Hey, love?"

She placed her book down on the towel, holding her page and lifting her head back to look at him, "Yeah?"

He grabbed his chest as if he had been stabbed, "me chest is feeling a bit uncomfortable." Emily fell into a brief panic.

"Oh no! Are you okay? Let's get you out of the sun… here I'll help you to the house."

His plan, backfiring quickly, he replied, "No, no, I'm certain I'm alright, I just think I need to take me medicine. Will you be a mate and run in and fetch them for me please?"

Emily sprung up like a trampoline.

"Of course, I'll be right back. But you should really lie down inside if you're feeling pain."

Usually Emily would put him through a series of test to assure he was alright, but his pride made dealing with him impossible because he never answered any of her medical questions honestly. He grabbed her as she walked by, pulling her on top of him and giving her a kiss as the weary beach chair did its best not to collapse.

"Thanks, love, I love you."

"I love you too. I'll be right back, and please try to take it easy. You don't need to be straining yourself trying to look at every half naked girl that walks by."

Like a well-trained spy, his eyes followed her through the back-door until she was out of sight. He darted from his chair, only to be out of breath by the seventh step. He didn't even ask the kids if he could play, suspecting Emily would be right on his tail so time was of the essence. Jude got one good touch in, rain-bowing a kid before providing a pin point through ball for a kid he assumed was his teammate because they all celebrated together when he kicked it between the two shirts lying adjacent on the sand. Emily broke up the game fast, practically dragging him back to the beach house by the ear like some petulant child. She remained furious with him through the afternoon, giving him the silent treatment until dinner. But Jude figured it was worth it since it would probably be the last time that he'd ever touch a football.

After Jamaica, they traveled to Las Vegas where Emily was groped by an extremely overweight Elvis Presley impersonator in front of the *MGM Grand*. While there, Jude took the time to film a brief commercial for his new heart cancer foundation, encouraging males of all ages to be safe and get annual checkups. Emily also surprised him by collaborating with his agent to book a double dinner date in Las Angeles with his childhood hero David and Victoria Beckham. Emily didn't get much attention from Jude that night, as the date pairings seemed to read more like David and Jude than Emily and Jude. It was truly 'bromance' at first sight, as Melissa would say. Emily found it hysterical at the way Jude laughed at every joke David told and agreed with every word out of David's mouth. If she didn't know any better, she would have thought he was trying to get into his pants.

They then went on to steal a few days in San Palo, where she had to virtually tie him to the hotel bed so they didn't have a repeat of the Jamaica football incident. Football was being played and watched down every street, and with each kick of the ball it had him frothing at the mouth to play. To suppress his football desires, Emily secured tickets to a River Plate versus Flamingo match, followed by a romantic meal at one of Brazils' finest restaurants *Figueria Rubaiyat*, and a night of love making back at the hotel.

They lied in the tropical hotel room, their bodies naked and the moon's beam keeping them warm. Neither could sleep, and with Emily's head rested peacefully on his chest above his surgical scar and their legs entangled under the sheets, she spoke,

"Do you think we would have spent every night feeling like this?"

"Like what?" he replied softly, stroking her hair to a soothing rhythm.

"Happy. I mean, do you think we would have ever grown tired of each other like every other married couple?"

They both continued to stare out into the moon's smile.

"I reckon we wouldn't. Because unlike all those other people, Emily, you are all I shall ever need in this life."

She rolled over on top of him, her breasts brushing up against his chest like two smooth pillows, and the sheet creeping up her back, temporarily exposing the bottom of her butt and their bare legs. He stared at her, as she smiled back at him with robust affection. He moved two runaway strands of hair from her face and tucked them securely behind her ear.

"I guess in a way, you're me heaven—and who could possibly grow tired of heaven.

Spain was their next destination on their month foray. Emily's semester of Spanish came in handy within the first minutes of their arrival when one of the flight attendants had lost their bags. Thankfully Emily could conjure up enough Spanish to say, "nuestro equipaje es de color negro con nuestro nombre en èl." She figured she had said, 'our luggage is black with our names on it' or 'these black luggages make fine hats.' She felt since they eventually found their bags it was safe to assume it was the first one. Their stint in Spain was even shorter than Vegas due to Madrid being so overpopulated with tourist this time of year.

Emily wished she could go back in time to Egypt, Jamaica, Spain, Brazil, and Paris, to feel his then strong arms wrap around her like a cocoon. But as she looked over at him from across the hospital room she understood that those days were over. She placed her coffee on the table beside her, no longer warm and appetizing. Her eyes wandered the room in frustration as her anger with their current predicament began to mount like an internal *Jenga* puzzle. She never considered herself to be a cynical person, but once you've become a doctor it's hard not to believe in the ugly facts of life, and the facts of science as a whole. All the get well balloons dangling throughout the room and the signed jersey from all his past teammates were all nice gestures, but in her mind futile. The simple medical and physical fact remained, he was dying and there wasn't a thing all her years of studying medical books could do about it. The small hospital room suddenly became even smaller out of her defeat and bitterness. She debated going on a walk to cleanse her mind but in the end sided against it because she didn't want to leave his side in case he woke up needing her. Her mind was just so convoluted. She was furious with herself for not being able to help him, and she was even more furious with the powers that be, if there is one, for putting him through this.

She struggled to get comfortable. Sitting in the same chair for over ten hours probably didn't do much for her posture either. In an effort to take her mind off her now cramping back, she opened one of the thirteen magazines Melissa had brought over for her. Melissa constantly persisted, 'If you're going to be cooped up anywhere, then you better have some good literature to get you through.' Not only did Emily consider Melissa's selections to not at all be literature, but she also found them redundant. There were issues of *People magazine, O.K.,* and *Cosmopolitan*. '*I mean who really cares if Angelina and Brad adopt another ethnic child or the many circumstances for Robert Paterson and Kristen Stewart's divorce? Maybe they realized that neither of them could act*', Emily thought. '*Oh no… developing an opinion was the first stage of getting sucked in*', she fretted. But just as she was giving up on the magazine and made the wise decision of attempting to get some sleep, Michael walked in. It was one-thirty in the morning and he looked just as beat as she did.

"Hiya, how's he doing?" he said making his way across the room to the empty chair beside her. He studied Emily's face, able to tell from it the decline in Jude's condition. Her face possessed the same defeated expression but now more sadistic then the one he had witnessed hours ago during his last visit.

"He finally got to sleep about an hour ago. He still wasn't able to keep anything down though."

He looked sympathetically at Jude as his emotions began conjugating in thought.

"Blimey…that can't be good."

"I'm afraid not." She attempted to change the subject, to a less depressing one. "What brings you here so late? Shouldn't you be at the hotel with Amy? I'm sure he won't be waking up anytime soon."

Michael leaned over in his chair, stroking his peppered grey stubble as if it were fully grown.

"Ah, I don't know. I couldn't sleep so I thought I would come down here and see him. You know he's a stubborn lad, I had to make sure he's not giving the nurses hell."

She gave a breviloquent smile at his attempted humor.

"He's so happy that you and Amy are here. It really means a lot to him."

"Of course, as soon as you phoned us we were on the first plane out of Brittan. He's like a brother to me. I'm pretty much the closest thing to family he has left. But I reckon he's much happier knowing you're by his side." She smiled faintly before looking back at Jude solicitously.

"How are you holding up?" asked Michael, concerned from her demeanor.

She hesitated before replying as if unsure of her answer.

"I'm hanging in there. It just kills me seeing him like this. I just wish I could do something, anything, to help. He doesn't deserve this. I feel like a worthless wife..." Her voice trailed off as her depression came storming back in full melancholia.

"You truly don't understand do you?" asked Michael, his voice now fierce and spilling over into an unapologetic rage. Emily was taken aback by his sudden anger. "He passed up an opportunity of remission for you."

She was dumb founded at his words.

"What are you talking about? The doctors said it was too late for any type of surgery."

"That's what they originally concluded, but right before you two took off they offered Jude a second option that could have removed the tumor. A new procedure that was still in the testing phase, one he would have been the first human trial for. Even though they said it was unlikely the surgery would succeed and if they didn't the repercussions would be immediate fatality, on the twelve percent chance they did succeed he would have had a shot at chemo and possible remission." Michael became chocked up at the missed opportunity, his voice resting in-between anger and sorrow. "And I wanted him to take that chance. A chance that could have worked...I just know it." The end of his words sunk into complete despair, as if saying them out loud could have willed the surgery into a success.

Emily suddenly became paralyzed at hearing Jude was offered surgery and a slim chance of survival.

"I didn't know..." her voice saturated in compassion and confusion.

"That's because you don't get it! He just couldn't bear the thought or take the chance, that it may be the last time he would ever see you. Instead he chose to live freely with you with whatever time he had remaining. Can't you see? That over life itself—he *chose you*. To this very moment every second he remains breathing is because of you."

Her eyes fell to the floor in shame.

"I'm truly sorry, Emily, but I've known him since he was a we lad at the Academy. And when his parents passed all he did was drink, shag, act like an ass, and piss his privileged life away. I tried for years to get him on the proper path, but there was nothing I could do. Now you want to know helpless? That's being helpless! Watching someone you love who has all the talent in the world piss their life away. But then you came along, and within a summer changed everything. You made him happy and gave him something to believe in again, you made him into the good man I always reckoned he could be. So you see, you didn't just help him Emily...you saved him."

Emily didn't move. Instead she sat there bleakly staring at Jude, unable to face Michael.

Michael took a breath, toning back his rage.

"Look, I don't mean to be hard on you, I just had to say something. Since we've flown in all you've done is complain about how you can't help him, when in reality you've helped him more than anyone ever has. You are his life, Emily, and he needs you now more than ever." He paused giving them both time to collect their thoughts. The tension was overwhelming.

"I'm sorry, Emily. I hope I haven't upset you?"

"No. You're right. I know I have to be strong...I...I just love him so much and don't want to lose him." She let out a humorous smirk, overcoming the tears in her eyes. "It's kind of funny. I remember a time when the last thing I wanted was a man in my life, and now I can't picture my life without him in it."

"That's what love will do to you," replied Michael, his tone now evolved to one of comfort and understanding.

Michael could tell how heavy their conversation was weighing on her, so he did what he could to lighten the mood.

"But let's not talk about all that now. Tell me how Paris was? You lot must have enjoyed yourselves since you spent three weeks there."

They both were surprised at how much they loved Paris. Everything about the majestic city relaxed and enthralled them. Every night they would go on a walk through the city and each time they fell in love with something new. The regal gold and black colors embedded in the city's DNA like some marvelous impressionist painting, gave them a sense of tranquility. The temperature was always welcoming and knew the precise way to sweep across their skin. The canals flowed freely and spirited like tiny pockets of life throughout the city. On several occasions after dinner they would take a ride through canal Saint-Martin. The boat would sway gently side-to-side like a cradle as the Gondolier guided them romantically through the canal, allowing them to taste every bit of beauty that Paris had to offer. Emily would lie in Jude's arms and gaze up at the European stars, sending them both into a world far beyond reality where they had not a care.

They must have walked the equivalent from France to Italy in true Olympic marathon fashion, because they never used any transportation other than the canals during the evenings. During the days they walked along the vintage cobblestone streets, passing bakeries smelling of fresh begets and scrumptious pastries, just the sweet scent alone was enough to put anyone in a diabetic coma.

People were constantly coming and going for all different reasons. The majority of which were sat outside cafes, which weren't hard to locate since there seemed to be one on every corner as if to remind everyone of coffee's existence. And they always made an effort to travel to the town square where there was always something going on. They caught a Victor Hugo poetry reading in Chantilly, a local playhouse's rendition of *A Midsummer Night's Dream* in Chartes, and they got a really poor portrait of them sketched in Senlis, where their heads were enlarged to the size of hot air balloons. Emily and Jude had literally been around the world, but no place had grabbed their spirits and captured their hearts like Paris.

The night before the heart stopping shrimp risotto, Emily and Jude nestled upon a bench at midnight in Rèpublique overlooking the Saint-Martin canal. The stars glistened through the water as the midnight's breeze whispered words of love and content through their ears. Jude could see Emily shaking, the hairs on the back of her neck at attention from the chill. He took off his black cashmere Polo sweater leaving him in his white undershirt. He wrapped it warmly around her, holding her close while she studied the stars as they rested peacefully beneath the full moon.

"Jude?" she said, her head comfortably settled on his shoulder. He leaned over slightly kissing her on the top of her head before replying, "Yeah, love."

"Are you scared?" They both continued staring off into the stars as if they possessed the answer.

"Of dying? No. Of losing you? Only every second."

She planted her head in his chest, cuddling him unyieldingly.

"I love you, Jude. Whatever happens, I will always be with you." Her words were like a summer breeze, both welcomed and comforting.

They sat a few more moments in a peaceful bliss, before Jude whispered, "I love you." She returned his words by tilting her head back on his chest, closing her eyes, and puckering her lips inviting his kiss. He leaned over accepting, and Emily followed it with an, 'I love you' of her own. In spite of their content silence, Jude could sense she was still disturbed over something. He often wondered how he was able to make out whenever she had something on her mind. It was like a sixth sense that he only possessed for her. Maybe it was because he knew her better than she knew herself? Or perhaps it just comes with being in love?

"What is it, love? I can practically hear you thinking, like some epic monologue."

Emily turned her nose, cursing the fact that he always could see right through her. She always considered herself to be a master spy when it came to hiding her true feelings. After all, she did manage to hide not talking to Jude from Melissa for over a month. But she gave into his question as if submitting to torture.

"So you don't think about dying at all? You're just fine with it…not a care in the world? Because I think about it all the time Jude, and it's driving me crazy knowing that any second could be your last."

He let out a fed up sigh through his nostrils like some bewildered animal.

"I don't know, Emily! Why do you have to go on and say something like that and ruin the night. To be honest I try not to think about it. I just want to enjoy me time with you, whatever remains of it. Is that such a bloody crime?"

She was dissatisfied with his answer, and growing sad at the thought of losing him. Her voice developed into humble reasoning, "I wasn't trying to ruin the night. I've enjoyed the past few months we've spent together, but the thought of you one day not waking up next to me really bothers me is all."

Jude got up and walked over to the bridge's old wooden railing, peering into the canal. For the first time since hearing the news, she could see his mind roaming and knew he was just as distraught at the situation as she was. She followed him, placing her arms around his waist and resting her head on his back. Her spectacles gave him a slight pinch as they dug into his muscles.

"I'm sorry. I didn't mean to kill the mood. Forget I brought it up."

He rotated in her arms, her spectacles now pinching his chest. "Emily, look at me."

She looked up able to feel the compassion flow from his blue eyes to hers.

"The thought drives me mad as well. But I don't think about it because I don't want to waste a single second being upset or feeling blue for meself when I could be spending that second being happy with you."

He relaxed his forehead on hers. The tips of their noses touching, feeling each breath the other took. The exhaustion from the conversation now coming full circle: "Love, I don't know if life is greater than death. But I do know having loved you surpasses them both."

The moon looked down with envy as she closed her eyes and kissed him slowly, only hearing the sound of his faint breath and the peaceful trickle of the canal's beauty. At that moment, they were immaculate. They were boundless. They were love, and together they appeased love as if mastering the very symphony of the emotion.

"What are you lot talking about?" asked Jude, his voice constricted and raspy like a lifelong smoker. His body was withering down right in front of them as his strength slowly crept from his muscles. It took every part of him not to scream in agony as he turned in the hospital bed to face Emily and Michael.

"Emily was just filling me in on your trip to Paris. How are you feeling, mate?"

"About as good as I look."

"So like shite huh?"

Jude could still appreciate Michael's sense of humor and if he wasn't certain his appendix would burst from the pain he would have laughed.

"Well done, cheers for that, mate."

"I'm just taking the piss, you look well."

"Now I know you're lying."

Michael tried to give him an assuring look but it failed, "No really, you're the dog's bollocks."

"Michael, I'm dying, I'm not some fourteen-year-old kid with self-esteem issues. I don't need you to big me up."

Emily intervened like a mom, breaking up two brothers, "Okay you two let's cool it, Jude needs rest."

"Yeah, Michael—I'm dying, don't wind me up," he said instigating the matter.

Michael smiled at Jude's spirits.

"I'm glad to see you're still yourself through all of this."

"Well, I did have some old bloke that used to go on and on about staying strong through adversity."

Michel was touched by the backhanded compliment and for a brief moment saw Jude as that troubled, rebellious, eager sixteen-year-old he first took under his wing. He recalled all the things Jude had accomplished in his life and was proud of the man lying in front of him.

"Oi, I'm not that old…just agedly challenged."

Emily pieced together that this was a moment between lifelong friends and decided to excuse herself, "I'm going to give you two a minute. I'll be right outside if you need anything, Jude."

Jude closed his eyes for several seconds, regaining some strength to speak.

"You know that part in *Episode One* when Darth Maul kills Qui-Gon before Obi Wan can do anything about it?"

Michael's lip rose sardonically, "Uh, yeah…where are you going with this, mate?"

"What I'm trying to say is, besides that being me favourite scene, I know I don't say it much, hell, I don't think I've ever said it, but I love you, Michael. I didn't want you going on not knowing that." Michael wanted to speak but didn't because he feared it would break Jude's train of thought, and he wanted to hear this. "I'm not trying to go all bent on you, mate. I just want you to know I appreciate all that you've done for me life. I wasn't the easiest lad to look…" Jude lost his breath momentarily but regained it, "…to look after." *'Try a pain in the ass,*' Michael thought. "But you were the closest thing I had to a father after me mum and dad died. And despite what you may think, I didn't ignore all those lectures over the years, I like to think it's because of the morals you taught me that I turned out in the end to be not such a bad bloke."

"Well, it's good to know you listened to something I said, you could have fooled me. But you're a good lad, Jude, always have been. Your parents would be proud of the man you've become. And I have always loved you like you were family."

Jude raised his fist to him, "as far as I'm concerned we *are* family, mate."

Michael gave him a fist bump, which somehow seemed to be the only manly way of expressing their true affections in fear there was a hidden camera in the room.

"Can you do me a favour?"

"Name it."

"Could you send Emily back in, and fetch me a coffee from the cantina? None of that rubbish that the nursing staff tries to pass off as coffee."

"Sure mate, I'll be back in a jiff."

"Oi! One more thing—" Michael turned to look at him.

"Yeah..." he answered obediently.

"I watched *Scarface*."

"And?"

"*Phantom Menace* was better, so it was shite."

Michael just laughed and shook his head in agreement, "Well done."

Michael left the room with an eerie sense of closure and Emily reentered with a strong sense of satisfaction at Jude's maturity level he had just shown towards Michael.

"Hey, love. Come over here so I can see that beautiful face. And also because I don't think I can roll back over on me own." He was only half kidding about that last part. Emily pulled the chair directly up to the bed, her knees brushed against the white cotton sheets. She aesthetically ran her fingers through his wild dirty blond hair, his face instantly gaining some color from her touch. "Here I am," she said smiling.

Jude found himself drowning in her eyes, becoming swept away by their allure.

"You know something, Emily? You have this way of making me forget what I was going to say. As soon as I feel your touch I forget all else exists." Each of his breaths now came as a struggle and from the corner of her right eye she could see his hand trembling.

"I'm going to get the nurse," said Emily petrified. She attempted to get up from the chair but Jude delicately grabbed her arm.

"No. It's alright. Just sit with me for a bit, yeah."

She sat there in silence holding his hand, both his hands now shaking as if he were trying to roll a seven.

"Love..." his voice fell even lower, she leaned in closer placing her ear adjacent to his lips. "Promise me..." He took a deep breath feeling his air becoming too costly to use. "...promise me you'll keep on living." She felt the tears coming and in spite of how hard she neglected them it was a fight she would inevitably lose.

"Don't talk like that!" she pleaded.

"You're a proper doctor, Emily, and I'm no idiot, we both knew this was coming so let's be adults about this. Now promise me."

Her eyes so overwhelmed with tears she could hardly make Jude out. She took off her spectacles and made a frivolous attempt to dry her eyes but the tears kept running like a forgotten facet. "...I promise."

"I mean it, Emily. Don't stop living. Keep fighting for your dreams, experiencing new things, and standing up for yourself. You're a lot stronger than you know."

"Jude...please don't go...I love you!"

"Hey...hey love, that'll be enough of that." He wiped her tears from her eyes with his thumb. "Do you see me crying?"

He continued his attempt to wipe the endless flow of tears from her eyes, but his shaking hands only smeared them.

"Yes…" she said almost cracking a smile.

"That's not the point. I'm not crying as much as you because I'm alright love. I'm happy."

"What? I don't understand."

His muscles ached to form a smile but he did so nonetheless.

"Because I'm the luckiest bloke in the world. How many can say they have found, loved, married, and truly lived as one with their true love? In this massive universe I was fortunate enough to run into you on the street that day. I look at you with no regrets or doubt, but with gratitude that fate provided me the chance to love you."

"Then we are both lucky, because I love you, Jude! You're the best thing that's ever come into my life, and I will never stop loving you."

"Nor will I, Emily…nor will I."

"Please don't go, we still have time…" her voice beseeching him to hold on.

"I'm afraid not, love. For what it's worth, having loved you I've lived enough for a thousand lifetimes. Now kiss me so I forever remember your perfection."

There was so much she wanted to say to him, so many things to still share, and so many nights to still spend. But all that came out of her mouth through the pool of tears was, "I love you." She bowed forward kissing him slow and profound like a timeless dance. Her lips exceptionally salty from the tears, but his somehow grew stronger from her touch. Her hands wrapped around his head pulling him tighter to the point their cheeks adjoined. She felt his breath on her tongue as it fluttered in and out calmly. Her heart was racing a hundred miles a second as she embedded every prolong second of the kiss in her memory banks. She was determined to not let the kiss end, holding on desperately to his warm lips as they grasp onto the only thing he ever came to understand. Perhaps he was already gone, or maybe her mind just refused to feel him fading, but within an imperative second, he was gone. His cozy lips gave way and faded back into his face, and the sound of the flatline echoed a cry for something that was once very much alive.

The doctors and Michael hurried into the room. Michael dropped the cup of blistering coffee as he saw Jude lifelessly cocooned in Emily's arms, he too was unsuccessful at holding back the tears. Emily rebelled to release him and instead fastened her grip around him immensely. She was weeping inconsolably and kissing him repeatedly, begging for him not to go, "NO...NO..., PLEASE DON'T LEAVE ME...PLEase...please..." her voice fading into her tears.

Michael eventually pulled her off and secured her in his arms. She cried on his shoulders until she no longer had the energy to do so.

X X

Emily: Dearest Emily

"**A**re you alright Mrs. Macavoy? You have been staring at your cup of coffee for over two minutes," said the Armani-wearing lawyer sitting across from her and Michael. She had forgotten she was even holding the cup. These mental lapses were becoming somewhat of a daily routine since Jude had passed ten days ago. Whenever she felt herself missing him her mind would trail off into the memories they once shared. Much to her pleasure, when they would occur during work they didn't hinder her performance, but instead motivated her to be an even better doctor, remembering her promise she had made to him. In fact, Dr. Landry felt her medical skills grew tenfold since her return to the hospital. It was as if Jude's love was the missing ingredient that created the successful well-rounded person Emily always had the potential to become. The precise one her mother and father had always envisioned her to be. At the rate she was excelling she would either, have Dr. Landry's job in two years or her choice of joining any top hospital staff in the United States. She was granted more responsibility than any other residency student, and some of the patients she assisted with actually preferred her treatments over the certified physician that Emily was working under.

For the past few days she refused to even acknowledge that the funereal had actually taken place. She preferred to believe that he was back in England, training and goofing off on the couch playing video games or watching *Star Wars*. She put a smile on for the world the best she could, but in her inside resided an empty hole that only Jude could fill. To define her emptiness as simply 'missing him' would be dissatisfaction to the abundance of love that she still possessed towards him. She didn't just miss him; she missed her other half, for he had become a part of her. He completed her in a way one needs a vital organ to survive. But she was true to her promise and kept on living. She not only became a substantially better doctor but she made a valiant effort to make time for Melissa and some of the new friends she made at the hospital. She took nothing for granted, cherishing the little things in life, like days off and good pizza. She eventually bought a puppy to help fill the void left from pining for Jude's safe touch at night, and named him, Kenobi, feeling it would have made Jude happy.

Surprisingly this was the first time she had ever met Jude's lawyer, however the same couldn't be said for Michael. Mr. Stanley Cole had received plenty of calls on Jude's behalf, mainly to bail him out of lockup. Like for the time Jude decided to show a little public display of affection when he peed on a police car in London, and for assaulting a Preston North End supporter in a nightclub for protesting Blackpool are shit, are just a few instances that come to mind. Stanley was considered one of the best celebrity lawyers in the UK, and the U.S. for that matter. He has offices in his hometown of Newcastle, London, and their current location, New York City.

"I'm sorry, I'm listening. Please go on," she said indifferently.

Stanley straightened his brown and grey striped tie before proceeding in his heavy Jordi accent.

"As I was saying, this should be a rather brief process. Will readings usually are, especially when widows are involved. Let's see, where to begin? Oh yes!" he said flipping through the tiny stacks of papers cluttering his desk. "Jude starts by stating, '*If Tiffany is in the room tell her to get the F…*' I will let you both use your imagination at what his choice of word is, '*out—because she's not getting shite.*' As I look around the room obviously she's not here so let's move along to the good stuff shall we? He goes on to state, '*To me love, Emily Macavoy. I leave you all me possessions and pounds. Please keep up the work on the Jude Macavoy Heart Cancer Foundation and take a few of me pounds and start a football academy in Blackpool. Somewhere where the lads can learn properly and stay out of trouble. Clearly we cannot have an American running this project. I love you Emily but you still call it soccer for Christ's sakes, so collaborate with Michael, who I know will do a brilliant job running the whole thing. You both should obtain fifty percent of the academy's proceeds. And for me best mate and brother, Michael Vaughn, I leave you me original Blackpool training kit and me complete Star Wars Blu-ray collection.*' And that's it. Like I said, quick but gripping stuff. Mrs. Macavoy and Mr. Vaughn I'm deeply sorry for your loss. He was a good lad. He wasn't just a high profile client but a friend. Now if there's nothing else, you can see Ms. Stacey outside who will write you up and attend to validating your parking."

"I'm sorry, mate, are we rushing you? Are you missing the first half of X-Factor or something? Actually yes, there is one more thing." Michael leaned over unzipping the black and orange Blackpool athletics duffle bag he brought with him, pulling out an old brown Nike shoebox.

"Emily, Jude asked me to give this to you once he passed. He instructed me not to open it, so I don't know what's inside. But here you go."

She accepted the box and immediately began examining it as much as she could without opening it. A part of her wanted to open it now, but if Jude didn't want Michael to see it, '*then there was no way he wanted his ignorant lawyer to witness its unveiling,*' she thought.

Michael and Emily shared a taxi to Grand Central Station, first to drop Emily off for her train back to New Haven and then to LaGuardia for Michael's flight back home. As they pulled up to 42nd and Park Avenue there began a heavy downpour. Before exiting the taxi she secured her purse strap over her shoulder, clamped the shoebox under her arm, and prepared her hair for the quick dash through the New York City rain. Michael leaned over and gave her a hug.

"Take care of yourself. I'll phone you sometime next week so we can begin plans for the academy. I think I know just the spot Jude had in mind."

She pulled away placing her hand on the door handle.

"Sounds good—I'll talk to you then. Have a safe flight and give my love to Amy for me, okay."

"Will do—" As she was about to shut the cab door behind her he stopped her, "Emily?"

"Yeah!" her volume rose to be heard over the New York traffic and the pellets of water crackling the roof of the taxi.

"Thanks for everything… I mean with Jude. I know he lived and died happy because of you. You were his miracle."

The rain continued to fall, dripping from the rims of her spectacles making it impossible to separate the rain from the tears that began to spill. Her lip quivered slightly as if she wanted to speak, but a plethora of thoughts were running through her head.

"I really miss him…" she said sadly. The hole left by Jude was tugging at her heartstrings, she longed for his touch now more than ever.

"I'm certain he's missing you right now as well. I'd bet my life on it."

She smiled half-heartedly and waved goodbye before closing the door and disappearing into the heavy rain.

After the conductor came by and took her ticket she diverted back into her seat staring bewilderedly out into the passing scenery, as tall aged buildings and graffiti dressed walls whizzed by. The train car billowed from left to right, reminding her briefly of her and Jude's canal rides. Not able to shake the cognizance of him she grabbed the shoebox from under her seat and placed it on her lap. She opened the box. First seeing the robust collection of loose-leaf paper, over five hundred sheets, all written on with either pencil or pen. There was also his black and white composition notebook that he wrote to her in during their year together, filled with letters to her, each entry signed and dated, she couldn't believe he continued writing even after they had broken up. The final item in the box was a white envelope sealed and addressed to Emily. She opened it gingerly, careful to not rip the paper.

Dearest Emily,

I already miss you madly, so much so I cannot begin to form me feelings into words. If you are reading this then I am no longer breathing, but that doesn't mean I'm no longer with you.

In this box you will find every letter, every note, and every thought I have ever written you. Most are from the notebook we kept for one another while the rest I composed more recently to help you get through the rest of your life and to constantly remind you that I love you madly.

Never forget the promise you made to me. You must continue being the greatest doctor in the world, continue smiling, continue living free, and for the love of God continue trying new things. But most importantly, continue enjoying life. You will one day meet someone new, and that's alright, just be sure he treats you well. Because you deserve the best Emily, you are an angel, you are perfection, and you are the epitome of beauty.

Know that each day I will be looking down on you smiling—being proud of you and the love we once shared. The greatest love is love everlasting, the kind that guides the heart and frees the soul, and that's what you gave to me every day, and it's what we will continue to forever share.

If you ever need to speak with me I'm right here among these papers, right beside you. I love you Emily and I miss you.

> *All Me love for now and forever,*
> *Jude*

Her smile illuminated the train. She held the box close to her heart, embracing it tight as if it were him. She smiled out into the newly formed clouds as the rain clouds strangely washed-away back into the sky, leaving the sun shining bright, and somehow she knew Jude was smiling back at her. She rested her head upon the cold window and whispered, "I love you too, Jude. Thank you for everything..."

She went back to the night when they stood boundless, overlooking the Paris canal. Within that kiss they were untouchable to life, circumstance, and eternity. And gazing out the train's window she knew, that no matter how far apart they were, whether it is this life or the next, their love would forever be—boundless.

Charles A. Bush

Charles Bush lives in Philadelphia, where he writes novels. In addition to earning his bachelor of arts in English at Cabrini College, he is currently obtaining a postgraduate degree in English literature and creative writing at The University of Oxford.

You can follow Charles Bush on his Amazon author page, his Facebook page (Charles Bush), and on Twitter (@CharlesBush10).

35969499R00147

Made in the USA
Lexington, KY
01 October 2014